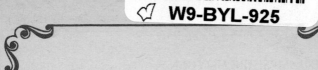

She started to get up, but Jack moved quickly, rising in one fluid motion to his feet and holding his hands out to her.

Heart pounding in her breast, Sarah placed her hands in his and felt fire shoot from his fingers into her veins, flaming into her, heating her cheeks, pushing her heart into her throat as he pulled her effortlessly to her feet. She stood scant inches from him, gazing up into his night-darkened eyes and quite unable to look away.

She could kiss him now. She had only to rise on her toes, and her mouth would meet his . . . .

By Michelle Martin
Published by Fawcett Books:

THE HAMPSHIRE HOYDEN
THE QUEEN OF HEARTS
THE MAD MISS MATHLEY
THE ADVENTURERS
THE BUTLER WHO LAUGHED

THE BUTLER
WHO LAUGHED

Michelle Martin

FAWCETT CREST • NEW YORK

A Fawcett Crest Book
Published by Ballantine Books
Copyright © 1997 by Michelle Martin

All rights reserved under International and Pan-American Copyright Conventions. Published in the United States by Ballantine Books, a division of Random House, Inc., New York, and simultaneously in Canada by Random House of Canada Limited, Toronto.

http://www.randomhouse.com

Library of Congress Catalog Card Number: 96-90773

ISBN 0-449-22528-3

Manufactured in the United States of America

First Edition: May 1997

10 9 8 7 6 5 4 3 2 1

* Prologue

THROUGH A CAPRICIOUS twist of fate, John Rawlins was born the third son to the Duke of Merifield. His birth, however, was not celebrated by pealing bells and a dramatic fireworks display, as the births of the duke's first two sons had been, for Jack was born on the wrong side of the blanket. He was the culmination of a long affair discreetly conducted by the duke and Catherine Rawlins, a housekeeper at one of the nobleman's many estates. The duke—peeved at Catherine for being so reckless as to conceive a child—demoted her to one of his minor estates in Staffordshire before the Duchess of Merifield could detect her housekeeper's interesting condition. Publishing herself as a widow, Catherine worked here and raised her son. Being a practical woman, despite her earlier indiscretion with the duke, and knowing her son would have to make his own way in the world, she trained Jack in service as she and all of her family had been.

It was not until Jack was twelve that he first saw his father. During the whole of the duke's visit—an impromptu hunting party with a dozen of his cronies—father and son never exchanged a word, nor did the nobleman acknowledge Jack by look or deed. Jack was simply a comely page boy who carried out the orders of his masters.

When he turned fourteen, however, fate intervened in Jack's life once again. The duke brought a second hunting party to Staffordshire. This time Jack served his father on horseback and in the field, scooping up the dozens of birds massacred in the name of sport. The duke was so taken by Jack's abilities with guns and horses that he impulsively decided to remember his parental obligations to the boy and provide him with an education. Jack was given a new wardrobe, a generous allowance, grimly instructed not to reveal his parentage—on either side—to anyone, and sent off to school in Scotland, to avoid meeting those who might detect a resemblance between him and his illustrious father. As Jack showed well as both a scholar and an athlete (in contrast to his elder legitimate brothers), the duke's benificence was touched once again. He sent his secret son to the University of Edinburgh with the same grim condition of revoking his financial support should Jack ever breathe a word about his parentage.

It might be assumed that any child born to a servant would be grateful for these advantages, but Jack Rawlins was not. True, he enjoyed the education provided by books and tutors, but the schooling he received at the hands of his fellow students darkened his naturally generous heart and illuminated his reluctant mind to the rigid truths of his world. Raised a servant, he had been ignored or cuffed by his betters. Self-control had been a daily lesson. Yet he found himself held in awe by his Scottish classmates, for that self-control, along with a keen mind and an impressive pair of fives, intimidated them. They made him their leader, aped every fashion or mannerism he adopted, and could not seem to do enough for him. Excluded in his childhood and raised to a pedestal in his youth, Jack quickly learned the bitter truth: He would never belong, not to his mother's class, nor to his father's. His birth and education had irrevocably removed him from both.

Upon his majority, John Rawlins possessed a gentleman's education, the superior manners of a servant, a thorough knowledge of the Haute Ton's hypocrisy, nearly one hundred pounds that he had saved from his allowance during the course of his education, a strong prejudice against his father's class, and his first and only letter from the Duke of Merifield. In this brief document, his father declared himself to have satisfied all of his parental obligations to Jack. The duke wished his unacknowledged son success in whatever future course he chose, and recommended establishing himself in the clergy, the law, or the navy—a career long favored by the younger sons of the Merifields.

Jack chose the army.

Upon *his* majority, Fitzwilliam Hornsby, the wholly legitimate eighth Viscount Lyleton, received, in accordance with his grandfather's will, six thousand pounds a year and Charlisle, a vast estate in Somersetshire. Charlisle, in addition to rolling pastures, verdant farmland, towering woods, and lush gardens, all described rhapsodically in the better travel guides, was particularly noted for its fine mansion, built in the Elizabethan style at the beginning of the seventeenth century. Its pale yellow Bath stonework glimmered in the sunlight. Its high ceilings, marble and wood floors, and elegant apartments would have pleased the most fastidious taste. Wordsworth, upon touring the property one idyllic summer, had likened Charlisle to "a beauteous sun, glowing amidst a pastoral scene so alluring to the eye, that sylvan Diane hath often wandered there."

Who could ask more of a country seat than this?

Fitzwilliam Hornsby, "Fitz" to his friends, of whom Jack was one, had visited Charlisle exactly once in the three years since attaining his majority, and then only after being threatened with vivisection by his estate manager. The viscount deplored the country with its dirt and dogs and peasant habiliments. Fitz was a devotee of Town life—appearing in the newest fashion in neck cloths, promenading down Bond Street, and gambling at Watier's until dawn. Had he been asked to state his greatest ambition in life, he would have said, "To cut a dashed fine figure in Town."

Unlike many, the Viscount Lyleton was a man who achieved his lifelong ambition at an early age.

Fitz had but one complaint against the onerous weight of his legacy—his parents. Somehow the Earl and Countess of Lavesly had failed to take in the fact that the viscount was four-and-twenty, a young man of independent means, a leader of fashion, not some child bound to his parents' leading strings. Their treatment of him, he declared to any who would listen to him, was the shabbiest thing imaginable. Why, only last month they had delivered a lengthy and rather cutting lecture that took in his wardrobe, his gaming, his hours of repose (which took up most of the daylight), his friends, his stable of hot-blooded bonesetters, and his complete lack of a wife.

This last seemed to irk the earl and countess no end, but in vain did they remonstrate with their son. If the viscount could claim any other ambition, it was not to marry until he was at least thirty, and as he grew closer to that age, he seriously considered upping it to forty. It was not that Fitz disliked women. He thought they were rather good fun and often entertaining, particularly when they could not say enough about his newest coat or the rakish style he had affected with his black locks.

But as for marriage, the viscount would rather wear sackcloth and ashes to Carlton House, forswear Watier's, and give all of his horses to some penniless Scottish farmer than enter the wedded state. Fitz might not be clever, but he had a keen sense of survival. He noted all of the matchmaking mamas on the Marriage Mart throwing their daughters at his rich and handsome head, and he ducked every one of them. Occasionally being called onto the carpet by his doting parents was a small price to pay for his freedom, and Fitz considered himself one of the more fortunate of his crowd.

This opinion suffered a serious revision one black May in 1813 when the Earl and Countess of Lavesly informed their flabbergasted offspring that, beginning in late June, he was to host a summer house party of over two dozen guests, whom they had taken the liberty of inviting to Charlisle. Worse, they meant to be on hand to see that he did not shirk his duty by even an hour. He was to rusticate in earnest.

Fitz could not but suspect some ominous purpose to these arrangements. He tried to take a firm stand. "No, dash it, they can go to Hades for all I care, but they shall not pollute Charlisle!" hung upon his lips, but was choked back by the basilisk glare of his father. It had the effect of turning his spine to jelly and his heart to ashes.

The viscount resigned himself to his lot. His written instructions to his country staff were minimal. He gave them the number of guests to expect and bade them make everything ready. He spent the rest of the merry month of May in a black and, depending upon the amount of wine he had consumed, self-pitying mood. A letter, arriving at the end of the month, sunk him even further into gloom. This single sheet of correspondence not only put Fitz off all future romantic interludes, it also adversely affected his appetite and sleep. More than one friend commented on his weight loss and fevered gaze.

"In fact," said John Rawlins as he surveyed Fitz in the morning parlor of the viscount's Berkeley Square town house, "you look damned haggard, young Hornsby." His expression became grim. "What's wrong now?"

Fitz groaned and dropped his beautiful head into his hands once again. "I'm sunk, Jack. The devil's got me by the coattails, and I can see no way to shake him off. You've always been my guardian angel. You've got to help me!"

"Fitz," sighed the guardian angel with a weariness that came from the soul, "I have been back in England only three months and already I have extricated you from the mercenary clutches of a cardsharp and a misunderstanding with the Bow Street Runners! I told you the day I settled in Devonshire that I had no more appetite for saving anyone's neck but my own. I'm done with futile heroics. I don't want to leave my orchards and fields and woods. I don't want to rescue you. I mean to live my life as I choose and the rest of the world be damned!"

"But, Jack, it's hellfire and damnation if you don't rescue me!" the ashen viscount cried. "I swear, I'll not call on your aid for the rest of this year if you'll only help me now with this Templeton."

Jack sighed heavily. There were few who could withstand that pathetic gleam in Fitz's black eyes. "Very well, I will *look* at the letter."

"You are too good!" said Fitz, nearly overcome with emotion. He handed his friend the distressing document.

Jack slumped down in his chair and thrust his long legs out before him. He wore a dusty riding coat, breeches, and top boots—hardly appropriate attire for the fashionable London parlor of one of the ton's leading beaux—but he had arrived in

London on horseback from Devonshire not a half hour earlier, and he and Fitz had never stood on ceremony with each other.

The document in question was concise and to the point. Sir Marcus Templeton stated that he was in possession of a letter written by Lord Lyleton to Aldora Higgins, an opera dancer of considerable beauty but dubious morals. In his missive, Fitz had declared both his undying love and his fervent promise to marry said opera dancer. As the young woman's newest protector, Sir Marcus offered Fitz two choices: marry the girl or buy the girl off . . . through him.

"Did you really write such a letter?" Jack demanded with disbelief.

Fitz groaned and wrapped his arms around his aching head.

Incredulous, Jack regarded his hapless friend. "You are the most marriage-shy man I've ever met! How could you propose to this girl?"

"I think it was the brandy." Fitz moaned. "And her perfume. Gad, Aldora's perfume would make any man's head swim."

With an oath, Jack rose from his chair, mangling the letter in his fist. "And here is one of the greatest blackguards in all of England to take advantage of your temporary delirium. The gall of the man!" he said, throwing the crumpled letter into the grate beside him. "The hypocrisy! Sir Marcus Templeton has compromised more girls in this country and produced more by-blows than the Duke of Clarence. How dare he take you to task for corrupting this opera dancer! The girl undoubtedly had a dozen lovers before you succumbed to her charms." Jack paused. "We could prove that in court, you know."

The viscount jerked his head up, a look of horror on his handsome face. "Good God, no! No court case. No publicity! Have you any idea the miserable hellhole my life would become if my parents ever found out about Aldora?"

"It doesn't bear thinking about," Jack agreed.

"But surely you, Jack . . . I mean, you're so dashed clever . . . surely, you can think of some sort of scheme to save me from this damned Templeton."

"Blackmail *is* a devilish problem," Jack conceded, taking his seat once again.

"It's put me off marriage for life, I can tell you."

"I don't wonder. Still, I think yours is a problem that can be rectified."

Fitz jumped in his chair, hope beginning to glimmer in his black eyes for the first time in a fortnight. "My dear fellow! Could you? Would you?"

Jack accepted the inevitable. "Yes, I shall."

"Oh, Jack, you are the cleverest man in the whole of England! What must we do?"

John Rawlins sighed. He should never have rescued Lyleton from that pummeling by a mutual school acquaintance in Scotland so long ago. "Your parents, for all their high-handedness, have provided us with the perfect opportunity to retrieve your letter. All you have to do is invite Sir Marcus to the summer party at Charlisle. Say that you want him to produce the letter there, and if it is genuine, you will pay him off."

"But I don't want to pay him off!"

"You won't have to, because I, my dear Fitz, shall steal it from Templeton at the first opportunity. Without the letter, he has no hold on you."

"Steal it? Under the noses of over two dozen of the stodgiest members of the Haute Ton? How?"

Jack winced. It seemed his life had come full circle. "A servant—let us say a butler—has access to every room in a country house at every hour of the day. It should be a simple matter for me to pose as Charlisle's butler, wait my chance, search Templeton's room, retrieve the letter, and send the blackguard packing."

The Viscount Lyleton stared at Jack as if just comprehending the full breadth of his friend's magnificence. "You would do all that for me?"

For the first time that day, Jack's expression softened. "I am confident that you would undertake an even more ridiculous scheme if I were ever in trouble. Mind you, the success of this venture rests solely on you remembering to call me Rawlins instead of Jack."

"I'll call you Empress Josephine if it gets me out of Templeton's clutches."

"Is there a chance any of your guests would recognize me from Edinburgh?"

Fitz shook his dark head in disbelief. Who would have thought his friend could be so dim? "Jack, the Haute Ton scarcely acknowledges Scotland's place in the empire! None of them would think of crossing the border. You shan't be recognized."

"Very well," said Jack. "The first order of business is to send Charlisle's butler off on what will hopefully be a brief holiday."

✳
Chapter 1

"CHARLISLE IS A pretty place, is it not, Sarah?" said the duchess.

"Indeed," her youngest daughter cautiously replied. The Duchess of Somerton had never made a casual remark in her life. There was purpose behind her admiration of Charlisle, and Sarah was not eager to uncover it.

"I understand Lyleton also has a fine town house in Berkeley Square," remarked the duke, his leonine features in profile as he examined the fireplace mantel where a ceramic shepherdess was being wooed by a ceramic shepherd. He set the duo back down with a faint shrug. "It could become the center of Town life with a little work. Lyleton is quite popular in his own circle, you know."

"I believe the viscount is fond of society," Sarah agreed, becoming honestly worried now.

"Young, attractive, rich, a decent background," the duchess stated. "Lyleton's bride will be a lucky woman indeed, don't you think, Sarah?"

Lady Sarah Thorndike surveyed her mother with the greatest alarm. She had heard similar versions of that ominous query too many times in the past not to suspect its deeper meaning now. "I have not yet even met our host, Mother. How can I have formed any sort of opinion on the luck or the lack thereof of his future wife?"

"Nonsense, Sarah," said the duke. "You've been out for three years now."

The duchess was seen to shudder at this.

9

"You should be able to judge a young man," continued the duke, "a mere thirty seconds after entering his house."

"Although he has not moved in *our* circle, you have undoubtedly heard of the viscount," the duchess stated, her pale blue eyes boring into her daughter. "Town is forever buzzing of his exploits, I believe. You must have formed an opinion of the young man."

"Must I?" Sarah asked faintly.

"You know I cannot abide evasion in anyone, particularly my own children," said the duchess, who was always formidably forthright. "I asked you a simple question, Sarah, and I expect a simple answer. What is your opinion of Lord Lyleton?"

"He's . . . a bit of a dandy, don't you think?" Sarah hazarded.

"Why, any young man of spirit is a bit of a dandy nowadays," said the duke. "Age and maturity will soon shake it out of him."

"The Earl and Countess of Lavesly were quite taken with you, Sarah," said the duchess.

"But how could they be?" her daughter cried, more and more perturbed by the tenor of this conversation. "They've never seen me before. I just curtsied to them in the hall five minutes ago."

"I have never believed in being obscure in an important conversation," said the duchess, her sharp face rigid, her carefully dyed auburn curls quivering slightly. "You should know, Sarah, that your father and I have been in negotiation for some time with the Laveslys. We reached agreement last month on the marriage contract. You are to marry the Viscount Lyleton by Michaelmas."

"But I don't want to marry Lord Lyleton!" Sarah burst out.

There was a moment of crystalline silence in the sitting room. Sarah hurriedly stared down at the pale green wool carpet.

"What you want is of very little concern to us," the duchess grimly stated.

"Your lack of a husband is making us the laughingstock of

the ton," the duke complained. "It will not do, Sarah. You have had three years to find a husband to your liking. You must trust us now to act in your best interest."

Sarah's head came up at this. "I *did* find a husband to my liking two years ago!"

"Sir Geoffrey Willingham was a wholly unsuitable choice," the duchess snapped.

"He was a good and honorable man of whom no one could say ill," Sarah bravely countered. "He was sincerely fond of me, and I quite liked him. We would have suited each other admirably and you would then have been spared being made the laughingstock of the ton."

"That is quite enough!" said the duchess.

Sarah took a hasty step back.

"Sir Geoffrey Willingham," said the duke in a tone of utter disgust, "was a penniless and obscure knight without any sort of decent family background. He had nothing to recommend him. Nothing. Your alliance with such a man would have exposed us to the contempt of the ton. You are Somerton's daughter, Sarah. You will marry for wealth, or position, or not at all."

"No daughter of the Duke of Somerton has ever married anything less than a son of an earl," the duchess informed her ashen daughter. "The eighth Viscount Lyleton brings both a good title and a large fortune to this union. *He* will suit you admirably."

"Yes, Mother," Sarah whispered, her head bowed in defeat.

"The affiliation is not everything we could wish, it is true," the duchess admitted with greater composure now that she had made her irksome daughter submit. "The Laveslys have held their current title for only two generations. They are the merest upstarts. But Lyleton is personable, attractive, and well liked. He will be an acceptable connection."

"That is the impression you are to create during the course of this summer," said the duke as his daughter regarded him with shuttered blue eyes. "You and Lyleton are to rub together, get to know each other, reach agreement on whatever particulars you want to raise about the marriage, and then wed in the fall. Why, the announcement won't even be in the papers for another month!"

"How very considerate of you," Sarah whispered through a dry throat.

"You will exert yourself in the next few weeks in getting to know young Lyleton," commanded the duchess. "He, certainly, will not be remiss in paying you those attentions due a young woman during a public courtship."

Now it was Sarah who shuddered. Public did not even cover the most rudimentary aspects of the situation. Charlisle was filling up with some of the stodgiest members of the Haute Ton ever assembled under one roof—the Merbleses, the Braithwaites, and the Throwbrights among them. Sarah shuddered again. That aspect alone had made her dread this sojourn. The prospect of being openly courted by that tulip of fashion, the Viscount Lyleton, turned that dread to pure, unadulterated nausea.

"I think I will lie down in my room before dinner," she said in a strangled voice.

"Very wise," said the duchess. "You must look your best tonight. I suggest you wear the white muslin with the blue ribbons. A simple strand of pearls. No brooch. And have Jenkins fashion your hair *à la Sappho*. It is very becoming to you."

"Yes, Mother," Sarah said, then escaped the sitting room, which lay between her parents' bedrooms.

Head swimming, she stood in the sunlit hallway a moment, unable to get her bearings, and dazedly wondered if she could board a fast ship to America before being overtaken by her parents' henchmen.

"Might I be of some assistance, Lady Sarah?" a gentle voice inquired.

Eyes still a little unfocused, Sarah looked up to find one of the most handsome men she had ever seen standing before her. He was tall, broad of shoulder and chest, his immaculate clothes revealing a muscular frame. His hair was dark brown, his gray eyes kind, and his expression one of concern.

It was hard for Sarah to find her voice. Could this be the Viscount Lyleton? She had heard him called beautiful, but this gentleness, this lack of ostentation, the relief she felt in the strength he exuded, were more than she could have hoped for. Perhaps the fate her parents had so ruthlessly arranged for her would not be so terrible after all.

"Are you Lyleton?" she asked hopefully.

He blinked. An amused smile touched his lips. "Hardly, my lady. I am Rawlins, the butler."

Oh, good God, she had been admiring the butler! A blush flooded Sarah's cheeks. Trust her to confuse a servant with a viscount. How her parents would roar! Still, her mistake was wholly understandable. She was quite certain that butlers weren't supposed to come in such striking packages. It was most unkind of him to lead her on like that. How dare he not be doddering and balding and fat! Sarah realized that she was staring up at Rawlins, mouth agape. She hurriedly closed her mouth and searched desperately for something to say. "Were you in the hall just now?"

"No, my lady. I was outside assisting the Dowager Formantle from her carriage. It required several minutes to accomplish the task."

Despite the horror of her impending nuptials, Sarah smiled. She had met the Dowager Formantle. She suspected it would take a pulley and tackle to get her out of even the most commodious carriage.

"I congratulate you on accomplishing so formidable a task, Rawlins. I have known lesser men to fail. The Christmas ball at Carlton House comes most forcibly to mind." A giggle escaped her. "She got wedged in the carriage door. It took nearly twenty minutes to extricate her."

"You witnessed the debacle?"

"I was cheering her on."

"I am certain the dowager was grateful for your support," Rawlins remarked, a twinkle in his eyes that Sarah found wholly charming.

She took a deep breath and brought herself to order. Just because Rawlins was proving to be delightful company was no reason to lose her head. She was chatting familiarly with a butler not three feet from her parents' door. If they found her like this, they would roast her on a spit and serve her for dinner. It was time to retrench. "I will now present you with a problem of lesser scope, Rawlins. Do you know which room I am in?"

"Yes, my lady. You are in the Rose Suite, at the end of the west wing overlooking the rose garden."

"It sounds charming, but where is it?"

Again that touch of a smile. "If you will permit me, Lady Sarah, I will escort you there."

"Yes, thank you, and after you have been so good as to lead me through this maze of a house, do you think you could smuggle a large quantity of hot chocolate to the Rose Suite?"

He stared down at her. "Hot chocolate, my lady? In this heat?"

"I find it a very soothing libation, particularly when laced with brandy. Don't forget the brandy, Rawlins. I am in great need of soothing," Sarah said with a slight shudder as she contemplated her future as the Viscountess Lyleton.

"Certainly, my lady," Rawlins replied. He turned, stiff and erect, and began to walk down the hall.

Sarah followed a step behind, confused by his suddenly icy demeanor. Had she said or done something to offend him? They turned to the right, down a passageway lined with Elizabethan and Jacobean portraits. "Have you been with the viscount long?" she asked, uncomfortable in the silence and unable to remind herself that he was a butler and had no need of conversation.

"On the contrary, my lady," he coolly replied, never once glancing down at her. "I have been here only a few days. Charlisle's butler, a most capable man by the name of Greeves, is on leave for several weeks attending to some family business in Essex, and I have stepped in as his substitute."

"It sounds a very lengthy leave."

"The viscount is a most generous employer."

"Well, there's hope in that, I suppose," Sarah muttered.

"I beg your pardon, my lady?"

"Don't mind me, Rawlins," Sarah said with a melancholy little sigh. "I always talk to myself. There are few others who

14

would enjoy the conversation." He had made *that* clear enough.

The butler led her around a corner and opened a broad door with a formal flourish. "The Rose Suite, Lady Sarah."

"Thank you, Rawlins."

"I will bring your hot chocolate and brandy within the quarter hour."

"You are an angel of mercy," Sarah replied. She gazed hopefully up at him, but his expression remained aloof. He must think her a peagoose. "Make it a large cup, will you?" she said, turning and walking numbly into her room.

"Very good, my lady," Rawlins replied, closing the door behind her.

"Good heavens, Lady Sarah, what's hobbled you?" cried Maria Jenkins, Sarah's maid, as she turned from a commodious wardrobe. "You're as white as a sheet!"

"Ah, the perfect remedy for removing freckles: abject terror," Sarah said, sitting down with a thump on the foot of the bed.

"I'll ring for some brandy," Maria began, reaching for the bellpull.

"It is being attended to," Sarah said. "Have you met the butler?"

"I have drooled over the butler, my lady," Maria said with a grin.

Sarah was able to conjure an answering smile. "He is very attractive—and very confusing. He began by being the most charming creature imaginable, and then suddenly turned cold and forbidding. I don't know whether to be cross with him for being so unsettling, or grateful to him for being so distracting."

"And what need have you to be distracted?" Maria demanded, pulling Sarah's cold hands into her own. "What has happened, my lady?"

Sarah began to tremble and found she could not stop. "I have been sold off, Maria," she whispered. "My parents have just informed me that I am to marry the Viscount Lyleton."

Maria's grip tightened. "That popinjay? What could the duke and duchess want with him?"

"My scandal-free removal from their guardianship."

Small and thin, with graying brown hair and a good twenty years on her mistress, Maria Jenkins gave Sarah a fierce hug that effectively cut off all supply of oxygen to the lady's lungs. "Those ogres!"

"Now, now, Maria, those ogres pay your wages."

"There's no defending their decision, my lady."

"Oh, of course there is," Sarah said wearily, as she eased herself from Maria's firm grasp and began to listlessly wander the airy rose-papered room. She had long ago become adept at accepting the inevitable, no matter how unpleasant. "I should have been married off in my first Season. It's a wonder I've lasted this long."

"Oh, dear. With his reputation, I wonder if you'll suit?"

"I have been instructed to throw myself into Lyleton's company the whole of this summer and make myself most agreeable. Why else do you think we've come?"

"And if you dislike the bandy rooster, what then?"

Sarah stared at her and then turned away. "The marriage contract is signed, Maria."

"*Marry* Sarah Thorndike?" Viscount Lyleton cried in the utmost horror. "*Marry* . . . are you mad?"

"It is you who are mad for even questioning such a match," the Countess of Lavesly snapped, her impressive figure trembling with barely suppressed anger before her bothersome son.

"Good God, boy, don't you know what this means?" the earl erupted. "We'll be related to the *Somertons*. There isn't a door in England that won't be opened for us!"

"That's all well and good for you," Fitz retorted, still so stunned by the previous announcement that he had quite forgotten his usual deference with his parents, "but *I'm* the one you mean to saddle with the wench!"

"*Fitzwilliam,*" intoned the countess, "I will not have you expressing yourself in such a common and disgusting manner!"

"But hang it, Mama, I don't even know the girl!"

"And why else do you think she's been installed here for the whole of the summer?" demanded Lord Lavesly with the utmost satisfaction.

His son turned green. "B-B-But I don't *want* to get married! I'm too young."

"Nonsense," said the countess with a flick of her silk shawl as she walked across the room. "Your father was two-and-twenty when he married me, a good two years younger than you are now."

"A wife is just the thing to make a man out of you," said the earl, clapping his son on the back.

"A wife will steady you," the countess appended.

"A wife will ruin me," Fitz muttered.

The viscount was not a clever man, but he knew a stacked deck when he saw one. He strode to the sideboard in the paneled library where his parents had trapped him, poured himself a healthy glass of canary wine, downed it in a single swallow, and turned to regard the earl and countess.

His father had retained a trim figure despite his advanced age of forty-nine, which only his graying black hair revealed. His mother topped her husband by a good two inches and, with her blond curls (which she carefully dyed, though she rigorously denied this) and perfectly oval face, had long been one of the ton's acknowledged beauties. Both were determined to advance in the world. Fitz had always known they meant to use him to do so, but never had he imagined it would be through a forced marriage. Templeton's letter was nothing to this! "What have you arranged?" he asked through dry lips.

"That's my boy!" said the earl jovially.

"You are to court Lady Sarah at every opportunity this summer," the countess informed her son with a certain self-satisfaction. She had always known this conversation would go her way. "Your engagement will be announced in four weeks' time. You will marry in the fall. I doubt if you will find any of the arrangements an inconvenience to you. Lady Sarah's dowry is so vast that even *you* cannot lose all of it at Watier's."

Fitz bristled at this. "I've had a dashed good run of luck at Watier's lately."

"That, of course, is music to any mother's ears."

"You'll be the envy of every young buck in the ton," Lord Lavesly exulted. "The daughter of a duke is quite a prize."

"We intend," the countess added, "for you to make the best use of such an opportunity, Fitzwilliam. It is now in your power to assure the wealth and position of your own family. Why, with your new connections, I wouldn't be surprised if the Laveslys are elevated to a dukedom in the next twenty or thirty years."

"Yes, by God," said the earl, glowing with secret plans. "We'll show the Haute Ton what kind of blood runs in *our* veins."

The Laveslys prattled on and on about the social heights they intended to reach riding on their son's coattails, while Fitz stood ashen and numb before the horrors of impending matrimony.

Charlisle's guests settled into their rooms with far less distress than Sarah and their reluctant host. The bellicose and unwieldy Dowager Formantle—exhausted from the exertions of travel and the climb upstairs—spent a mere quarter hour harrying her maid in the disposition of her wardrobe, jewels, and other personal effects. Out of general principle, she spent another quarter hour hectoring her son, George, and daughter-in-law, Susan, and then took to her bed for a well-deserved nap.

Blissfully freed from her iron grip for at least two hours, and possibly more, George and Susan Formantle escaped outside to explore Charlisle's fine gardens and share a rare afternoon of privacy and pleasure.

Also joining Sarah in the west wing was Mr. Freddy Braithwaite, who found himself rooming beside his sister, Corliss. This suited him perfectly, for these siblings were fond of each other. More to the point, their parents—Friday-faced harpies, according to their impertinent offspring—were housed a good mile off in the east wing of the house. There was every chance Freddy and Corliss would have to be in company with the dreaded Mr. and Mrs. Braithwaite only at meals.

Mr. Beaumont Davis, though placed in a rather small room at the north end of the house, was perfectly satisfied with his

18

accommodations, for there was a writing desk directly before a window, and this window looked out upon lush gardens and meadows that were already inspiring several odes in his brain. Mr. Davis was a poet who shunned masculine pursuits—to his father's disgust—in quest of beauty—to his mother's delight.

Housed in the east wing, his parents—Lord Franklyn and Lady Julia Merbles—were singularly ill suited to each other. He had been captured by youth and beauty and a decent fortune. She had been captured by a title. They quickly discovered they had nothing in common. Indeed, they disagreed on every topic and on every question regarding their son's upbringing. As Lady Merbles was a lovely and tenderhearted woman, and Lord Merbles was a hard-drinking and often grim gentleman, Beaumont had quite naturally entered his mother's camp at an early age and, despite the continual sneers and taunts of his father, saw no reason to leave it.

Lord Cyril Pontifax—who seldom had two guineas to rub together—joined Mr. Davis in the north wing. His room, too, was small, but he had no complaint. He was in a large, comfortable house, with food and wine for the asking and several wealthy young women—Sarah Thorndike not the least of them—who might, with judicious wooing, end his habitual poverty once and for all.

Also in the north wing were Miss Fanny Neville, a pretty blonde, Lord and Lady Danvers, a charming couple in their early thirties, and the generally unpleasant Sir Marcus Templeton, who found nothing to like in his room and demanded an immediate replacement. Among the rest of the company were Lord and Lady Doherty. They were Sarah's only hope for respite from the trials this summer promised. Lady Charlotte, a brunette, with fine dark eyes, was Sarah's oldest and dearest friend. She was also seven months pregnant. Lord Phineas, the responsible party in this case, had had the great good sense to marry Charlotte a year and a half earlier, and she had insisted from the outset that her best friend and her husband must be best friends as well. There was little difficulty in this. Both Sarah and Phineas loved Charlotte, both were intelligent, well-informed, and possessed a lively sense of humor. Charlotte's happiness was assured.

But her happiness was not universal at Charlisle. The servants—male and female—were all in a dither. Their former master—the viscount's maternal grandfather—had died four years earlier, and they had been left quite alone ever since. Though they had had ample warning to prepare the house and themselves for the summer onslaught, it was still a shock to be suddenly scurrying in all directions, catering to some of the most important and demanding members of the ton, running upstairs and downstairs and then back upstairs again, with seldom a moment to catch their breath.

"And I was told the country life was peaceful!" exclaimed one of the newer additions to the household, a young footman named Earnshaw.

"You were misled," said Jack, as he supervised Earnshaw and two other footmen in the setting of the mammoth dinner table, "at least for this summer."

He disliked how easy it had been to assume a servant's mantle once again. Edinburgh and Portugal might never have been, save for the soul-weariness that haunted him. Nor had he anticipated the unappetizing crew now ordering him and his staff about with a high-handedness that made his blood boil. Fitz had been vague about Charlisle's guest list, and Jack was now suffering the consequences. All of his worst opinions of the ton had been confirmed a scant hour after it had descended on Charlisle.

"Mr. Rawlins," called Mrs. Clarke, Charlisle's housekeeper, as she bustled into the room, two maids in tow. She was a plump and cheerful woman in her late forties. "Lady Winster is asking for you."

Jack manfully suppressed a groan. He had been fending off Lady Winster's ilk since he was fifteen. "Thank you, Mrs. Clarke. Gentlemen," he said to the footmen, "you will continue with your work. I will return in the quarter hour to inspect your progress."

He left the dining room without pleasure. He had not been thinking of the dangers posed by women of Lady Winster's stamp when he had decided to undertake this masquerade on young Hornsby's behalf. He had not thought he would be serving a duke so like his own father in temperament that Jack felt himself become invisible whenever he was in Somerton's presence. Nor had he thought that any member of the Haute Ton could lead him into indiscretion.

Lady Sarah Thorndike, however, had caught him unawares, making him actually forget for several treacherous minutes the reserve that a servant's upbringing and war had made natural. Her wan expression as she stood in the hallway that morning must have reminded him of the desperate souls he had met on the Peninsula and that was why he had reacted so unaccountably. The spoiled daughter of a rich and powerful duke could not have known a moment's trouble her entire life. He had no reason to feel sorry for anyone who had enjoyed the best of everything from the day of her birth. She had been pale because she was dieting or was hungover or was one of those silly girls prone to the vapors.

Her amiability must have had an ulterior purpose. Her unexpected whimsy was a fluke. He should not have let her make him forget who she was and who he was and what his purpose was in this house. That he should let her first touch and then amuse him! Because of some rattlepated ninnyhammer, he had let down his guard and nearly jeopardized his efforts on Fitz's behalf. Thank God, she had recalled him to the facts of his life. Thank God, he had had the sense to pull back quickly before he had done any further damage to his chosen role. Lacing hot chocolate with brandy indeed! He was thoroughly acquainted with young ladies of *her* stamp. He would not forget himself again.

*

Chapter 2

LADY SARAH THORNDIKE and the Viscount Lyleton came face-to-face for the first time at dinner that night. Each was horrified. Fitz found that his future bride was a girl of medium height with red hair, bleak blue eyes, and more than a smattering of *freckles*! He shuddered inwardly. He would never live this down at Watier's. There was, moreover, a certain strength in her chin that boded ill. He pictured himself living under the sign of the cat's foot, forced to abandon all of his pleasures for the narrow, steady course his parents had long insisted upon.

For her part, Sarah beheld the realization of every horror story she had ever heard about the viscount. He was undoubtedly a beautiful young man. But that beauty was almost entirely disguised by the mass of black ringlets so elaborately styled on his head and the foppish clothes covering his decent figure. His shirt collar points were projected well up on his cheeks. A corset had narrowed his waist. His blue frock coat was so tightly cut, it was a wonder he could move his arms at all. His knee breeches of pale pink silk were staggering to behold. And rather than white silk stockings, his were a powder blue to match his coat! The superb execution of this amazing costume could only have been accomplished by placing himself into his valet's hands for a good two hours prior to dinner.

With one glance, Sarah found that her future husband was a Bartholomew baby, a park saunterer, the antithesis of everything she had ever longed for in a mate.

They sat down beside each other at the long dining table, labored to find something, anything, to say to each other, and failed miserably. The twenty-six other people at dinner were

22

far less tongue-tied. Lord Roger and Lady Penelope Danvers were flattering their dinner partners and trotting out the delightful stories that always made them so popular at these social functions. The very loud Dowager Formantle was haranguing George and Susan on their singular refusal to provide her with a grandchild after nearly a year of marriage.

Beaumont Davis, his romantically long blond hair tumbling frequently into his face, was quoting some of his newest verses to his dinner partner, Miss Fanny Neville, who was wholly uninterested, for on her other side was seated Sir Marcus Templeton. Every inch a muscular, robust *man* (as opposed to the willowy Mr. Davis), he offered proof of his masculinity by describing a boar hunt in which he had been gored in the leg.

Freddy and Corliss Braithwaite were engaged in an animated conversation about who among their relatives was the most disagreeable. Lady Charlotte and Lord Phineas Doherty, though well past their honeymoon, were still generally oblivious to the people around them.

In the midst of these and many other conversations, as dish after dish was paraded through the dining room by a multitude of liveried and bewigged footmen, Sarah and Fitz sat mute and miserable, each unable to tolerate more than a bite or two of food. Sarah at first thought herself rescued by Lord Cyril Pontifax, who was seated on her left and wholly inclined to engage her in conversation. His naturally curly brown hair was styled to rakish effect, he had a good figure that was clothed without the extremes of fashion paraded by the viscount, and he was adept at weaving flattery into any story he told.

Pleasure, however, quickly turned to suspicion by the fifth course. Lord Pontifax had developed the rather distasteful habit of warmly clasping her hand during his more and more frequent praises of her sparkling blue eyes, charm, character, and intellect. Suddenly, Sarah remembered a few choice tidbits about Lord Pontifax.

He came from a good family that had run through its fortune generations ago. His connections at Oxford and his wealthy godfather's good graces had introduced him to a host of rich and reckless young men, who were more than happy to put him up entirely at their own expense whenever he chose to visit them. Only last year, Charlotte had warned Sarah against Lord Pontifax, calling him a wastrel and a fortune hunter. Watching him now, Sarah could only admire her friend's foresight. She turned, almost with relief, back to her future husband.

"I understand, my lord, that you have one of the best stables in all of England," she ventured, though she had often heard the viscount derided for buying flash not substance.

"Oh, I daresay there are half a dozen stables its equal or better," Fitz glumly replied. His stomach roiled, and he pushed away his plate of aspic.

"Do you attend the races?"

"Good God, who doesn't?"

Sarah was startled into a smile. "My parents disapprove of females attending such sporting exhibitions."

"Oh, well, *females*—" said Fitz. He searched around for even one more word that might be added.

Sarah, too, was racking her brain.

"More wine, my lady?"

Sarah looked up to find the icily impassive Rawlins standing at her elbow. "Thank you, no," she replied with equal chill. She'd need her wits about her if she was to escape this evening unscathed. Rawlins moved on to Lord Merbles as she looked rather helplessly at Lord Lyleton. "I . . . um . . . I understand the Americans are breeding a new horse for light carriage and saddle work. They call it a Morgan."

"The Americans," sniffed Fitz, "wouldn't know decent horseflesh if it walked up and bit them. Arabians and Thoroughbreds are the only horses worth talking about."

"Is that the newest fashion in neck cloths?" Sarah rather desperately inquired, as she gazed at the yards of cloth wrapped so lovingly around his throat.

She could not have chosen a better topic. "Indeed it is," the viscount said, preening a bit. "It's called the Rosebud. All the Bond Street beaux are mad for it, but none have the knack of tying it just right." He thereupon launched into a twenty-minute explanation of how the Rosebud, in all its intricacies, was to be properly pressed, tied, folded, and shaped.

Sarah gazed at him all the while with a mixture of horror and disbelief, which finally turned to amusement. The viscount *was* a Jack-at-warts, just as Lady Jersey had once reported to her, but he was a sweet boy for all that. If only she didn't have to face spending the rest of her life with him, she might actually begin to enjoy his conversation, for she had always delighted in the absurd.

After several hours, and several more courses, the party at last rose from the dining table. The men retired to Charlisle's library for port and cigars, the ladies walked into the main drawing room, a sumptuous affair of white and gold with over a dozen vases filled with summer blooms. Sarah, however, could not enjoy this respite, for her mother claimed her company for a good quarter hour, during which she impressed upon Sarah in no uncertain terms the effort she was to make to win Lord Lyleton's affection when the gentlemen rejoined them.

She was then captured and bludgeoned by the Dowager Formantle, who demanded in a voice that carried across the room and out into the garden to know why Sarah persisted at being unmarried at such an advanced age as one-and-twenty. She was then passed over to Lady Penelope Danvers, who declared that she was enthralled by Sarah's simple strand of pearls, claimed she'd never seen better, and launched into a discussion of Lady Corelgate, a notorious gamester, who had through the years sold off all of her jewels to pay her debts, replacing them with paste replicas that were so badly done she was becoming the laughingstock of the ton.

A headache throbbed at Sarah's temples. She had but five minutes to claim some peace with Charlotte before the gentlemen entered the drawing room, laughing loudly among themselves, a few still smoking their cigars, while others indulged themselves in delicate pinches of snuff.

"Do try some of my sort, Your Grace," said Lord Danvers to the Duke of Somerton. "It is really something out of the ordinary."

The duke eyed the offered snuff with some caution and took a delicate pinch.

"No one can sway my godson from the wretched girl's

25

side," Lord Merbles was mournfully informing Lord Phineas Doherty. "A cleric's daughter. A *cleric's*! Like Virgil, I have mourned: 'Ah, Corydon, Corydon, what madness has caught you?' "

"And Horace has your answer," Lord Doherty replied with a grin. He looked unerringly across the room at his wife. His smile gentled. " 'Happy, thrice happy and more, are they whom an unbroken bond unites and whose love shall know no sundering quarrels so long as they shall live.' "

"I tell you, Freddy," Fitz was saying to Mr. Braithwaite the younger, "Brummell has grown old and stale. The Rosebud will sweep the ton, you mark my words."

A baleful glare from the duchess nudged Sarah forward. She reluctantly, and as slowly as she dared, made her way toward Lyleton's side. Halfway there, however, she chanced to overhear Mr. Beaumont Davis, whom she did not know, quoting Andrew Marvell to Miss Corliss Braithwaite, whom she did know.

" 'As lines, so loves oblique, may well / Themselves in every corner greet; / But ours, so truly parallel, / Though infinite, can never meet,' " Mr. Davis rhapsodized.

"Actually," Sarah intervened, "it's 'As lines, so loves oblique, may well / Themselves in every *angle* greet.' "

Mr. Davis forgot his Byronesque posings so much as to actually turn on her with eager green eyes (he normally made them droop, much to his father's disgust). "Yes, by heaven, you are right! Do you know Marvell?"

"I have studied him a little," Sarah conceded.

"He's just being rediscovered, you know. I like him well enough, but he's nothing, of course, to the god Byron."

"Ah," said Sarah, and sighed inwardly. Unlike so many of her sex, she had not been swept away by *Childe Harold's Pilgrimage* or its posturing author. Mr. Davis, on the other hand, had the burnished eye of a rabid disciple. "Do you follow Byron's work?" she ventured.

It was all the encouragement the resident poet needed. For the next twenty minutes, while Miss Braithwaite (who was not poetical) eagerly made her escape, Mr. Davis quoted poem after poem to Sarah, explaining each line, enthusing over each phrasing, until Sarah began to feel her eyes glaze over. She was rescued, just as Mr. Davis began to recite the first canto of *Childe Harold*, by Lord Cyril Pontifax, who claimed a previous engagement with Sarah and triumphantly carried her off to the other side of the room.

"I feel like a knight in shining armor rescuing a fair damsel in distress," he declared. "Though that Davis is far from being a dragon. The way he affects a limp when his legs are as sound as mine!" (Lord Pontifax was particularly proud of his legs, which were beautifully shaped and had often been admired in the ton.) "I might just as well put on a blindfold and call myself Homer."

Sarah could not help but smile. "He's merely a boy in love with words," she replied, watching Rawlins pass by with a physical grace she was quite certain servants weren't supposed to possess.

"You are too generous, Lady Sarah, but that is hardly a fault in your sex. In truth, it is a blessing for such rough louts as myself who are of a lesser race and know it. Would to God that Davis fellow knew his place."

Sarah now regarded Lord Pontifax from under hooded eyes. "And just what is his place, my lord?"

"Why, in the schoolroom with the rest of the children!" Lord Pontifax stated, laughing at his own wit.

"Lady Sarah?"

Sarah looked around to find Rawlins regarding her, his handsome face forbiddingly impassive. "Yes?"

"The duchess asked that I remind you of the promise you made her earlier this evening."

"Ah. Yes. Thank you, Rawlins," Sarah said gratefully. Even Lyleton was preferable to her current company. "You will forgive me, Lord Pontifax, but I must attend to another matter."

"Adieu, for now, then," said his lordship, catching her reluctant hand in his and raising it to his lips.

She hurriedly escaped him and thrust herself into the midst of the company before she had even determined where Lord Lyleton could be found. She began a methodical search through the glittering throng, but was soon distracted by the curious actions of one Bigby, a stocky young footman who was weaving toward her, a tray of filled wineglasses precariously balanced on one hand. His cheeks were ruddy, his gaze unfocused. She knew the signs all too well. He had been tippling, and before him loomed the Laveslys and imminent disaster.

She would have to act quickly. She placed herself between the Laveslys, knocking them to either side, and directly in Bigby's uncertain path. The rest was inevitable. The footman collided with her, his tray falling to the floor with a resounding crash that silenced every conversation and drew every eye in the room to her.

"Oh! How clumsy of me!" Sarah cried. "I do beg your pardon, Bigby. It was entirely my fault. I must have tripped."

"I'll clean it up at once, my lady," Bigby declared, beginning to bend down.

Sarah desperately grabbed his arm and hauled him upright. Her experience of inebriated gentlemen during her three London Seasons had left her well versed in the effects of too much alcohol. If Bigby stooped over, he would fall and never get back up.

Rawlins materialized at her side. "Is there some difficulty, my lady?" he coolly inquired.

"The man is drunk!" Sarah said in an urgent undertone. "You must get him out of the drawing room at once before the Laveslys or my parents notice his intoxication."

Rawlins drew himself to his fullest height. "None of my staff would ever forget himself so much as to—"

"Well, Bigby has!" Sarah hissed. "He nearly threw that entire tray of wine at the Laveslys!"

"I'll clean up this mess, Mr. Rawlins, never you fear," Bigby cheerfully assured the butler.

Rawlins's expression was glacial. Like Sarah, he could not have missed the smell of wine on the footman's breath. His hand snaked around Bigby's upper arm in what was apparently a most painful grip. "You will come with me, Bigby, to fetch the necessary implements."

He dragged the footman off, leaving Sarah to turn apologetically to the Laveslys, and her grim parents, who had joined them. "I am so very sorry, Lord Lavesly, Countess," she said in all sincerity. "I have never been so clumsy. It was disgraceful of me to bump into you like that. I hope you will accept my abject apology."

The countess smoothed back a curl. "Accidents will happen," she said frostily.

"It was unforgivable of you, Sarah!" her mother admonished.

"The whole room was staring at you," said the duke.

"I only hope Fitzwilliam did not take the wrong impression from your unaccountable behavior," said the Earl of Lavesly.

"I am certain the viscount is too good a man to hold this one incident against me," Sarah said humbly.

As Earnshaw and a parlor maid had appeared and begun to clean up the mess from the wrecked wine tray, the Laveslys and the Somertons turned away to try to save this difficult situation through conversation. A quick glare from the corner of her mother's eye reminded Sarah of her original purpose in crossing the room. She was supposed to attach herself to Lyleton's side. There was only one problem: She couldn't find him anywhere.

Rawlins, however, was an easier matter, for his height and the breadth of his shoulders set him apart from the other men in the room.

"Rawlins," she said, when she had reached his side.

He sent away the footman he had been instructing and turned to regard her. "Yes, my lady?"

Sarah wanted to stamp her foot. Never had she known such an aloof man! And after all she had just done for him, too. "Would you be so good as to have someone bring me a small glass of brandy? I will be with the Viscount Lyleton . . . wherever he is."

"He is standing by the Ming dynasty vase a few yards to your left. You are in further need of . . . soothing, my lady?"

Wholly surprised, Sarah looked up with an unconscious smile that quickly faded. There was something of disdain in his eyes. "Yes," she said quietly, and turned away.

She stood with Fitz for the next hour, struggling to create a conversation neither one of them wanted to engage in. Finally, the Dowager Formantle demanded card tables, and Sarah was saved, but not by the dowager. The Dohertys urged Sarah to play at their table; Freddy Braithwaite, whom she had known since her debut, insisted on partnering her; and Corliss requested that Lord Lyleton join her at another card table at the opposite end of the room.

There was nothing her parents could do about this arrangement except cast Sarah an occasional grim glance. For her part, Sarah spent the rest of the evening thanking her friends over and over for their kind auspices on her behalf and carrying almost every hand she played.

She was able to return to her room, therefore, in an equitable mood. True, the Laveslys nudged Lyleton to her side to escort her upstairs along with the other guests retiring for the night, but that was tolerable. She and the viscount discussed the cards they had been holding minutes before. He bowed to her when they reached the Rose Suite, she curtsied, and that was that.

She heard his sigh of relief as he turned to escape to his own room. It was as hearty as her own. "Poor boy," she thought. "He is just as miserable and trapped as I am."

Maria was waiting for her, taking her shawl while Sarah sat at her dressing table and removed her earrings, pearl necklace, and bracelet. Maria then handed her her habitual evening cup of hot chocolate. Just as Sarah took a grateful sip, there was a sharp rap on the door that both knew too well. Maria hurriedly hid the cup behind jars of lotion and bottles of perfume on the dressing table as the Duchess of Somerton swept into the room wearing a magnificent dressing gown of blue brocade. The duchess disapproved of between-meal sweets.

"Ah, there you are, Sarah," she said. "Danon has made you a new freckle wash. You will begin using it tonight."

"Yes, Mother," Sarah quietly replied, taking the lotion her mother's maid had prepared.

"You will see to it, Jenkins," the duchess sternly informed Maria.

"Certainly, Your Grace," said Maria with a curtsy.

The duchess placed two regal fingers beneath Sarah's chin

and tilted her head up. She scrutinized her daughter carefully, and then sighed. "If only you had Arabella's bone structure."

"I'm sorry, Mother," Sarah replied. She had heard the complaint many times before.

"Or even Frances's nose," the duchess said, removing her fingers from Sarah's chin. "There is no distinctive quality to your face. Certainly, no brilliance to your skin. Your teeth are good, I grant you. And the color of your eyes is rather fine. But as for the rest . . ." The duchess sighed again and looked her youngest daughter over from head to toe. "An adequate figure, I suppose, but really, Sarah, when will you learn to hold yourself with that air of superiority that so distinguishes the Somertons from everyone else?"

"I am sorry, Mother."

"Perhaps marriage will impart those qualities you have so singularly failed to adopt thus far. I will leave you. Don't forget the freckle wash."

The duchess was gone. Sarah and Maria regarded each other a moment.

"The last time we used Danon's freckle wash, it burned your face," Maria said.

"I remember," Sarah replied with a sigh. "We'll continue to use Dr. Withering's cosmetic lotion and pretend that we are using the freckle wash. We'd best take a little out of the bottle each night, just in case Danon comes snooping."

"And she will."

"But only on Mother's orders."

"No distinctive quality indeed," Maria said with a sniff. "Why, you've more quality—"

"And more freckles."

"—than any other girl in the house." Maria stopped and suddenly laughed. "Drink up your hot chocolate and to bed with you."

"Yes, Maria," Sarah said fondly.

*

Chapter 3

OF CHARLISLE'S TWELVE footmen and twenty-three maids, only seven were present in the servants' hall, quietly taking their tea before the next flurry of activity struck. All glanced surreptitiously at Jack as he strode from his small sitting room and joined them at the table. From his first day at the country estate, rumors had been rampant among the staff about his background and taciturn nature.

Whatever his background, though, his beauty and the power he wielded in the household commanded every servant's attention. The female staff artfully posed themselves to catch his eye, while the male staff, who were his purview, racked their brains to see if they had somehow left a task uncompleted. Mr. Rawlins had sharp eyes. The senior parlor maid—Lizzie Benton—was present, and so it fell to her to pour Jack a cup of tea.

"Here you are, Mr. Rawlins." She handed him the cup with a flirtatious smile, the other girls jealously watching her. "Nice and hot."

"Thank you, Benton," Jack replied, scarcely glancing at her.

Mrs. Clarke bustled into the hall from the kitchen. "That French chef the Laveslys installed has finally brought some order to the place," she said gratefully, as she seized upon a teacup. "I wasn't sure he had it in him."

"There was only the language barrier to overcome," Jack said dryly. "A few boxed ears soon resolved the matter. Mrs. Clarke, might I have a word?"

"Certainly, Mr. Rawlins." The housekeeper took the empty chair on his right. Happily married to the head coachman, she had no need to earn the butler's admiration. Jack, therefore, enjoyed her company with a tremendous sense of relief.

"This morning," he said, "I chanced to overhear the Duchess of Somerton reproving two parlor maids for giggling and gossiping together as they worked in the Green Saloon."

"The Kiley sisters, no doubt," said Mrs. Clarke, nodding.

"The same. I hope you will speak to them."

"Within the hour, Mr. Rawlins. They're some of the village girls I've taken on for the summer and not yet fully trained in their posts, I fear."

"From what I have seen, they do good work. It is their manner only that needs correcting. I've a similar problem," he said, directing a stern glance at Bigby, seated at the opposite end of the table, "among some of my own staff."

"It's the previous lack of employment that's done the mischief, I'll warrant."

"And the often onerous duties imposed by Charlisle's guests," Jack added.

"I've never seen such a collection of brittle-tempered people in all me life," remarked Bigby, trying to draw the attention of the pretty parlor maid beside him away from Jack. "They've none of them a kind word to say to themselves, let alone us."

"Now, now, it's not so bad," said the girl, reluctantly turning toward him. "There's some it's an actual pleasure to serve."

"Name one," Bigby said.

"Lord and Lady Doherty, that's two," the maid retorted. "And Lady Sarah Thorndike always has a kind word to say."

Jack pricked up his ears at this, for Sarah Thorndike had unaccountably been on his mind since their first meeting. He had convinced himself that her amiability *then* meant that she intended to flirt with him during the summer, perhaps even pursue him as Lady Winster did.

But she had not.

Her friendliness had continued as a matter of course with all of the servants, save him. With him, she was cool and withdrawn. He could not but consider her manner with him a deliberate snub. The thought rankled, particularly as he peered down the table at Earnshaw, who was always running errands for her and laughing at whatever jests she uttered for his ears only.

"I've heard," said an upstairs maid, "that she's to marry the viscount!"

"We've *all* heard that," said Bigby. "Why else is the viscount sunk into a fit of the blue devils? And I don't blame him, poor man. Who'd want to marry a plain, freckle-faced girl like her?"

"Why, you rag-mannered oaf!" Jack erupted from the head of the table. "Last night that *girl* selflessly saved you from immediate dismissal. She deserves far more from you, Bigby, than cutting remarks and mean-spirited slurs. Do not forget that I have placed you on probation. You will remember your position and the civil tongue that goes with it."

Every servant at the table stared at him in amazement. Jack found that he was equally amazed. Where on earth had that tirade come from? Why had he, of all people, defended the spoiled daughter of the Duke of Somerton, when she was no different from any of them?

She was demure to the point of blandness. She had lived in ease and comfort all of her life, pampered and sheltered, every whim catered to. And *she* was to marry Fitz. Jack shook his head. A proper young woman forever doing her parents' bidding, one who agreed with whatever was said by the company in which she found herself, was to marry Fitz Hornsby.

She would ruin him, that was clear enough. Any daughter of the Somertons must dislike Fitz's exuberant pleasures of wardrobe, gambling, and stable of Cleveland machiners. She would make him old by his next birthday; a sad prediction, for the viscount had a certain *joie de vivre* that was contagious. . . . Not now, of course. Now Fitz was wholly downcast and much of the cause could be laid at Sarah Thorndike's door. Already she seemed to be hounding the poor fellow. She was seldom from his side.

Realizing that he was still the center of attention in the servants' hall, Jack rose from his chair. "You will none of you gossip about the personal lives of those we serve. Now, I suggest we all get back to work."

A bell from Lady Winster's room rang imperiously once, twice. Jack looked at it and sighed. He left the hall without a word, followed by eight pairs of knowing eyes.

It was the knowing glances directed at her by every guest every minute of the day that upset Sarah most.

"I am going mad," she informed Charlotte Doherty, "and in public, which is even worse."

"It must be very trying," Charlotte sympathetically replied, as they walked arm in arm through the western rose garden.

"I've been at Charlisle only three days," Sarah grimly continued. "How is it that everyone, even the servants, seems to know that Lyleton has been ordered to court, win, and wed me?"

"I believe the Laveslys have not been entirely circumspect in their conversations with their guests."

"Nor have my parents been precisely subtle in maneuvering Lyleton and me together at the least provocation," Sarah muttered. "It's all so embarrassing."

"Now, now, there's nothing shameful about two people being brought together to wed," Charlotte said bracingly. "It happens all the time, and often in public. At least everyone knows about it sooner or later."

"What would the ton be without gossip?"

"Precisely. My advice to you, my girl, is to buck up. Don't let those prattle-boxes get you down. Show them what you're made of."

"Freckles, mostly," Sarah retorted.

"Yes, and pride and common sense. Put them to good use. Charlisle's guests can't disturb you if you refuse to let them do so."

"That's true enough."

"Besides, you haven't looked as if you were withering away in Lyleton's company."

Sarah smiled at that. "He is the silliest and perhaps the sweetest boy I've ever met. From what I can tell, he has a complete horror of marriage, and from what I've seen of his parents, I don't blame him."

"There, you see?" Charlotte said triumphantly. "Already you have at least one thing in common."

Sarah's smile faded. "But little else, I'm afraid. He knows nothing of politics or poetry, Charlotte. He has no knowledge of how his own household is run. He has little understanding of why we are at war with America. Why, he even claims to dislike Shakespeare because it's too hard to understand the fellow!"

"He is not your intellectual equal."

"Even that I could withstand," Sarah remarked, her fingers brushing against a full red bloom. "But he's such a . . . such a *boy*, and I want a *man* for a husband, Charlotte, not some child-groom to raise with my own infants."

"Yet Lyleton *is* sweet, and I know your generous heart too well, Sarah, not to believe that you could form an affection for the . . . boy."

"I daresay I could, if he were intended as a friend. But I am more and more convinced that we would make each other miserable as husband and wife."

As she had come to the same conclusion herself, Lady Doherty could make no reply to this.

Nor, for a moment, could Jack think of anything to say as he rounded a tall hedge and stood facing the feminine pair. Fond as he was of Fitz, he had to agree with Lady Sarah's assessment of his friend. But how was he to reconcile the conversation he had just overheard with his initial impression of this ducal daughter? She was wholly different in this garden from what she had been in company these last three days, and he couldn't understand why.

As for Sarah, she could not hold back the blush creeping into her cheeks. Had Rawlins heard her insult his master by calling Fitz "boy"? A quick glance at his shuttered eyes told her all. He had. Her blush deepened.

"Yes, Rawlins?" Charlotte said into the uncomfortable silence.

The cool mask was once again firmly in place. "I beg your pardon, ladies. I was looking for Sir Marcus Templeton."

"I believe he is touring the greenhouse with Miss Neville and Lady Danvers," Charlotte replied.

"Thank you," the butler said with a slight bow, before turning on his heels and decamping.

"I wish I knew what I've done to make him so stiff and cold in my company," Sarah remarked, her brow furrowed as she watched him walk off.

"Now, now, I'm sure it has nothing to do with you, Sarah," Charlotte assured her.

"Lady Sarah!"

The two young women turned to find Maria trotting up to them, a parasol in hand. Sarah groaned.

"Mother has been spying?" she asked Maria.

"From her sitting room window," Maria replied, a suspicious gleam in her eyes. "The duchess asked that I bring you this parasol, my lady, as you have so unaccountably forgotten to wear a hat in this sun."

Sarah shook her head at the maid. "I would freckle in the darkest, dankest dungeon, Maria."

"But as the duchess is undoubtedly still observing you—" Maria said, holding out the parasol.

Sarah hurriedly took the parasol, holding it aloft to shield her from her further scrutiny.

"Perhaps you can solve a riddle, Maria," said Charlotte. "Does Rawlins bear Sarah any enmity?"

"No, my lady."

"There, you see, Sarah?"

"But why does he seem to dislike me so?" Sarah demanded.

"It's nought to do with you, my lady," said her maid. "He is cold and taciturn with everyone he serves or supervises. Still, if I were but a few years younger, I'd be setting my cap for Mr. Rawlins just now and make no mistake."

Charlotte laughed. "He is a most attractive man. I suppose the female servants are all aflutter over him?"

"Half of them swoon whenever he enters a room, and the other half lie in wait, hoping to trap him into private conversation. I'll give him this: He seems wonderfully adept at avoiding each and every feminine lure cast his way."

Sarah found this oddly cheering. "What sort of man is he, do you think, Maria?"

"Mr. Rawlins is not what I would consider a happy man, my lady," her maid answered.

"You think him unhappy?" Sarah crinkled her brow at this unexpected pronouncement. "I thought he just enjoyed nabbing the rust."

"I doubt if he finds pleasure in anything, my lady. He's always keeping to himself," Maria said as they began to walk back toward the house. "He makes no attempt at friendship with any of us and spends his off-duty time in his room reading, from all that I can gather."

"And to what do you attribute this solitary and unhappy character?" Charlotte inquired.

"Mr. Rawlins doesn't like the people he serves," Maria declared.

"A serious problem for a man in his position," Charlotte conceded.

"Perfectly understandable, of course," Sarah said, unhappily twirling the handle of her parasol. She had not been mistaken, then. He was critical of her. "There is nothing to admire and very little to like in the lot of us."

"Now, now, you're just feeling cross because Lord Pontifax and Mr. Davis insist on thrusting themselves into your company at the least provocation," Charlotte said with a smile.

"I have never in my life been so popular," Sarah agreed with a sigh, "and I don't like it. I was meant for the simple, quiet life, Charlotte, not this parade down Bachelor's Row."

"The summer won't last forever, my dear," Charlotte said, squeezing her friend's slim waist.

"Oh, don't say that! I wish it would last an eternity, because at summer's end I am intended as a bridal sacrifice upon the pyres of my parents' touching determination to be rid of me for good."

"I wonder which is the worse fate," Charlotte ventured, "to be confined by parental rule and ordered about as if you were no better than a scullion, or to live in your husband's house and undoubtedly act very much as you choose?"

"Why must you be sensible in the midst of my Cheltenham tragedy?" Sarah demanded as Maria held open the west door for them.

"I just think it's important to remind you that there are different ways to regard your situation, if you choose."

"Were you always so reasonable and clever before you married?"

"Indeed, yes," her friend said with a laugh. "You just weren't desperate enough to notice before."

"Blast!" said Mr. Braithwaite the elder in the midst of the après-dinner drawing room throng. "My man forgot to refill my snuffbox." He thrust the heavy gold bauble back into his coat pocket.

"Allow me to offer you some of my snuff," said the solicitous Lord Danvers. "It is my own recipe, and I flatter myself that it is not too indifferent."

Mr. Braithwaite helped himself to a pinch of snuff from the gold box. He sniffed appreciatively. "Why, 'tis excellent, Danvers! I congratulate you."

Lord Danvers bowed. "You are too kind, sir. If you would like, I can send my man 'round to your rooms with a sufficient supply."

"I wouldn't want to deplete your stores."

"Nonsense! I always travel with three or four jars of different snuff. Lady Danvers is forever tweaking me about it. I could draw on those jars for a year and still have plenty left for my friends."

Mr. Braithwaite took the glass of port he had requested from a tray that Jack extended to him. "I thank you, Danvers. Send your man 'round anytime. I'm fond of Hardman's '37 myself. This is very like it."

Jack glided through the crowd, frustrated that his duties were keeping him from making a thorough search of Templeton's room. Butlering demanded that he minutely observe his staff in the midst of the all the prattle that filled the air, his impassive expression firmly entrenched, even though he longed to bellow at the lot of them and demand that one of them, just one, say something of intelligence.

"Did you know," tittered Miss Fanny Neville to Sarah Thorndike, "that when she is in her private rooms, the Princess of Wales likes to sit before a fire and make wax models of His Royal Highness? Then she sticks *pins* into them until they finally melt away from the heat of the fire!"

"Princess Caroline is much aggrieved by her husband," Sarah mildly replied.

"No, no, *he* is the one who suffers!" Miss Neville riposted. "Prinny at least has the sense to wear a corset, whereas all of *her* fat flounders around in those gaudy costumes of hers. And the amount of rouge she uses! My dear, she could light up a room if all the candles were extinguished!"

Miss Neville laughed heartily at her own joke and—when Sarah excused herself to obey a parental summons—went off to repeat her witticism throughout the room.

Jack surreptitiously studied Sarah as he supervised his staff. The contrast with what she had been in the rose garden earlier and the demure young woman she presented now could not be greater. What could be the cause of so great a change?

"Ah, Sarah, there you are," said the Duchess of Somerton as her daughter approached. "I have just been telling Lord Lyleton of your great proficiency upon the pianoforte."

A soft blush suffused Sarah's cheeks. "Lord Lyleton is too wise, I know, not to regard with anything but suspicion the praises of a parent for a child. I am a competent performer, my lord, that is all."

"The duchess informs me that you also sing?" remarked the viscount, looking vastly uncomfortable.

"Usually for my own enjoyment. I see no reason to inflict my pleasure on others' ears."

"We must have a musical evening," the duchess announced, casting a swift, stern glance at her daughter.

"An . . . excellent suggestion," Fitz unhappily replied. He loathed musical evenings. "But how does one go about organizing such an event?"

"Perhaps I can help."

40

The trio turned to find Charlotte smiling at them. "I am always searching for some way to display my talents to the world," she continued.

"Sarah will help you plan the evening, of course," the duchess intoned, hiding her anger. She had meant for Sarah alone to organize the event and thus strengthen the general perception of her rightful claim to this house and its master.

"Yes, of course," Sarah murmured, desperately trying not to meet Charlotte's gaze, for she was convinced she would succumb to a fit of the giggles.

"I have always found," Lord Danvers was remarking to Mr. Braithwaite, "that the Turkish blends are too acrid."

"Princess Caroline," Miss Neville was saying with a titter to Susan Formantle a few feet away, "wears so much rouge that she could light up the whole of Drury Lane herself!"

"Self-absorbed, unthinking giglets and *twits*," Jack thought with the utmost disgust the next morning as he took his habitual predawn walk through Charlisle's lush gardens.

He shook his head with something like disbelief. Over two dozen people who spoke nothing but gossip and inconsequential chatter. They buttressed all of his worst opinions of the English aristocracy formed from a lifetime's service to and with them.

Jack, with a loan from Fitz, had entered the army as a lieutenant and been shocked to find, not glory or honor, but carnage and stupidity and the bestial treatment the common foot soldiers received at the hands of their aristocratic officers. They had been serfs, not soldiers. Wellington, upon taking command of the desertion-prone Peninsular forces, had termed his men "the scum of the earth" who had "enlisted for drink."

Jack had wanted to leave the army after only a year, but he believed he could not desert his men. It seemed he was the only officer interested in keeping them alive. Two years passed. Four. Five. And then had come San Miguel. Jack gasped as sudden nausea assailed him. San Miguel. Would he never rid his nightmares of that horror?

Despite all of his arguments, he had been ordered to attack

41

the French stronghold at that Portuguese town. More than half his men were slaughtered before the town—nearly destroyed by cannon fire—was finally taken. For the blood on his hands, he received a knighthood and an annual pension of fifteen hundred pounds a year. He quit the army that very day.

He had returned to England seeking sanctuary from violence and stupidity and looking for peace. He had found it on a modest Devonshire farm that he loved at first sight and purchased the same day.

How he longed to be there now, rather than trapped among people he had no reason to like and blithering conversation he could not tolerate. Even Sarah Thorndike . . . Jack stopped. Now, why should he single her out? She played the modest, demure young woman to perfection.

Jack stopped again. She *played* the role? He turned over in his mind the two faces she had presented yesterday: thoughtful, honest, and whimsical with Lady Doherty and the dutiful duke's daughter with everyone else. Jack caught his breath. She *had* been playacting! Whenever he had seen her in company with her parents, she had seemed to efface herself into the nearest wall. But with Lady Charlotte . . .

Jack stopped. Oh, what does it matter? He scowled. What did it matter if Sarah Thorndike *was* whimsical and knowledgeable and amiable and as unhappy as Fitz at being married off? What had any of that to do with him? She was a duke's daughter. He was a duke's son, yet their lives could not be more different, their advantages more disparate, their viewpoints more at odds. *She* had not been an outcast. *She* had not suffered the abuse he had known in service. *She* knew nothing of pain and privation and a heart deadened by war.

He had never cared a groat for any of her class—save Fitz—and he wasn't about to start now. Jack ruthlessly turned his thoughts to his present surroundings—the crisp clean air, the woods in which he now walked, the morning chatter of hundreds of birds. This blue sky, these trees, these birds were important, unlike Sarah Thorndike and the rest of that stiff-rumped crew. Slowly, the beauty all around returned him to a semblance of good humor. He was a gudgeon to cut up stiff over a pack of leather-heads who couldn't see past their fortunes and fashions. He hadn't cared a spangle for them before Charlisle, and he wouldn't let them put him out of humor now. He was a proper widgeon if he let it be otherwise.

The sound of hooves speeding over the ground turned him in time to see Sarah in a forest green riding habit galloping across the meadow to his right, as if the hounds of Hell were in close pursuit. She flew through the meadow and then up a grassy hill, moving with her horse as if they were one, her skill clear to any intelligent observer. She disappeared down the other side of the hill, and it was then that he saw a groom cantering after her on a bay gelding and seemingly in no hurry to catch her up anytime soon.

A curious performance.

Jack had never seen any tonnish female up and doing at such an early hour. Of course, it was always possible that Sarah Thorndike had not yet even been to bed—a much more likely explanation from his long experience of the ton.

Jack sighed and leaned back against a sturdy beech. He really must stop thinking about her. He studied the elegant scene before him. Sloping away from the woods in which he stood were Charlisle's formal eastern gardens, including a topiary garden. Directly in front of the estate was its Bath stone courtyard leading down into three terraces, each with a large fountain. These terraces ended at the tree-lined avenue that curved up to the front door. To the west of the house were lawns and gardens ending in orchards and rich pastureland. To the north lay formal gardens near the house and a faux Greek ruin, before pastures and hundreds of acres of fertile fields carried the landscape to the horizon. Behind him were some of the best woods in the country and a large, well-stocked lake now coming alive as the sunrise burst across the eastern horizon in a spectacular display that demanded his full attention.

"I had a letter from Arabella yesterday, Henry."

Jack turned in surprise to find Sarah and her groom riding side by side, less than twenty yards away from him, as they walked their horses back to Charlisle's stable. Jack hid himself behind a tree. He had no desire for company.

43

"How I wish I was more like Arabella," Sarah continued wistfully. "Perhaps my parents wouldn't despise me so much if I had her sweet temperament and much-praised bone structure."

"Now, now, my lady," said Henry, chuckling, "you've twice the heart of Lady Arabella and vastly more intelligence, and that counts for more than good bone structure any day."

Sarah smiled fondly at the groom. "Dear Henry, my staunchest supporter. Still, I would like to know a little of what Arabella feels. Every line of her letter was filled with the most complete happiness. It was such a pleasure to read."

"I trust Lady Arabella is well?" Henry asked.

"*Vastly* improved. The morning sickness has quite dissipated."

"Pity she doesn't have your mother's constitution. I doubt if the duchess even knew she was with child until her lying-in."

Sarah laughed. "An iron will and an iron constitution. I wish she had bestowed the former on me."

"Now, now," Henry chided, "you never give yourself enough credit. You're pluck to the backbone if you'd but let yourself know it."

"There's a rapper if ever I heard one. I'm so wretchedly timid I even disgust myself. You should have seen me last night, scuttling about trying to help my poor chambermaid with her toothache without being spied by my parents. I spend my life trying to avoid their charges of fraternizing with my so-called social inferiors, when the only honorable course is to stand up and tell them both that the servants I know are a better class of people than ever could be discovered in the ton! I am a mouse, Henry."

"You'll find yourself turning into a lion one of these days. You mark my words."

Their voices faded away as they moved farther down the field.

Jack leaned against a beech tree, frowning in puzzlement. It had been a singularly unusual conversation for the daughter of a duke to hold with a groom.

Chapter 4

"BLAST IT, JACK!" hissed Fitzwilliam Hornsby into the supposed butler's ear. "Why is it taking so long to pinch Aldora's letter? I'm going mad sitting at table with Templeton day in and day out while he smirks and winks at me and plans how to spend my money!"

Jack pulled Fitz aside so the Danverses could enter the breakfast room. "It is not the simple matter I had hoped," he replied in an undertone. "My household duties are more time-consuming than I had anticipated. And then there is Templeton's damnably persistent valet, who seems to be forever in his master's room. What little opportunity I've had to search for the letter has produced nothing save an unappetizing array of personal accoutrements."

"What can we do?"

"Demand that Templeton produce Aldora's letter this evening. If he cannot, throw him out of the house. If he can, I'll find some way to relieve him of his prize."

"Are you certain?" Fitz asked anxiously.

"When have I ever failed you?"

Fitz sagged with relief. "Then, I shan't worry about the matter any longer."

Jack was about to respond but caught sight of the Dowager Formantle advancing upon the breakfast room door. "I trust you had a pleasant night, my lady?" he asked her.

"Only if you like peacocks screeching at you for hours on end!" she trumpeted. "Have them removed from under my bedroom window, Rawlins, or I'll take a shotgun to them."

"Certainly, my lady," Jack murmured.

45

Fitz stared after the dowager. "It's a wonder you haven't run screaming back to Devonshire."

"I've been tempted on more than one occasion," Jack said with a grin.

"I don't know why you've stuck by me all these years."

"Don't you?"

"Haven't a clue."

True affection warmed Jack's countenance. "That is because you do not value yourself as you should, young Hornsby. You are the best friend a man could ask for. Your true amiability embraces even my poor company, your *joie de vivre* lightens my hard heart. You're the most loyal man I've ever met, and your absurd predicaments are a constant reminder not to regard life too seriously."

Fitz considered this. "I don't know whether to be flattered or affronted by that last one."

"Lyleton!" bellowed the Dowager Formantle from the far end of the breakfast room. "Stop your jabbering and get in here. We're all waiting on you."

Fitz cast a despairing glance up at Jack.

"Think of her as one of your absurd predicaments," Jack advised.

Groaning, Fitz walked into the breakfast room.

Sarah found herself surreptitiously studying Rawlins all that morning as he supervised activity in the breakfast room and later in the morning parlor. She chastised herself for not having done so before, for seeing only the wall and not the man. She concluded now that Maria had been right yesterday: He *was* unhappy, almost desperately so. She recognized it in him, because it was a part of her as well. Unhappiness had been growing in her breast for over a year now and showed no signs of abating. She knew how hard it was for Rawlins to be forever pretending in company to be someone he was not, because she was forced into the same painful deception. She understood how the idiocies of her class could grate on his nerves, for they grated on hers more and more.

No wonder, then, that he should be so terse with her as he

was with everyone else, or so aloof, when there was nothing to tempt him to come closer and everything to hold him back. Rather than being put off by his coldness, she should have been doing what she could to thaw it. With anyone else—servant or acquaintance—she would have done as much. Why hadn't she with Rawlins?

A blush crept into her cheeks, for the answer was clear enough. Her pride was at fault. She had been piqued that he seemed to disdain her. Pride was a terrible thing. It led to vanity and conceit and directly to the poor treatment of others; witness her studied coolness toward Rawlins.

This was intolerable. It could not continue. She had been wholly at fault, and she must make amends. Above all, she would watch and wait her chance to do him some good. Sarah had not set herself a very difficult task. There was an undeniable pleasure in watching Rawlins. Yes, he was handsome, but she had known many handsome men and had derived no pleasure from watching any of them. What was it about Rawlins that demanded her interest? Was it his unhappiness? His mask, which hid every thought? Or, perhaps, it was the blatant masculinity that his position and duties could not hide?

A blush flamed anew in Sarah's cheeks, surprisingly, for she had never before met a man who could make her blush.

Or was it that she had never before found a man who demanded such honest self-scrutiny?

Sarah had spent most of her life studying others. There was a certain safety in knowing the quirks and prejudices of Society, but seldom had she examined herself. She had done what was expected of her—sneaking in what happiness she could through the years—and had left it at that. It seemed Rawlins wasn't the only one to wear a mask. But, while he used his to hide from others, she had used hers to hide from herself. This was an uncomfortable truth!

Thoroughly distracted, Sarah gave but scant attention to Lord Lyleton and the Laveslys and all the rest, and escaped them as soon after lunch as was safe. She settled herself in a red leather armchair in the library, book in hand, trying not to perspire as poetry soothed her uncomfortable thoughts. The library's French doors were open wide to catch the faint breeze on this hot afternoon. A library had always been her sanctuary, but today its quiet was quickly invaded. Most of Charlisle's guests were playing croquet on the western lawn just beyond the library doors. Standing between the guests and those doors were Rawlins and a footman. She could see and overhear everything perfectly.

"Earnshaw," Rawlins was saying to the slim boy on his right, "Mr. Charles Braithwaite complains of an earache, and none of his valet's remedies have helped. You will go to the apothecary in the village and have him make up this solution, which I have long found efficacious in these situations." He handed a slip of paper to the footman.

"Certainly, Mr. Rawlins."

"You, there, lackey!" bellowed Sir Marcus Templeton from the croquet field.

Rawlins stiffened. He dismissed the footman. Earnshaw hurried away as Rawlins calmly walked toward Templeton. "Yes, Sir Marcus?"

"Don't 'yes, Sir Marcus' me, you damned whipstraw. We're all boiling in the sun, and you've done nothing about it."

Rawlins icily withstood Templeton's glare. "I beg your pardon, Sir Marcus. I was attending to some unfinished business. Do you require umbrellas? A canopy, perhaps?"

"No, you insolent mushroom. We want Madeira, isn't that right, gentlemen?"

The four men nearest him murmured their agreement and then turned with universal shrugs away from Sir Marcus.

"Well, what are you standing there for?" Templeton demanded of Rawlins. "Fetch us some Madeira and be quick about it!"

There was a dark flush in Rawlins's cheeks that had nothing to do with the heat of the day and everything to do with what Sarah believed to be a badly frayed temper. Still, he restrained himself admirably. She, on the other hand, strongly wished she could box Templeton's ears on the butler's behalf!

"Certainly, sir," Rawlins replied. He turned and walked back across the lawn and into the library.

Sarah colored. She had not counted on him taking this shortcut. She must say something to announce herself so he would know he was not alone in the room. "Not all of us are so abominable, you know," she remarked, studiously keeping her head in her book. She longed to remove her legs from the arm of the chair, but she would not let herself be embarrassed by a butler, however handsome.

There was a startled moment of silence. "I beg your pardon?"

Sarah turned a page in her book. "Oh, I grant you the lot of us are pretty worthless, some are downright mean, others abhorrent, a few more quite beyond the pale, but the intolerable ones, like Marcus Templeton, are wholly in the minority, I assure you."

"I fail to understand you, Lady Sarah."

Sarah hid her smile in her book and affected a melancholy sigh. "Shakespeare was right: 'Men were deceivers ever.' " She peeped over her book and saw a slight flush creep into Rawlins's face. How lovely that she could discomfit the impassive butler for once! When she felt herself safe, she set the book down in her lap and gazed innocently across the room at him. "It must be very trying working for people you dislike. Lyleton, I suppose, makes an amiable employer, but he does move in the more irritating circles. This house party must be quite wearing on your nerves."

Rawlins regarded her without expression. Then he turned to the nearby sideboard, which boasted a host of decanters, and began arranging glasses on a silver tray. "Every profession has its more . . . unsettling aspects, Lady Sarah."

"Some more than others." She considered his broad back for a moment. It seemed to bristle with antipathy, and she didn't blame him one jot. Templeton was a blackguard. "Why ever did you choose to become a butler if you have so little fondness for the peerage?"

"I have never said—" Rawlins began.

"Many sentiments can be expressed without words," Sarah countered. "You don't like us. I know why I don't like us, but why don't you?"

He turned to her, his eyes narrowed, as if he was puzzled, not by the question, but by her. "It has been my experience, Lady Sarah, that your class regards anyone not of their station as subhuman. Contrary to your opinion, the Templetons of this world are all too common and take many forms. Landowners who give not a thought to the poverty and misery they cause as they continue to enclose what remains of England's common lands and then charge exorbitant rents to their tenant farmers. Factory owners who treat their workers worse than Roman slaves." His expression hardened. "And then there are the aristocratic officers in Wellington's army who are well known for considering their enlisted men as little more than cannon fodder, easily expendable in the purchase of a hill or a village. You will never see a rifleman in the newspapers' lists of wounded and killed in action. They are not considered worthy of notice. Are those reasons enough, Lady Sarah?"

Ah, no man should have to live with such bitterness! "Clearly and concisely stated, Rawlins," she quietly replied. "There is not a single flaw in your reasoning. But my question still stands: Why have you chosen to serve those you despise?"

Again there was a moment of tense silence. "I entered the family business, as it were, my lady," Rawlins replied, turning back to the sideboard and calmly pouring out the Madeira.

"Was your father a butler?" Sarah asked with interest, sitting up in her chair.

His slight hesitation would have been unnoticeable to anyone less used to observing the people around her. "No, my lady, but my grandfather, uncles, and cousins are all in service to noble houses." Rawlins turned back to his task.

"With such a background, it is no wonder you are able to withstand even the brutish treatment of Marcus Templeton. How you must have longed to plant him a facer! I daresay there are many here who would have forgotten themselves so much as to cheer you on. He is not popular."

"But he is my superior."

"Only by an accident of birth, Rawlins."

"It has been my experience, Lady Sarah, that that *accident* is everything in this world."

"Yes, I daresay any man who was foiled in his elopement with Lord Wittleston's daughter would hold that belief."

Rawlins whirled around. "I never!"

"No, no, of course not. No butler would ever forget himself so completely."

Rawlins's clear surprise turned to an appreciative gleam in his gray eyes. "Ours is a rigid society," he solemnly agreed.

"Yes, I daresay you are given daily examples of *that*. All those fool essayists and pamphleteers who write about the fluidity of English society and how the world envies us for allowing any man with enterprise to rise to the highest station make me quite cross. Mr. William Wilberforce, for all his accomplishments and the good he has done this country, still knows what it is to be snubbed and shunned by those who consider themselves his betters simply because of the lucky happenstance of birth. Fluidity, my foot!"

The barest suggestion of a smile touched Rawlins's lips. "Are you a secret evangelical, then?"

"Hardly. Mother would clap me in irons. But I can secretly applaud the good Wilberforce has done and be glad that you were sensible enough *not* to elope with Lord Wittleston's daughter, not because I don't wish you to rise in the world, for I do, but because she is a notorious flirt and would only make you miserable. I used to think that discontented people like you and me ought to escape to America, which praises individualism and the common man in every penny paper they print. But then I chanced to meet an American one day—quite unbeknownst to my parents, of course—and he assured me that Americans are even greater snobs than the British. Old families with old money rule society there. They just lack the titles to go with them."

Rawlins was staring at her, his expression one of astonishment. "These are neither the philosophy nor the sentiments one would normally find in the daughter of a duke."

Sarah cast him a wry smile as she rose from her chair. "So my parents are forever telling me. I pray you, don't expose me to their further censure, shrug off Templeton's barbarism, and I'll leave you to continue your work unmolested."

51

She walked from the room, oddly aware of Rawlins's gaze warming her back, and glad that she had in some small measure made up for Templeton's boorish behavior.

All contentment was quashed in the next moment as the Duchess of Somerton walked out the music room door opposite the library and came face-to-face with her youngest daughter.

"Sarah!" she said sharply. "Where have you been?"

"I was reading in the library, Mother."

"Reading? When I have told you to keep yourself at Lyleton's side? Disobedient, willful child! You delight in flouting me at every turn!"

"There is no pleasure in it, Mother, I assure you," Sarah quietly replied. "Lyleton has gone off to the village with a few of the other men. I did not think it suitable that I join such a party."

"And so you spend your time shut away *reading* when there are dozens of people all around you that would provide suitable companions. What will they think of you when you deliberately shun them like this?"

"They are too busy enjoying themselves, Mother, to give any thought to me."

Angry pink stained the duchess's cheeks. "Nonsense! You are Somerton's daughter. Every eye is upon you. How many times must I impress upon you the august position you hold in Society? How often must I remind you that it is your duty to bring no blemish to that position?"

Sarah glanced at her book. "Alexander Pope is a blemish?"

The duchess slapped her, hard. "You will remember to whom you are speaking!"

"I can never forget it, Mother."

"Pardon me, my lady."

Sarah turned to find Rawlins in the library doorway, a full tray in his hands, a certain grimness to the set of his mouth.

"Some of the gentlemen requested Madeira," he informed the rigid duchess.

Sarah hurriedly stepped aside, and he passed by, tall and

graceful, the tray perfectly balanced in his hands. Why had he not gone through the French doors as before?

The duchess snatched Sarah's book from her fingers. "You will join the rest of the party at once, Sarah, and make yourself as agreeable as I desire you to be."

"Certainly, Mother," Sarah said, turning away, her cheek stinging, wondering if her skin still bore the imprint of her mother's hand. She could not recall the duchess ever striking Frances or Gerald or Arabella. But then, they had not been disobedient or willful. She, alas, seemed to have always been so and through the years had grown quite used to being cuffed by her mother. She could even keep her eyes dry now whenever she was struck. But her heart felt tight and constricted within her breast.

Still, she could walk outside and present an agreeable face to the party engaged in playing croquet even as she watched Rawlins pass through the men, calmly presenting them with the requested libation.

Sir Marcus Templeton took his glass with such violence, that some wine spilled onto his hand. "Took you long enough. Where did you go? Spain?"

"I am sorry for any delay, sir," Rawlins replied. When Templeton turned away from him, Rawlins shrugged and then walked off to attend to the elderly Lord Throwbright.

Tempted to join the butler instead of her peers, Sarah instead claimed mallet and ball, insinuated herself into one of the croquet parties, and gave the rest of them a good run for their money—there was, of course, a wager on the game—for she had some skill and had no need to lose. Lyleton was not present. She uttered a triumphant "Ha!" when her ball hit the final wicket and turned to the six others she was playing against.

"That's a guinea each, I believe," she said, holding out her hand.

The Danverses exuded cheery pleasure at being so soundly beaten; Mr. Freddy Braithwaite declared that he'd never seen a better hand with a mallet; Lord Phineas Doherty shook his head at her, called her a cheeky girl, and handed her a guinea; Charlotte declared that Sarah had no feelings for a woman in her delicate condition—which engendered a hoot from the youngest daughter of the Duke of Somerton—and Corliss Braithwaite pouted prettily as she handed over her guinea and said she had not known Sarah could be so bloodthirsty.

The other croquet parties were also breaking up. Jack and several footmen were moving among them now with glasses of lemonade. Jack was finding his duties onerous at present, for he badly wanted to stop and study Lady Sarah Thorndike and puzzle her out once and for all. That she should see his carefully hidden anger and go out of her way to cheer him! That she should suffer from such a mother and make so fast a recovery.

"I tell you, Merbles," ventured Lord Throwbright, mopping his brow, "this Bonaparte fellow will be hounding us for the next forty years, just like Pompey."

"Pompey? Don't you mean Cromwell?" said Lord Merbles in some confusion. He had been an indifferent student at school.

"I believe," interjected Jack as he handed them glasses of lemonade, "that Lord Throwbright is referring to the reconquest and settlement of Britain by Rome's Emperor Claudius in A.D. forty-three."

"Yes! That's the fellow!" Lord Throwbright said happily. "Married his niece. Shocking thing to do. Lucinda!" he called to his bride of two years. Lady Throwbright, a pretty young woman thirty years his junior, turned reluctantly to face him. "It is too damned hot out," he informed her. "We're going inside."

The Throwbrights were joined by half the party who declared themselves overheated and exhausted from the fervor of the game. Jack should have followed, but he sent Earnshaw in his stead, for Sarah Thorndike, the Dohertys, and the Braithwaites had decided to remain outdoors to enjoy the soft breeze.

"Lady Sarah?"

Jack watched Maria Jenkins approach her mistress, parasol in hand.

"Oh, lord," Sarah groaned aloud.

"The duchess asked me to bring this to you, my lady," Maria said, handing her the white satin, fringed parasol.

54

"The poke bonnet is not enough?" Sarah pleaded

"It has never been enough, my lady."

Sarah sighed heavily. "Too true. Was ever a countenance more plagued by freckles? They are already forming what I fear will soon be a complete map of the Caribbean Islands!"

Jack wholly failed to see Lady Winster summoning him.

Freddy Braithwaite, meanwhile, was staring at Sarah in amazement. "By Gad, you're right!" he said. "It's the most astounding thing I've ever seen!"

Maria Jenkins, Miss Braithwaite, and the Dohertys were lost to laughter as Sarah grimly regarded young Mr. Braithwaite, who stood only a few inches taller than herself, his pomaded light brown locks drooping in the heat. "Freddy," she intoned, "don't you ever want to get married?"

"Course I do," he replied, glancing at the giggle-prone others in some confusion. "Looking forward to it. Chance to better my fortune and all that. Mother's been hounding me for years to find a wife."

"Then, I suggest you button it!"

Jack hurriedly turned away to hide his mirth.

"Beg pardon, Sarah?" asked Mr. Braithwaite.

"Your mouth, you gaby," Sarah said with a grin. "It will sink you in every courtship if you aren't careful."

"But you said—!"

Sarah put her hands on both his shoulders. "Freddy, you mustn't pay any heed to what I say, for I always say the wrong thing. In fact, you should use me as a model of what to avoid."

"That is what Mama always tells me," said Corliss with a wicked grin. She was an attractive girl with hair the color of summer wheat and striking brown eyes. These, and her vast dowry, had made her quite popular during her first London Season.

"But dash it, Sarah, you're the only amusing girl in the ton," Freddy riposted. "Why, if I'd half the fortune Lyleton has, I'd pursue you myself!"

"Thank you, *no*, Freddy," Sarah said laughing. "Between the two of us, our tongues would get us barred from every house in the ton within a fortnight of the wedding." She stopped and considered this a moment. "Which might not be a bad thing. Have you ever considered a Gretna marriage, Freddy?"

"N-N-Now don't start getting sap-skulled on me, Sarah," Freddy stammered, nervously backing away. "You know my mother has a weak heart, and your parents would eat my liver if we ever eloped."

"Alas," Sarah said with a sigh. "So ends my last chance of escaping the viscount."

"But why would you *want* to escape Lord Lyleton?" Corliss demanded.

Jack recalled the overheard conversation in the rose garden. *He's such a . . . such a boy, and I want a man for a husband, not some child-groom to raise with my own infants.*

"If you are considering Freddy Braithwaite as a substitute, you *are* desperate," Charlotte opined.

"I beg your pardon?" said the gentleman in question with the utmost dignity.

Charlotte grinned at him.

"Just how desperate are you?" Lord Doherty asked Sarah.

"I'll show you. Oh, Rawlins," Sarah called to Jack. "Would you be so good as to find out which ships are sailing from Bristol to America, and when? On the secret, if you please."

"Certainly, Lady Sarah," he replied, a lurking smile in his eyes meeting her mischievous gaze and holding for a moment. She had had him fairly capped, but no longer. Sarah Thorndike, Jack decided, was a quizzling.

"She is *quite* desperate," Lord Doherty informed his wife.

The party was now distracted by a commotion heard on their left. Fitz, leading a party of four gentlemen all dressed in dusty riding clothes, rounded the corner of the house and came into view.

"We're to have some fun at last," he cheerily called out. "I've granted permission to a band of Gypsies to set up camp in the east meadow."

The news, alas, was delightful to only a few of the party, for the others considered their jewels, purses, and very lives now in the greatest jeopardy.

"What in God's name possessed you!" the Earl of Lavesly

demanded of his son an hour later in the library. "It was bad enough that you invited *Templeton* to stay, but to allow *Gypsies* on Charlisle's grounds? My stomach roils at the very thought."

"Should I ring for a stomach powder?" his son solicitously inquired.

"No, damn you! I want you to order those foreigners to be off and never come back."

"But I said they could stay."

"It is unthinkable. Unconscionable," the Countess of Lavesly declared, stepping into the fray. "When I consider what the Somertons must think now of your judgment and your character . . . You will send them packing at once, Fitzwilliam."

"Send the Somertons packing?" Fitz asked in surprise.

"No!" the countess shouted. "The *Gypsies*!"

"Well, I can't," Fitz retorted, startling both parents. "You know I'd do anything to oblige you, Mama, but I've already given them my word that they may stay a month, and you know that a Lyleton never goes back on his word."

It was one of the few times in his life that Fitzwilliam Hornsby had ever stood up to his parents. The success of this venture so surprised him that he could actually regard even Sir Marcus Templeton with complacency when the Charlisle party sat down to dinner an hour later.

*
Chapter 5

THE SOUND OF distant hoofbeats caught his ear. Jack turned slowly, scrutinizing the horizon until he saw Lady Sarah Thorndike galloping with a fierce speed that almost bespoke desperation—as she had done the three consecutive mornings before this. Whether far off in the distance or riding close by and oblivious to him, Sarah was up before dawn and running as far and as fast away from Charlisle as she could.

Certainly she had ample reason to dislike the house. In addition to her rigid and censorious parents, she was also hounded by an unappetizing pair of suitors—Lord Pontifax and Mr. Davis—who cleaved unto her as if magnetized. Mr. Davis wanted her as his muse, Lord Pontifax wanted her for her money. And then there was Fitz, who didn't want her at all, but seemed resigned to having her.

It didn't matter that Sarah had as little wish to be married as Fitz. Jack had seen the determination with which the Laveslys and the Somertons continually thrust the unhappy pair together. There could be no escape.

This was disturbing. From his boyhood, Jack could not tolerate seeing any trapped creature—a rabbit in a snare, a bird in a cage—and he was finding it difficult to watch now. Fitz was a good man and deserved some happiness in life. And Sarah, for all her public propriety, was a warmhearted young woman of whom Charlisle's staff could not say enough good. She deserved better than a forced marriage to a reluctant bridegroom.

He watched Sarah and her huge dun-colored hunter disappear into a distant wood. That she had calmly taken her mother's slap yesterday had told him much. Hers was a life very different from the one he had first imagined for her.

Sarah and he were alike in ways he would have thought impossible a week ago. Even with a ducal father who acknowledged her, she knew what it was to be an outcast. She had suffered abuse all of her life at the hands of those who should have protected her. She had known pain and privation of the keenest sort. Sarah made him feel a little off balance, as if the world had tilted slightly beneath his feet. He didn't know if he should be angry or sad that she seemed incapable of standing buff to her parents and refusing to ruin two lives with one bad marriage. He was unsure if he should be amused or troubled by the witty—almost bitter—quips she made whenever she was alone with him or with her particular friends.

Jack scowled. It was not like him to be so uncertain. He blamed Sarah freely for such discomfort. The scowl turned to an unconscious smile. She was the oddest creature.

Ever since that astonishing conversation in the library, she had tried to smooth for him the stings and snubs of those he served, apologizing, occasionally making some quip to get him to smile at their rag manners, not that he ever allowed himself to smile, of course. He understood the decorum his position required. Still, she had lightened his thoughts and his heart almost hourly it seemed. Like Fitz, she showed him the absurdity of life, and he was grateful. He conceived a sudden desire to do something more for Sarah than slip her an occasional glass of brandy. A debt was owing.

Sarah celebrated the anniversary of her first week at Charlisle by hiding in the shrubbery. Alas, the glint of her red hair in the sunlight gave her away. Beaumont Davis ran her to ground.

"There you are, my Daphne, my Psyche, my Celia!" he rapturously called, trotting up to her. "I have written you a new poem."

"Another?" Sarah asked faintly.

"You are my muse, dearest Lady Sarah," he said, fervently catching her hand in his. She just as fervently pulled it free.

"The words come so quickly, I cannot get them all down on paper. You have made of me a poetical god! Sit here," he said, tugging her toward a stone bench, "and let me do you homage."

He draped himself before her in his newest poetical attitude (he had practiced it all morning in front of his mirror), tossed his hair back from his forehead with one hand, and began to read.

" 'Lord Howard's Progress,' by Beaumont Davis," enunciated Charlisle's poet laureate. "Ah, Lady! on Olympus called of heavenly birth, Sweet Muse! brought here by Homeric decree!"

Sarah cringed. In only one week, she had already sat through the recitation of nineteen poems, all dedicated to her, and had been forced to read nearly a dozen others. What Mr. Davis lacked in originality and talent, he more than made up for in productivity. She could expect to be trapped . . . that is, seated here for the next hour. If only she was not so tenderhearted. If only she was not so concerned for the poor boy's feelings. If only she would take Charlotte's advice and tell Mr. Davis that she preferred Milton to Wordsworth (which she did), thought Byron an affected untalented ass (which she did), and preferred a good gallop across an open field to sitting still and silent on a summer afternoon listening to bad poetry (which she did).

"Pitiful though my songs may be, I yet call thee from thy graceful bower," Mr. Beaumont Davis rhapsodized, sweeping his blond hair back from his forehead once again.

It all came, Sarah supposed, of trying to avoid the Viscount Lyleton's company at all costs. Though he was vastly more entertaining than Mr. Davis, she thought it strategically best to avoid Lyleton whenever her parents weren't looking and pray that he would take her obvious lack of interest as a strong hint not to go down on his knee, however much their parents prodded him. He had stood up for the Gypsies, perhaps he would stand up for his freedom, and hers.

"Yet, soft! As I pass by that sylvan glade, I see thee emerge, like Diana from a forest mist," the besotted poet continued.

"There you are, Lady Sarah!" cried a jovial voice.

Sarah turned and suppressed a groan as Lord Cyril Pontifax strode up to them. There was no doubt he looked quite dashing in his brown double-breasted coat and high-waisted yellow trousers. But appearance wasn't everything. She saw the derisive gleam in his eye as he glanced at Mr. Davis. She had never liked confrontations, but this second suitor seemed to thrive on them, at least when combating a lesser foe like Mr. Davis. She wished Lord Pontifax anywhere but here.

"Your smile, so sweet, pierces my too human heart," Mr. Davis read—somewhat grimly—aloud.

"This is no day to be sitting quietly!" Lord Pontifax exclaimed with no apology for interrupting the poet. "Come, let us walk through Charlisle's park or perhaps take a boat out upon the lake."

"She doesn't want to go punting!" the resident poet said angrily, his face stained red. "She wants to hear my poem!" He held the pages before him like a shield. "Thy hand upon my pale brow bids me speak words yet unfathomed."

"Give over, Davis," Lord Pontifax scoffed. "Anyone can see Lady Sarah is bored out of her mind and longing for escape."

"Really, my lord, I must remonstrate with you—" Sarah began.

"Lady Sarah is a goddess!" Mr. Beaumont Davis fervently declared. "You defile her with your every breath. Be gone!"

Muscular arms akimbo, Lord Pontifax smiled derisively at the willowy poet. "As if *you* could chase me off," he sneered.

Mr. Davis's face grew a deeper shade of red. "You are an insufferable lout. I despise you!"

"And you—" his rival began.

"I beg your pardon, Lady Sarah."

Sarah turned to find Rawlins standing gravely at her elbow.

"The duke was desirous of having a word with you in the library, my lady," he continued.

"Yes, of course," Sarah said, rising with alacrity. "I'll come at once."

"Allow me to escort you, my dear," said Lord Pontifax, offering his arm.

61

"Nonsense!" Mr. Davis cried. "I am her first companion. It is *my* right to escort her back to the house!"

"I'm sorry, gentlemen," Rawlins intervened, his expression perfectly bland, but Sarah was not deceived. He knew exactly what he had interrupted. "The duke specifically requested that Lady Sarah and only Lady Sarah come to him."

"I shall go at once," said Sarah.

The two gentlemen vociferously protested this declaration. Jack wisely removed himself from the fray, looking on the trio from a few yards away with barely masked amusement. Both men were trying to press later afternoon engagements upon Sarah and she—to her credit—was politely fending them off.

"Gentlemen," she finally declared with just a note of exasperation, "my father will wait no longer." She hurried over to the butler as if toward sanctuary. "Take me away from all this, Rawlins."

" 'What?' " said he, a surprisingly mischievous gleam in his eyes as he regarded her. " 'Wouldst thou come when I called thee?' "

" 'Yea, signior,' " said Sarah with a startled smile, for he quoted from *Much Ado About Nothing*, one of her favorite Shakespearean plays, " 'and depart when you bid me.' "

" 'O, stay but till then!' "

" 'Then is spoken.' " She turned and gaily waved at her two suitors. " 'Fare you well now.' " Relief singing in her heart, she started quickly back to the house, Rawlins at her side. "Your timing could not have been better," she informed him.

"I hoped it would be so, my lady."

Sarah stared up at the butler, a good deal stunned, but not so stunned that she stopped walking away from her two tormentors. "You hoped . . . ? Did not my father summon me?"

"I am afraid you have caught me in a blatant falsehood, Lady Sarah. I have not spoken to His Grace the whole of this afternoon."

"Good God, Rawlins, do you mean to tell me that you purposefully set out to rescue me?" Sarah cried, her heart quickening.

"I chanced to observe Lord Pontifax looking into a number

62

of rooms," the butler replied. There was still a hint of reserve in his voice. "His was a determined search. I readily guessed its object, and thought you might be in need of some assistance."

"Oh, you *darling*! I've never been so grateful to anyone in my life!"

A small tinge of color crept into Rawlins's cheeks. "I am glad I could be of some service to you, my lady."

"Words cannot express the depths of your service, Rawlins. Any suggestions as to where I can best hide from the Terrible Two for the rest of the afternoon?"

The corner of Rawlins's mouth quirked up for a moment. "I believe the Dowager Formantle has organized several whist tables in the drawing room, my lady."

Sarah could not but pause at this information. To be trapped for several hours in the same room—perhaps at the same table—with the bellowing dowager was not for the faint of heart. But still, when she considered the alternative . . . "Desperate situations call for desperate measures, Rawlins," she said, as they came up to the west door of the house. "Thank you."

"You are very welcome, my lady," Rawlins said with a bow.

" 'Pray for me! and what noise soever ye hear, come not unto me, for nothing can rescue me.' "

He paused as if uncertain what to say or do. "Christopher Marlowe's *The Tragical History of Doctor Faustus*, scene sixteen?" he inquired.

She beamed at him. "*Very* good, Rawlins! Your knowledge of literature is most impressive."

"A butler is always prepared, my lady." He bowed, turned, and sauntered off in the direction of the library, as if nothing untoward had occurred. But it had.

Sarah watched him go, her heartbeat a little rapid, her face a little flushed. That he should have *chosen* to play Spenser's Redcrosse Knight to her Una! She could not banish the smile from her lips, even as she entered the house and turned toward the drawing room. That he should be so *aware* of her movements, so solicitous of her welfare!

63

"George, you blithering idiot, *spades* are trumps!" bellowed the Dowager Formantle.

Sarah girded her loins and entered the lion's den. Not even the determined Lord Pontifax would dare to accost her here, while Mr. Davis avoided the dowager as he would a Caliban. She would be safe. Rawlins, she decided, besides being amazingly handsome and surprisingly sweet, was a genius.

Several hours later, her headache diminishing, Sarah sat in her nightdress in the window seat of her room overlooking the western rose gardens. The window was open fully, and the cool evening air washed over her as she leaned back against the wall and gazed up at the stars.

This was one of the reasons she preferred the country to the city. Starlight was dimmed by city lights. Here, however, the stars shone with all their brilliance in the darkened sky. They were many and lustrous, and reminded her that there *was* another world beyond the walls of this house.

She tried to distract her thoughts by tracing with her eyes the constellations she recognized, but it was no use. With a melancholy sigh, she drew her legs up and wrapped her arms around her knees, her chin sinking down upon them.

Somehow she had always thought her life would turn out differently. She thought that she would have her own home and someone to love her and children who would see her more than the daily quarter hour her parents had allotted her the first thirteen years of her life. She had thought she would find someone *she* could love and be happy with.

Instead there was only Lord Lyleton: a dandy, a gamester, a poor judge of horseflesh, a Town beau, and her most reluctant suitor.

Hope had failed her as it always had. Her parents had indeed sold her, and it was entirely her own fault, for she had done nothing to prevent it. And what now?

This last sennight she had tried to resign herself to her fate, just as she had always done with everything else in her life. But for once, resignation had not come, would not come, and what did that portend? Only greater unhappiness in her marriage.

A movement in the rose garden below distracted her. In the faint light of a waxing quarter moon, she saw a man, his back to her, staring up at the stars as she had done. But not just any man: It was Rawlins. She knew him by his height, the breadth of his shoulders, the shape of his head, the way he held himself.

Rawlins. There was someone else who seemed unable to reconcile himself to his lot in life, or at least to the company he now served. Skilled and knowledgeable though he was, in some ways he was wholly unsuited to his post: he was too intelligent, too well read, too proud to long withstand the daily indignities he endured. Still, he had a great advantage over Sarah, for his position at Charlisle was only temporary. He would leave the house for good in a few weeks, just as the announcement of her engagement appeared in all the best papers.

She stared down at her toes peeping out from her nightdress as the minutes slowly ticked by. It had become habit—a pleasurable habit—to study the butler whenever he came into view. But that enjoyment had become more subdued these last few days, for she had detected something within Rawlins that harried away happiness and would not loose its hold. A line came to her from Goldsmith: "the silent manliness of grief." It was a phrase that had struck her some years earlier and had stayed, waiting for its mark. And here was Rawlins. It troubled her to see so good a man so very unhappy.

She glanced down into the garden. He was gone. Disappointment stabbed into her with a force that surprised and unsettled her. She sat at the window another half hour, staring out into the night, loneliness enveloping her.

With four sets of parental eyes, two determined suitors, and the surreptitious gazes of the other houseguests watching her every word and movement, Sarah had been unable to call a moment her own since her first day at Charlisle. Even her bedroom was not safe, for the duchess was prone to walk in on her without notice either to send her back into company or to harangue her for her singular lack of cooperation in what was really a very simple matter: her courtship and marriage.

65

As it had been throughout her life, riding was Sarah's sole source of escape. Desperation now had her regularly rising before dawn, dressing without Maria's help, and then hurrying out to Charlisle's stables, where Henry Jenkins—Maria's younger brother and one of the Somertons' senior grooms—waited for her with Dune.

Once free of the stable yard, Sarah would spur Dune to a gallop and—Henry following behind—she would flee Charlisle, and her parents, and the Laveslys, Lyleton, Lord Pontifax, and Mr. Davis, too. She rode as if the devil himself was chasing her. She pushed onward until her lungs were bursting and Henry was trailing far behind. Only then would she pull Dune down to a walk so they could both catch their breath and watch the sun rise over the green eastern hills.

When Henry finally caught up, she would turn Dune and slowly circle back the three or four miles to Charlisle, sometimes talking to Henry, sometimes staying mute and lost in her own increasingly dark thoughts.

"The day's going to be another scorcher," Henry said a trifle glumly as they began their slow ride back this morning.

"How long will the heat last, do you think?" Sarah asked, wanting his conversation today. The loneliness she had felt the night before was still with her.

"A good fortnight, I'll wager, my lady."

"Lovely. Something else to look forward to."

As they had earlier in the week, they passed within a half mile of the Gypsy camp and saw smoke from seven different fires curling up and fading into the morning sky.

"Have you visited the Gypsies yet, Henry?" Sarah inquired.

"I don't hold with throwing away good money," Henry self-righteously declared.

"But you don't have to spend a farthing just to *look*."

"Ah, *them*. *They* find a way to dip their hands into your purse, I warrant."

"Still, do you think some night you might escort—"

"*No*, my lady," Henry said firmly.

"Just for an hour, Henry?"

"No, my lady. I've no liking for the tongue-lashing I'll get

66

from the duke when he finds out I've taken you to a good-for-nothing Gypsy camp."

"But he won't find out."

Henry hooted at that. "Someone will see you leave the house, however careful you think you are. And that someone will tell someone else, who will tell that herring-faced valet of your father's, and *he'll* tell the duke, and then we'll both be in for it."

This was not idle supposition. Henry Jenkins spoke from vast years of experience as Sarah's groom, friend, and occasional cohort.

"Oh, but Henry—"

"No, my lady. The duke's cantankerous enough as it is this summer, without you rushing off on some harebrained scheme."

"It isn't harebrained. *Everyone* likes to visit Gypsy caravans."

"I don't."

Sarah sadly shook her head. "There is no adventure in your soul, Henry."

The groom guffawed. "That's only because you and your mad schemes beat it out of me long ago."

Chuckling, Sarah pulled Dune to a stop and jumped to the ground, though they were still half a mile from Charlisle's stable. "I'll walk the rest of the way, Henry. If this is the only cool air I am to know today, I mean to enjoy it."

"Yes, my lady," said Henry, taking Dune's reins from her. He set his horse off at a trot, Dune in step beside them.

Sarah watched them go and sighed, though she didn't know why. Looking at the undulating green earth all around, she sighed again—this time with pleasure. She threw the train of her burgundy riding habit over her right arm and began to walk on an invisible course that would lead her through a nearby stand of beech trees, away from Charlisle's stables, and toward its formal eastern gardens.

She had not gone more than five yards when she topped a slight rise and stared with surprise at the familiar broad back of a man seated on a fallen tree and staring up at the crescent moon, which had not yet set.

She gasped. "Rawlins!"

He turned his head and gave her a brief nod. "Good morning, Lady Sarah."

"What on earth are you—Oh, I beg your pardon. I did not mean to interrupt your solitude."

"That's quite all right, my lady," Rawlins replied, standing up. He was already dressed in his uniform of a high-collared, double-breasted tailcoat, a dark green today, cravat, fawn-colored breeches, silk stockings, and shoes with simple buckles. A soft breeze stirred his dark brown hair. "I was just preparing to return to the house."

Sarah blinked. Good God, did he actually mean to accompany her? She smiled up at him with particular brightness as she reached his side. "I thought I was the only one who liked predawn romps."

"Butlers do not romp, Lady Sarah," Rawlins informed her.

Sarah quite failed to suppress a gurgle of laughter. "They must, I am convinced of it! Once their employers remove to Town, the whole household undoubtedly breaks open a cask of wine and holds a vast three-day orgy to celebrate."

Rawlins's expression was severe. "Not in *my* experience, Lady Sarah."

"Oh, come now," Sarah said as they began walking toward Charlisle, "servants love a good party as much as their masters. Everyone needs a little fun now and then. What do *you* do for fun, Rawlins?"

"I?"

"You," said Sarah firmly, fighting back a grin.

He glanced across at her, and then looked stonily ahead. "I like to read, my lady, and I enjoy an occasional game of cribbage."

"Cribbage?" said Sarah with a wealth of disgust. "No wonder you never smile if you've only got cribbage for entertainment."

"If I do not smile, it is because the world offers little incentive."

"But it does!" Sarah cried. "Only look at this beautiful day. Is this not reason enough to smile?"

"I believe that war steals away such beauty."

68

"Well, then, what of the joys of literature?"

"One might also ask what of the privations of poverty?"

"Oh, I never knew a man so determined to be unhappy. Rawlins," Sarah said suddenly as a thought occurred to her, "do butlers ever laugh?"

"I beg your pardon?"

"I've never heard one do so, and I've seen dozens of butlers in my lifetime. Probably hundreds. Surely, butlers must laugh now and then, if only in private."

"Certainly not, my lady, it would be highly improper for any man in such a position to forget himself so badly."

"Fiddle," Sarah retorted. "I daresay it's being unhappy in your work that's caused at least some of the mischief."

"I beg your pardon?"

Sarah beamed at the butler. "You heard me. Anyone trapped their entire life in a job they loathe must be wholly unable to find anything to laugh at. Perhaps you should have gone to sea."

"Thank you, *no*, Lady Sarah. The navy offers a hard and often brutal life to the men who sail the king's ships. I count myself fortunate in my position."

"Not with this crowd you don't," Sarah said, with a grin that broadened as she detected an answering gleam in Rawlins's eyes. "No sane man would. However did Lyleton find you?"

"We have a . . . mutual acquaintance, my lady."

"Stole you away from some arch rival, no doubt. The duchess is forever stealing hairdressers and abigails and chefs from her rivals in the Haute Ton."

"The duchess would make a formidable opponent in any contest."

"Now, there's a keen observation, but don't count out the duke. He's *vastly* experienced in having his own way. I never seemed to acquire the knack. Inexcusable of me, I know, but there it is." She sighed. "I suspect we have something in common, Rawlins."

"Have we?" he inquired, glancing down at her as they entered Charlisle's topiary garden through a gate in a low hedge.

"Yes," Sarah said, plucking a small green leaf and methodically shredding it. "We both dislike the roles we have been assigned in this life."

There was a moment of startled silence. "And what is your role, Lady Sarah?"

"Why, the black sheep, of course. Or should I say black ewe? It's more technically correct."

"But perhaps less effective," Rawlins suggested. "The term sheep can be used generically."

"One of these days I will have to examine those books you read." Sarah glanced up at the butler's strong profile. For all his reserve, she felt remarkably comfortable with him. He gave an unexpected pleasure to the day, the war and poverty not withstanding. "Rawlins? What is your Christian name?"

He blinked. "I beg your pardon?"

"Your Christian name. You know mine; it is only right that I know yours. Come on, give it up. Every human being has a Christian name."

"Except, perhaps, for the Turks, the Egyptians, the Chinese, the Japanese—"

"Why, Rawlins," Sarah murmured wickedly, "if I didn't know better, I would swear you are laughing at me."

"I would never, my lady, forget myself so badly," Rawlins assured her.

"No, no, of course not," Sarah said, her eyes dancing with delight. Behind that handsome, impassive face lurked a devilish sense of humor, and she had discovered it! The world seemed suddenly a better place. "Your name, sir, and no more parries, if you please."

"It is John, Lady Sarah."

"John?" Sarah cocked her head as she considered this piece of information. "You may have been christened John, but I warrant there's a Jack capering behind that impenetrable facade."

Rawlins regarded her with some astonishment. "Decidedly *not*, Lady Sarah."

"No?" she said with an arch grin.

His gray eyes revealed a momentary confusion.

Rawlins and she separated at the house, he going downstairs, she going upstairs to bathe and change for breakfast. She found as the day wore on, that she could not be in a room with the butler without studying him and wondering about him. He seemed quite unlike anyone she had ever known, and she puzzled a good deal over why this should be so. It came to her finally that it was his eyes. Usually, they were veiled and unreadable, but occasionally the mask would fall and she would see the bitterness and the grief lurking there. And now there was something new: mischief and humor. What more might she discover through further observation?

Her parents, she knew, would be appalled if they found she was giving so much time and thought to a mere servant, but with Sarah it had always been so. There were few in her own class who captivated her, let alone earned her regard. Phineas and Charlotte Doherty were two of the very rare exceptions.

As was the fashion for many of their rank, the Duke and Duchess of Somerton had handed their children over to nurses and nursery maids upon their births and seldom saw them afterward. Sarah had been raised, not by her parents, but by servants. It was Nurse Beecham who had sat by her bed comforting her when she was ill. It was Henry Jenkins who had taught her to ride and love horses and accompanied her on all of her equine excursions. It was old Bill Regis, the Somertons' head gardener at Rolbrook, their country seat in Lincolnshire, who had taught Sarah about flowers and herbs and other plants, passing onto her his wisdom, which seemed to encompass all of life and death. It was Maria Jenkins who had supported her through the horrors of adolescence and her debut, laughing and crying with her and keeping her on course.

She privately considered these people to be her true family. Their values, way of life, and good hearts were more suited to her own than those of her parents. She found that they were the people who interested her. They were the people whose opinions she valued and with who she liked to talk.

She told herself that John Rawlins was no different.

*

Chapter 6

THAT EVENING, JACK watched as Sarah avoided the ardent gaze of Beaumont Davis, sidestepped Cyril Pontifax, and found sanctuary in the company of Lord and Lady Doherty in a far corner of the drawing room. She said something that made this loving pair laugh and then began an animated conversation.

The contrast could not be greater with her deep melancholy of the night before, when she had sat at her bedroom window, red hair tumbling over her shoulders, her face inexpressibly sad, as she gazed up at the stars. Seeing her then, he had had to turn away, unable to look upon so much unhappiness, unwilling to acknowledge how closely it mirrored his own.

"Ah, there you are, Rawlins, you naughty fellow," said Lady Winster, rapping him flirtatiously on the shoulder with her fan.

He masked his distaste and turned to the lady. Any man yet breathing must own she was a handsome woman. Tall, voluptuous, with large green eyes and full lips, Lady Winster had been one of the ton's leading beauties since her debut over a decade before. She had married Lord Winster at the end of her first Season and in the course of her marriage had taken literally dozens of lovers, from Prince George (it was said) on down to the attractive footmen she liked to hire.

She had made it clear from her first day at Charlisle that she wanted to add Jack to that list. He had nothing against bedroom sport, and she promised with those eyes of hers that he would enjoy sport of the very best. But beauty was all Lady Winster had to recommend her, and that was far from being enough, particularly when he observed the cruel delight she took in openly flirting in front of her husband with any and every man who caught her eye. Jack preferred a far different sort of bedfellow.

"May I get you anything, Lady Winster?" he inquired without expression.

"Yes, of course you can! I want the key to your heart."

"It was lost long ago. Will there be anything else?"

"Well, then, I'll settle for the key to your room," her ladyship said with a saucy smile.

"Abigail!"

They turned to see Lord Winster striding toward them, pale and tight-lipped. His brown hair looked as if his fingers had raked through it more than once. He might have been an attractive man in his youth, but marriage had hardened his features and his spirit.

"Oh, what is it, Edmond?" Lady Winster demanded, cross at having her flirtation interrupted.

"An express has arrived for you, my dear, from one of your many admirers."

There was a certain tone to Lord Winster's voice that hinted his wife should abandon her current pursuits for the letter waiting in her room, or suffer the consequences.

Ah, well, thought Lady Winster, the summer was yet young and anticipation did add spice to any affair. "I'll go at once," she said, her hand trailing down Jack's arm as she walked off.

Lord Winster stood his ground, his hazel eyes grimly measuring Jack, his attitude both belligerent and defensive.

Jack could not but pity the gentleman. Lord Winster was one of the few men of his class who actually cared that his wife was an adulteress. Each affair of hers cut him to the quick. Every knowing glance from the men at his club infuriated him. Every manservant who claimed his wife's bed deepened the thick pool of his humiliation.

Jack wished he could say something that might alleviate Lord Winster's current agony, but he could not. An assurance that her ladyship had not and would not succeed with him, besides being impertinent, would only be met with disbelief. Lord Winster knew his wife too well to doubt her success now.

73

"May I get you anything, my lord?" Jack quietly inquired.

"You can by God stay away from my wife!"

"That I can promise you."

Lord Winster scowled at him, clearly unconvinced, and stalked off.

Jack watched him go. He was but one of so many in this house trapped in an unsuitable marriage. Property and fortune and even occasionally a pleasing form were the ties that bound the ton in marriage. Witness the Winsters and the Merbles. Witness Sarah and Fitz Hornsby.

Family interest was bringing those two together, though beauty was not lacking. Fitz, of course, was admired everywhere, but Sarah had her own charms, no matter what Bigby or the duchess said. Her red hair became a flaming halo whenever caught by the sunlight, her blue eyes were wonderfully expressive. She had a pleasing, graceful figure. There was even a certain delight in the anarchic sprinkle of freckles across her nose and cheeks. Her laugh was infectious. Her smile could make you forget every past and current misery.

It came to Jack that Lady Sarah Thorndike was in fact a very attractive young woman.

He observed a stern look pass from the duke to Sarah. She left the Dohertys, walked obediently up to Fitz, and entered into his conversation with Freddy and Corliss Braithwaite.

When Fitz and Sarah were married, as they must be, would she become another Lady Winster, going from man to man to find the pleasure and happiness lacking in her own marriage?

Jack angrily pushed the thought aside. Her future was none of his affair. But the thought became a gnat that hounded him the rest of that evening, returning bitterness to his heart.

"*Why* does Lady Doherty insist upon championing Alexander Pope?" Beaumont Davis demanded an hour later.

"Because she likes Mr. Pope," Sarah replied with a smile. "You do not?"

"I abominate him and all those smirking intellectual poets like Dryden and Donne and the lot of them. They have no sensibility! Give me the heartrending verse of Crashaw, Marvell,

Wordsworth, and of course the immortal Byron, and I am a happy man." The willowy poet suddenly sagged against Sarah.

"Mr. Davis, are you ill?" she cried.

"I beg your pardon, Lady Sarah," Mr. Davis said, hurriedly righting himself. "A sudden dizziness overcame me."

"And no wonder," Sarah scolded. "You must eat more than dry biscuits and soda water, Mr. Davis! Byron uses them for a reducing diet and with good reason, but you've no need to reduce, I do assure you."

"You are very kind," said Beaumont Davis with a wan smile. "I know it is only your unexampled concern for my health that makes you speak so harshly of the god Byron."

"Harsh? Mr. Davis, it is not harsh to be truthful, and the truth is that the god Byron tends toward fat. Any of us tend toward fat when we frequent as many parties and dinners in the ton as he has done."

"Would not *he* consume dry biscuits and soda water if *he* were visiting Charlisle now?"

"Yes," Sarah said with a grin. "I daresay he would, and offend the viscount's chef no end."

"Then, *I* shall continue to do the same."

"But, Mr. Davis, it is not kind of you to deliberately offend Lyleton's chef."

The poet flushed. "If *you* will take me to task, my *dear* Lady Sarah, then I must in some way be in error." He considered a moment. "I shall only eat biscuits for breakfast and dinner. At luncheon, I will permit myself a little meat and salad."

"An excellent scheme," Sarah said approvingly.

"Sarah!" intoned a stern voice.

She found the Duke of Somerton scowling at her not two feet away. "Yes, Father?"

"You will oblige me with a word or two of private conversation." The duke glanced at the wan poet. "You will excuse us, sir."

"Oh, certainly——" Mr. Davis began, but her father had already led Sarah away to a potted palm near the drawing room's French doors.

"I strongly disapprove of you encouraging that wet goose," the duke stated.

"I don't encourage him, Father. I don't let him throw himself at my feet as he longs to do."

"Do not be impertinent, Sarah," he snapped as he fixed her with an icy blue gaze. "Whenever I look for you, that cawker Davis is hanging on your lips or that peacock Pontifax is trying to lure you out into the gardens."

"But he never succeeds, Father."

"He shouldn't be given the opportunity to try!" the Duke of Somerton exploded, and then hurriedly lowered his voice. "I speak for your mother as well when I tell you that I must condemn your current behavior."

"Father, you both asked me to be agreeable to the Charlisle party," Sarah said reasonably. "Mr. Davis and Lord Pontifax are a part of that party. Now, I don't enjoy their company any more than you enjoy seeing me in it, but short of causing a scene, I can find no way to hint them off."

"Flummery," snapped the duke. "The way to hint those fellows off is to keep yourself at Lyleton's side and demonstrate to the entire party that he is your choice among your many suitors."

"Only three suitors, Father, and one of them most reluctant."

"Are you saying Lyleton is being behindhand with you?" the duke asked grimly, directing a darkling glance at the viscount whispering in Rawlins's ear.

"Oh, no!" Sarah replied hurriedly, not wanting to land the poor boy in hot water. "He does his duty by me every day, but he doesn't seem to relish it, Father. In fact, he seems as reluctant to enter into this engagement as I am."

"Reluctant or no, he will marry you," the duke said, blue eyes boring into her.

"Yes," Sarah murmured, her gaze dropping to her satin slippers. "I know he will."

The duke harrumphed, led her back over to Lyleton, whom she had escaped but minutes before, cast Rawlins a dismissing glance, which the butler heeded without a blink, and informed the viscount that his daughter had been longing for his company.

Fitz paled at this, but manfully informed the duke that he was always happy to converse with Lady Sarah, then stood mute for the next five minutes, trying to think of some topic of conversation. The duke stalked away to find the lovely Lady Throwbright, with whom he hoped to pursue more pleasurable occupations.

"We must say something, my lord!" Sarah whispered. "Everyone is watching us."

Fitz started. "Oh. Yes. Of course. Sorry. Um ... er ... That's a very pretty bracelet, Lady Sarah."

"Thank you, my lord," Sarah replied, glancing at the sapphire bracelet on her wrist. "I bought it in Bath last year."

"Bath? Do you ... *like* Bath?"

Having a fair understanding of Lord Lyleton's character at this point, Sarah could honestly reply, "Not really. I find it very dull."

"Oh, so do I," cried Lyleton with relief. "London's the only town to live in."

"Even in the summer?"

"Well, one can always go to York in the summer for the races, don't you know," said the viscount. With but a little encouragement, he spent the next half hour recounting his history of attendance at the York Races, pleasing their parents with his animated conversation and her seeming interest in it.

"There you are!" said Sir Marcus Templeton, as Fitz reluctantly entered the library shortly after midnight. "Took you long enough."

"The countess wanted a word with me," Fitz said, avoiding his persecutor's hard gaze.

"Close the door, you fool, and lock it! We don't want to be interrupted now, do we?"

Fitz glumly did as instructed, then summoned up his courage and advanced to the middle of the room. He had a part to play, he might as well begin now. "Do you have the letter?"

"Of course I do." Sir Marcus rummaged in his coat a moment and produced a single sheet of paper.

"I trust this is not a copy as the last one was," Fitz remarked coolly.

"It's the original all right, and no mistake."

"I'll not be blackmailed with false goods, Templeton."

"And who said anything about blackmail?" Sir Marcus said expansively. "You are merely purchasing an item you find of interest. Besides, the copy I showed you before wasn't false goods, it was simply protection." Templeton held the sheet of paper out to Fitz, but when Fitz tried to take it, he snatched it back. "No tricks, now."

Fitz paled. Did he know? "No, no, of course not," he said hastily.

Templeton placed the document into his trembling fingers, a derisive expression on his swarthy face as Fitz miserably read every damning line he had written last winter.

There could be no doubt. The letter was his. This was his handwriting. This was his signature. Here were the florid out-pourings of love and the ardent offer of marriage. Fitz groaned inwardly. He must have been tap-hackled that wretched night.

"Very well," he said, "I concede that this is indeed my original letter."

"Of course it is," Templeton said, snatching the letter back, folding it, and replacing it in his coat pocket. "And you may have it for only ten thousand pounds."

"Ten?" Fitz stammered. "Your May letter demanded only five."

"Your heel-dragging has doubled the price. Purchase your indiscretion, my lord, or marry the girl. It's your choice."

"I'll pay," Fitz glumly replied.

Templeton waited expectantly. "Well?"

Fitz affected surprise. "What? You expect me to pay you now? Don't be ridiculous. I haven't got that kind of blunt at Charlisle."

"I'll accept a draft on your bank," Templeton very generously offered.

Fitz shuddered. "No! Nothing in writing ever again. I will

have to contact my banker in London. He'll send a courier with the money, though it's likely to take several days."

"I can wait," Sir Marcus placidly replied. He walked to the library door and unlocked it. "I'm quite enjoying this summer sojourn." He sauntered out of the room, leaving the door open.

Fitz slumped into a red leather chair and groaned. He was covered in cold perspiration. Why hadn't Edinburgh prepared its young charges—especially *him*—for the rigors of blackmail and its fiendish practitioners?

There was a whisper of movement. The library door closed once again.

"He has the original?" Jack quietly inquired.

"Of a certainty."

"Excellent."

Fitz glared up at him. "What's so bloody excellent about it?"

"We now know the letter is on the premises. I'll search Templeton's room again. It has to be there. The sooner I find that damned letter and you destroy it, the sooner Greeves can return to Charlisle and I can go home to the peace and quiet of Devonshire."

"I have never understood your preference for country life."

"Yet you like me anyway," said Jack with a fond smile.

Fitz grinned up at him. "Only a fool would disown his guardian angel."

*

Chapter 7

A GOOD TWENTY of Charlisle's guests were partaking of afternoon tea and conversation on the southern patio, a gentle
breeze keeping them from becoming overheated, when Lord
Cyril Pontifax was seen galloping up the avenue. He threw
himself from his horse before the gray had come to a complete
halt and then ran up to the surprised party, his riding clothes
dusty, his brown hair windblown, his attractive face flushed.
Many were prepared to object—and strenuously so—to this
appalling quirk of fashion, but his lordship forestalled them all.

"Have you heard the news? There are special editions of the
London papers all over the village," he crowed, pulling several
crumpled newspapers from his coat and waving them in the
air. "On June twenty-first, seventy thousand British, Portuguese, and Spanish troops under Wellington defeated fifty
thousand French under King Joseph and Marshal Jourdan at
some place called Vitoria. The papers say it's more important
than Salamanca. They say"—he hurriedly scanned one newspaper—"that it's 'the most complete defeat of the enemy yet
experienced in the Peninsula'! Wellington is now free to drive
through the Pyrenees and into France!"

Everyone cheered and hugged each other and called for
champagne. They then settled into excitedly discussing this
newest battle in England's long war against Napoleon Bonaparte. For the first time, it actually seemed that victory was in
reach. The factories springing up around the country could be
turned from supplying the war effort to world commerce.
Importation of foreign goods and exportation of English items
would no longer be dangerous. Smugglers would soon be

unable to charge their exorbitant rates for brandy. The joys of Paris and its superior fashions were once again within reach.

Jack and two footmen moved through the chattering throng with trays of champagne, silent and almost invisible in the commotion, for all were on their feet and talking at once.

"Look at this, look at this!" demanded the Earl of Lavesly, shaking one of the papers in the air. "The French were so eager to flee our troops that they left everything behind: their guns, their baggage, even Jourdan's marshal's baton!"

"Hurrah!" cried several people nearest him.

"That will make Boney sit up and take notice," Freddy Braithwaite said.

"We shall hang banners and garlands and colored lanterns all over the outside of the house," Fitz declared, exceedingly grateful for this distraction from his own troubles.

"Wellington knows his Shakespeare, by God!" thundered the Duke of Somerton. " 'When the blast of war blows in our ears,/Then imitate the action of the tiger.' And he has, by God, he has!"

"If I were but twenty years younger and in better health," said the white-haired Lord Throwbright at his side, "I should have been in the midst of Wellington's ranks, saber in hand, shouting 'Once more unto the breach, dear friends, Once more!' "

"Here, here," said several gentlemen standing nearby.

"But the papers say Wellington only had ninety guns and the French had one hundred and fifty-three!" Sarah exclaimed to Lord Phineas Doherty, as she quickly scanned the newspaper she had snared from Lord Pontifax. "We had the French outmanned, but they had us outgunned. How could we win?"

"Position is everything, Sarah," Lord Phineas replied, pulling the paper from her hands. "You see? It says here that Wellington first captured the heights commanding the river Zadora. He took that advantage and then drove into the French center. Divide and conquer, my dear. It's an old strategy, but an effective one."

Several gentlemen overheard this remark and clustered around Lord Doherty to laboriously debate Wellington's strategy. Sarah found herself squeezed out and was just looking for someone to talk to when she spied Jack standing a few feet away, staring out at the terraced gardens, his profile to her, his expression bleak. The mask had crumbled. His fist was clenched white as it pressed against a granite statue of a Greek nymph.

Sarah was at his side before she even realized she had crossed the patio. "Jack, what is wrong?" she asked in a low voice, unaware she had spoken his first name.

He righted himself, the reserved mask sliding back over his face. But there was misery in his eyes. "Nothing at all, Lady Sarah," he said.

"But there is! Why has news of such an important victory made you so sad?"

"Who would not be sad," he retorted, "knowing the carnage such a *victory* entailed? Neither side could have escaped the battle at Vitoria with under five thousand men killed and wounded."

Sarah felt the blood drain from her. *"Ten thousand . . . !"* Unconsciously, her hand gripped his arm. "Good God, so many lives?"

Jack closed his eyes a moment. He heard once again the deafening cannon, the screams of wounded horses, the agonized cries of dying men. He could smell the gunpowder blanketing the field of battle and see the shocked, terrified eyes of his raw recruits, red blooming on their chests, their bellies.

With a wrench, he pulled himself back to Charlisle. "That does not include the thousands missing and maimed," he said bitterly. "Arms and legs amputated like pruning trees, the body parts stacking up in bloody heaps in what we British so laughingly call a surgery. The unrecognizable dead rotting in the field beneath the sun. I see nothing to celebrate in such a *victory*." He turned back to the gardens, pulling free of her hand.

"How do you know this?" Sarah whispered, feeling as if she was standing on that bloody field. "How do you know this face of war?"

Without moving, Jack seemed to collect himself. "I have had friends who have gone to the Peninsula, my lady. Many died, including two cousins who were ... butchered ... at Salamanca and buried there, far from their homes and their families. Abandoned—"

"Do not," Sarah implored. "Do not torment yourself so."

"Those friends who returned were sadly altered, and not simply because their bodies were scarred and maimed. Their eyes ... They told me much of what they had seen." Recollecting himself, he turned back toward her again. "I beg your pardon, my lady. May I get you"—he stopped, as if surprised as he looked down at her—"would you like some champagne, Lady Sarah?"

"Thank you, no," Sarah replied, turning to stare at the merrymakers behind them. "As you say, there is little to celebrate." She was silent a moment. "I understand now the other reason why the newspapers do not name the enlisted men killed and wounded. There would be so many pages, name after name after name, that the populace could not but rise up against so much carnage and demand an end to the fighting."

"There is no need for rebellion," Jack said quietly, wanting suddenly to smooth away the taut crease in her brow. "The war will end within a year."

Sarah stared up at Jack. "Are you certain?"

"Quite. Victory was assured the day Bonaparte decided to invade Russia. He stretched himself too thin *and* met with disaster. He has not had time to recover. Vitoria has just notified the diplomats that it's time to start readying their quills for the peace treaty. It will probably take Wellington a few months to work his way through the Pyrenees, but after that, he'll have an easy walk into France. Bonaparte has lost ... for now."

"For now?" Sarah asked in the greatest alarm.

Jack met her gaze, feeling grim and not caring if she knew it. "The self-made emperor is too besotted with power and too convinced of his own military brilliance to stay long in a peaceful attitude. He will try to reclaim all he is now losing. It is inevitable."

Sarah was silent a moment. "Why do men love war, Rawlins? Why do they court death and destruction so assiduously? Women do not. Giving birth, we understand the value of life.

Burying our children, we know the pain of death. Why don't men?"

Jack quietly regarded her. He had never known anyone who would think, let alone ask, the question that had long plagued him. "I believe the cause is ambition mixed with a certain masculine myopia," he replied. "We men mouth the principles and ideals of peace, but see only the glory of conquest and the thrill of aggrandizement. We are urged on by the lust for greater power, which blinds us and enables us to use our brothers' blood to claim a patch of ground we think will help us achieve those goals. A blinded intellect can muffle any outraged cries of the heart."

"Pray God, I raise sons who will shun war," Sarah whispered.

Jack's expression softened as he looked down at her. "Do not despair, my lady. There is hope yet. Blood lust is not inevitable. A love of life may contravene it."

"You do not love life, Jack, yet you are no friend to war. What weapon did you use to combat the blood lust?"

He turned away and looked up at the dark blue sky. How many times a day in Portugal had he longed to see this shade of blue that only English skies possessed? "It was a combination of weariness and futility, my lady."

"A powerful antidote," Sarah quietly agreed. She knew both too well.

A stern glance from her mother drew her away from Jack and back into the excited party. It was an effort to smile and attend to what was said to her, for reality had claimed her and would not loose its hold. She fled the gabbling crowd as soon as was conceivably proper for the peace her room offered. Maria was not waiting for her, and she did not summon her. Instead, she sat in a window seat for nearly a quarter hour staring down at the exquisite rose garden, thick blooms embracing the sunlight. So much peace and beauty before her, while so many lives had been shattered. No wonder there was grief in Jack's eyes.

Finally, she rose and washed her face, and then rang for Maria. Her maid bustled into the room a few minutes later.

"I think the rose muslin for tonight, my lady," Maria said, opening the large wardrobe.

"Yes, thank you."

"I've been meaning to tell you, Lady Sarah," Maria continued, carrying the gown over to the bed and laying it out, "your sapphire bracelet has gone missing."

"I wouldn't worry," Sarah replied, hugging a bedpost. "It's bound to turn up. Things always get misplaced at country house parties."

"Very good, my lady," Maria said, handing her a pair of stockings.

Fitz had ordered a feast to celebrate Wellington's great victory, and the kitchen rose admirably to the occasion. Chickens, turkeys, geese, and pheasants were slaughtered for the repast. Mutton, ham, and lobster supplemented these. There were three different soups, a wide variety of vegetables from the kitchen garden, two salads, stewed oysters, cranberry twist, lemon possets, quinces, and vast amounts of fresh fruit.

The dinner conversation was all of Vitoria. Sarah consequently had little appetite, which left her plenty of time to converse with her dinner companions and study the others at the table. They were, for the most part, an unappetizing crew. How had Jack described it? Ambition and aggrandizement and the lust for greater power . . . all were displayed here tonight. Ambition of the lowest sort, aggrandizement of the most cold-blooded, power of the meanest order.

There were the Laveslys at opposite ends of the table, their family's relatively recent elevation making them censorious and rigid and eager to climb further. The Dowager Formantle sat between her son and daughter-in-law, her ferocious grip on the young couple squeezing the blood out of their lives. The Danverses were busy flattering and charming everyone around them, knowing full well that the Haute Ton considered them on a par with court jesters: well suited to amusement, but otherwise beneath their notice.

She glanced across the table at Sir Marcus Templeton. Swarthy and robust, a loud drunk, and Sarah thought, narrowing

85

her eyes, a very dangerous man. She had always distrusted anyone who pushed their horses too hard, and she had heard it said that Templeton had killed more than one horse beneath him. It was no wonder the Viscount Lyleton regarded him with scared black eyes whenever they were in conversation, edging away as quickly as propriety allowed. He felt the danger, too.

Lyleton. Sarah glanced at him as he sat beside her cheerfully demolishing a soufflé and telling Corliss Braithwaite on his left why Nugee, or at least Stultz, should be called upon to redesign Britain's military uniforms. The viscount. Her husband.

Sarah shuddered. Try as she might, she could not accustom herself to that thought and the life it foretold.

Familiar laughter brought her head up, and she glanced down the table at the Dohertys. Charlotte was glowing as her husband whispered something in her ear. Charlotte was always glowing, and Sarah thought it had less to do with impending maternity and more to do with the happiness she had known from the first day she had met Phineas Doherty.

Charlotte had finally been allowed to follow her heart. Was it wicked to wish that she could do the same?

Sarah sighed. There was much to think on, but her father was scowling at her and so she hurriedly engaged the viscount in conversation once again. She inquired how many fobs a Bond Street beau needed to be considered truly fashionable, and Lyleton set off at a furious pace.

It was in the drawing room a few hours later that a picnic at the nearby ruins of an ancient Roman villa was proposed. The younger guests deemed this a delightful scheme, the elders smiled indulgently, and so it was decided.

"The carriages must be festooned with ribbons and garlands!" declared Miss Fanny Neville, one of the instigators of this scheme.

"I shall write an ode to Vitoria for the occasion," Mr. Davis announced.

"Oh, good God," said Lord Merbles in disgust. "If you are so enamored of Wellington's deeds, let me purchase your pair of colors and you can, by God, give the man more than puffed-up poetical praises."

"I am not a warrior," Mr. Davis haughtily retorted.

"That's clear enough," said his father with a sneer.

"And we must drink only Portuguese wines tomorrow," Miss Neville continued.

Lord Lyleton required a few hints from his parents before he recollected that it was he who must order the carriages and the picnic hampers for the morrow. Fortunately, this required only a word to Jack, who assured him that he would attend to all the details, and Fitz could return to his hand of cards without giving tomorrow's excursion another thought.

"It is your play, I believe, Lady Sarah," he informed his partner.

She attended her cards, and it was very soon apparent that they would carry the game, as they had the last two. They were, she was unhappy to find, well matched when it came to whist.

"Very pretty indeed," Lord Danvers said admiringly as they counted their points and Fitz began to reshuffle.

"If I didn't know better," Lady Danvers said, and winked, "I would swear you two had been partnered for life."

The cards flew out of the viscount's hands and scattered across the table, which made the Danverses laugh heartily.

"I believe," Sarah said, fighting back a blush as she helped Lyleton collect the cards, "that no one could play ill with the viscount, for he is so very skilled at the game. Whatever mistakes I make, he is able to rectify."

The viscount cast her a grateful glance. "As if you'd made a single mistake the whole of this evening," he scoffed. "You would capture many a gentleman's fortune if you ever played at Watier's, Lady Sarah. Rawlins!" he called with some urgency. "More wine."

Another game and wager lost, and the Danverses declared they had been plucked enough for one night. They rose and ventured over to the Laveslys, who were telling Lord Pontifax of a dinner they once gave Wellington in town, while Sarah and the viscount regarded each other warily.

"Do you go much to the theater, my lord?" Sarah finally inquired, well aware they were being surreptitiously observed by most of the room.

"On occasion," he replied. "I'm not fond of that fellow, Kean, I confess. All that raging up and down the boards. And why women find him attractive, I'll never know. The fellow's practically a dwarf!"

Sarah hid her smile. "I believe it is the passion of his acting that draws so many of my sex to admire him."

"No doubt, for I'd stake my life not a one of them can understand a word he's saying! Why must he always play these damned Shakespearean roles that make no sense and always end in death and destruction? Give me a comedy any night of the week. Or a prizefight! I've never spent a jollier night than at one of the exhibitions at Jackson's Saloon."

"They are very popular in the ton," Sarah gravely agreed, though her mouth quivered slightly. "Do you ever go to the opera?"

"Not for the singing, I can tell you!"

A gurgle of laughter escaped Sarah before she could stop it. "You like the dancing, then?"

"*Much* more entertaining," Fitz assured her with a charming grin. "Never seen so many dashed pretty girls all in one place in my life." His grin faded as he recalled the difficulties raised by one of those pretty girls.

"Ah, my Diana, my virgin goddess of the wild!"

Sarah stifled a groan as she turned to find that Beaumont Davis had claimed the third chair at the table. "Hello, Mr. Davis."

"She speaks!" Mr. Davis cried. Lord Lyleton regarded him with undisguised astonishment. " 'Sidnaeian showers/Of sweet discourse, whose powers/Can crown old Winter's head with flowers.' "

"Crashaw," Sarah explained at the viscount's alarmed glance.

"I have watched you all this night," Mr. Davis said. "My eyes could fix on no other object. Your grace, your smiles, touched my heart like jagged stars falling from the sky."

"Are you foxed?" Lord Lyleton demanded.

Mr. Davis stiffened poetically. "You, sir, are a barbarian."

"And you, Davis, are a widgeon."

They turned as one to this newest interloper. Sarah suppressed a second groan when she saw that it was Lord Cyril Pontifax who claimed the fourth chair at their table. She was surrounded.

"Will you not allow me to play the knight-errant and rescue you from this slayer of verse, my dear Lady Sarah?"

"Any man who seeks to elevate himself by damning the company in which he finds himself, only sinks himself lower in everyone's estimation," Sarah retorted.

"Your tea, Lady Sarah."

Sarah looked up to find Jack setting a teacup before her. "Thank you, Rawlins." She took the cup from him, thoroughly puzzled, though not showing it. She had not asked for tea.

"May I get you gentlemen anything?"

The gentlemen demurred, and Jack walked away to attend to the other guests. Sarah pensively sipped at her tea, well aware whose company she would rather be in at this moment.

"Please believe me, Lady Sarah, that I did not mean to offend you to any degree," Lord Pontifax hastily assured her. "I only meant that I believe myself alone in being able to truly value all that you are and want only the privacy in which to assure you of my deepest regard."

"She doesn't want the regard of a barbarian," Mr. Davis declared. "Her soul is too sensitive, her heart too tender, to withstand your bombastic proclamations."

The viscount's eyes met Sarah's. They shared a secret smile and the same thought: so much sound and fury signifying nothing. The matter had already been resolved against the two men if they did but know it. "Actually," Lyleton said, "what Lady Sarah really wants is some worthy opponents at whist."

"Slander!" cried Mr. Davis.

"Ah, Fitz, you do not know the lady's soul as I do," Lord Pontifax kindly informed the viscount.

"Has your headache improved, Lady Sarah?"

Sarah looked up to find Jack once again at her elbow with a most solicitous expression on his face, and a certain satirical gleam in his gray eyes. A headache? Oh, he was a devil! And a prince among men.

"I'm afraid it's very much worse," she replied, affecting a pained expression.

"Perhaps you should retire, my lady," he gravely advised. "The lights and the conversation here may only exacerbate the condition."

"Thank you, yes," Sarah said, rising, the three gentlemen at her table hurriedly scrambling to their feet. "I believe it is best that I return to my room."

"Sweet Helena, cherished Chloe, are you ill?" Mr. Davis cried. "I will send for the doctor at once."

"That is hardly necessary."

"Let me give you my arm and help you upstairs," Lord Pontifax urged as he advanced on her, Mr. Davis scowling ferociously at him.

"Thank you, no!" Sarah said in some alarm, grabbing Jack's arm. "I would not disturb your evening for anything. Rawlins may attend me. Really, gentlemen, I am quite all right."

"I hope you feel better in the morning," Fitz said enviously. If only a host could plead a headache and escape!

"Thank you, my lord. I'm sure I will be."

Jack led her from the room with as much haste as Sarah's supposed headache allowed. The entry hall was silent and empty when he stopped.

"You are a godsend, Jack," Sarah said feelingly.

" 'But now my task is smoothly done; I can fly, or I can run.' "

Sarah grinned up at him. He knew Milton, too. " 'Servant of God, well done, well hast thou fought the better fight.' " Reaching the stairs, she reluctantly pulled her arm from his. "You are becoming quite adept at rescuing me, Jack."

"Thank you, my lady," he replied, amusement lighting his gray eyes. "It is a pleasure to serve you."

Sarah turned and frowned at the drawing room door. "Never in my life have I been bedeviled by so many marriage-minded men. I've a good notion to run away and live with the Gypsies."

"If I may be so bold, my lady, I fear there is a flaw in the scheme. Your hair," he said to her inquiring gaze, "it would make you stand out in any Gypsy camp."

"I'll dye it."

"And your blue eyes?"

"An indiscretion on my mother's part."

A muscle jumped in the butler's cheek. "And the freckles?"

"If I stay out long enough in the sun, there'll soon be so many of them that they'll join together into a universal tan, don't you think?"

Jack smiled with a warmth that was wholly arresting. "I think—"

"Ah, there you are, Mr. Rawlins," said Mrs. Clarke as she bustled into the hall. "That French chef is throwing another one of his tantrums, and I can't understand a word he says. Will you come and translate?"

Jack seemed to withdraw into cool reserve. "Certainly, Mrs Clarke. Good evening, Lady Sarah."

"Good night, Jack," Sarah said, wishing he would smile at her once more tonight, but already he was gone.

✳

Chapter 8

"So I GAVE him a sweeping right to the jaw," Henry Jenkins continued with pardonable pride, "smashed a left to the ribs, followed that up with a wicked uppercut to the chin, and down the young cockerel fell like a stone. Took ten minutes to revive the boy."

"Oh, well done, Henry!" Sarah exclaimed as they walked their horses to the crest of a northern hill. It was hours yet before the picnic caravan was to set out. Charlisle lay spread below them, Elizabethan gold glowing in the early morning light. "That should teach Templeton's groom not to disdain age and experience in the future."

"He'll not make the same mistake with me, at least."

"You should have a son, Henry, to pass on all your skills and knowledge."

"I'm working on it."

"Set up a flirt, have you?" Sarah said with a grin. "Who's the lucky girl? Come on, now, 'fess up."

"It's Lizzie Benton, the viscount's head parlor maid. She's got the makings of becoming a good housekeeper."

"And is that the only reason you like her?"

"Oh, no, my lady. She's got a kiss that turns a man's legs to jelly."

"Henry!" Sarah gasped, and then dissolved into laughter.

"Good morning, Lady Sarah."

Sarah stopped laughing and stared in astonishment at John Rawlins, who stood only a few feet away, his brown coat held in one arm. She had been so wrapped up in her conversation with her groom that she hadn't observed him walking from the

92

small copse on their right. Now she could look at nothing else. He seemed a part of nature, standing there so tall and proud, the light breeze lifting a lock or two of his dark brown hair, his dark waistcoat emphasizing the breadth of his chest, the sun warming the strong planes of his face.

"Good morning, Rawlins," she said hurriedly. "Are you walking back to Charlisle?"

"Just now."

"Would I be intruding? May I join you?"

"Certainly, my lady."

Before he could change his mind, Sarah jumped down from her horse and handed the reins to Jenkins. "I'll walk back, Henry. Off you go, and luck to you with Miss Benton."

"Thank you, my lady," he said with a grin. Then he cantered off.

She was alone with Jack, and for a moment was uncertain what to say or do. He took a step toward Charlisle, and she quickly moved to his side.

"I trust your headache is improved?" Jack asked.

"At least until I return to Charlisle," Sarah said with a smile. "Do you always go for a morning walk?"

"Yes, my lady," he replied as they continued down the hill, side by side. "The natural world—the orchards and fields, the woods and the animals—always seems so much more real to me than the inner workings of a large house. It provides a necessary perspective."

"Exactly!" Sarah said excitedly. That they should be alike in this as well! "Whenever the pomposity of the ton and the ruthlessness of my parents get too much for me, all I have to do is walk outside and breathe in the air, walk through the gardens and see the real beauty in this world, sit in the woods and feel their truth, and I am revived and myself again."

Jack came to an abrupt halt and stared at her, his gray eyes alive with wonder. "Yes," he finally said.

A little color stained Sarah's cheeks. She hurriedly continued down the hill, Jack falling into step at her side. "I've actually become something of a gardener, thanks to Bill Regis."

"Who?"

"The head gardener at Rolbrook, the Somerton country seat in Lincolnshire. I spent so much time out of doors in my girlhood escaping my governess, that Bill took me in hand and began to teach me about plants and gardening and . . . life. I think I liked sinking my hands into the earth best, feeling its richness between my fingers. You would like gardening, I think."

"Would I?"

"Yes, you've got the hands for it." And when had she noticed his hands? When had she given any consideration to their gentleness and their strength? "Perhaps that's what you should have been instead of a butler," she hurriedly added.

"You may be right," Jack said quietly.

She loved the way his low voice slid up and down her spine. "There's still time, you know," she remarked, a trifle breathlessly. "The knowledge comes easily if you've got the knack. There's no reason to stay in a job you dislike."

"Nevertheless, I do not see myself forsaking my current position in the near future."

"Oh, I do wish you'd reconsider. I once toured one of Father's mills in Yorkshire. I'll never forget the eyes of the workers. So much misery. Your eyes are very similar. You should not rest in unhappiness, Jack. You have the intelligence, the youth, and the ability. You should leave it."

"Do you always worry about the happiness of mere domestics?"

"Do not denigrate yourself or those with whom you work," Sarah said angrily. "You are not a *mere* anything. The American Declaration of Independence has a phrase I shall never forget: 'We hold these truths to be self-evident, that all men are created equal, that they are endowed by their Creator with certain unalienable rights, that among these are life, liberty, and the pursuit of happiness.' Are you not a man? Are you not therefore my or anyone else's equal? Do you not also have an unalienable right for happiness?"

"And do not *you* also have an unalienable right to happiness?" Jack riposted.

94

"Ah, well, the Americans spoke only of men, after all."

"I find it curious that you urge me to leave unhappiness behind, but will not take your own advice, even though you have a great capacity for happiness."

"Have I?" Sarah asked. "I would not have said so. But then," she added, looking away, "there has been little opportunity or reason to examine the issue. I think instead that I have a great capacity for selfishness, for I have so much and find myself always longing for something more."

"That is not selfishness, Lady Sarah. That is good sense prevailing in the midst of madness."

"Do you say the Haute Ton is mad, Jack?"

"As a hatter, Lady Sarah."

She chuckled. " 'Tis heresy to say so, but I've long believed the same. I have yet to comprehend why anyone would value champagne-polished Hessians over kindness and bonhomie."

"It is difficult to hold fast to one's sanity when one is surrounded by all the denizens of Bedlam insisting that *you* are the one who is insane, not they."

"Exactly. Sometimes I wonder if it is wise to keep up the struggle. Giving in to the general view would be so much easier, you know."

"Perhaps you need only meditate a little longer on the pursuit of happiness to find the best course."

Sarah considered this as they reached the patio that led up to Charlisle's north entrance. She was about to say she could not pursue something when she had no idea where to find it, but stopped herself as a phrase settled on her tongue. " 'Give me liberty or give me death,' " she murmured, and then smiled up at Jack. "Another American radicalism. Perhaps I *should* consider emigrating."

"It has its advantages, my lady, although I think the American Declaration of Independence flawed in one important aspect: men are equal only before God, not while they stand on this planet."

"But—"

"Do but think, Lady Sarah," Jack said, his gaze grave and measuring as it met hers. "May a dairymaid marry a prince?

May a cobbler marry the daughter of a duke? No. Society puts equality in its place."

Sarah pensively shook her head. "Ah, the wise and practical John Rawlins. You're right, of course. Even my paltry life is proof that money and position are everything."

"I will not allow you to denigrate yourself in such a fashion," Jack said, grimly. "You are not a *paltry* anything."

Sarah blinked up at him in utter surprise.

"There you are, Rawlins, you delightful fellow!"

They turned to find Lady Abigail Winster walking gracefully toward them, her eyes fixed solely on the butler, her white muslin morning gown blowing against her body in the soft breeze and clearly outlining her wholly attractive figure. Untempted, Jack calmly slipped on his coat as she drew before them.

"You did not bring me my morning tea, you naughty boy," Lady Winster said chastisingly.

Sarah clenched her jaw.

"I'm sorry, my lady. Other duties interfered," Jack replied. "I asked Earnshaw to attend you. Did he fail to do so?"

"Oh, no, he was there, prompt as anything. But he lacks your multitude of charms, Rawlins." This last was said with a certain lascivious gleam in Lady Winster's brown eyes.

"I'm sorry if he did not please you, my lady. If you will excuse me, I must inspect the wine cellar."

Jack walked off, the two women watching him go.

"God, he's gorgeous," Lady Winster remarked. "I'll have him and soon."

"Lady Winster!" Sarah gasped, horrified.

Lady Winster smiled at her derisively. "You're old enough to know the ways of the world, miss. That fellow has undoubtedly bedded half the women in the ton if I know anything of our sex, and I do."

"I think you wholly mistake Rawlins's character!"

"I was not speaking of his character, only his very palpable masculine charms and the determination of our sex to enjoy them. Surely, *you* are not immune to his allure?"

Sarah flushed. "Rawlins is very handsome, I grant you. But I would never think—"

"When you are married, you will think much more freely, I promise you," Lady Winster said, and then sauntered off in the direction Jack had gone.

Sarah stared after her, appalled. Lady Winster meant to take Jack to her bed! And would he go? She could not think it possible, for he so disliked their class. But he *was* a man, and Lady Winster was so very beautiful, and determined, how could he resist?

"Monstrous! Monstrous!" she said under her breath. But whether she meant Lady Winster or the pain she felt at thinking of John Rawlins in any other woman's arms, Sarah did not know and did not want to find out.

"Mr. Rawlins, we are a hamper short!" cried Mrs. Clarke, looking a trifle harried as footmen hurried back and forth between the hall and the waiting carriages.

"On the contrary, Mrs. Clarke, we are a hamper over," Jack assured her. "I took the precaution of advising the kitchen to make too much, rather than too little. The extra hamper is already outside."

"Thank God," exclaimed the housekeeper with palpable relief.

The picnic at the Roman villa was generally agreed to be a success. For those who wished to tour the ruins, there were rocks aplenty to study and marvel over. For those who preferred lounging beneath a shade tree, there were Jack and four footmen to attend their every whim.

There were only two who were really unhappy in the party: Sarah and Fitz. All Sarah wanted from the excursion was the freedom to cogitate on liberty and happiness. Instead, she was hounded from beginning to end by Mr. Davis and Lord Pontifax, who made her yearn for both American commodities, and by the Duke and Duchess of Somerton, who were ringing a peal over her head for encouraging the Terrible Two and ignoring the viscount.

The viscount, in turn, was bedeviled by his parents, who

could not understand why he was dragging his feet on such an important matter, and by Sir Marcus Templeton, who was making the most cutting remarks about his riding attire and horsemanship. The Dowager Formantle was demanding he dance attendance on her, and Miss Fanny Neville was trying to flirt with him! It was a most trying day.

Still, the food—everything from cold salmon to pear tarts—was satisfying, the site both attractive and interesting, and the entertainment a refreshing change from what the party had known thus far.

When they returned to Charlisle later that afternoon, they all had but one complaint: the heat. The drive to the villa had been perfectly charming, but by mid-afternoon, the breeze had gone and the sun had beat down mercilessly upon them. Returning, they all gratefully collapsed within the cool of the main drawing room, loudly calling for lemonade and their baths and a fresh change of clothes. Footmen and maids were kept running for the next two hours.

Alas, the day's trials were not yet over for Fitz. No sooner had he stepped from his bath, than his parents erupted into his room and harangued him for the next half hour as his valet helped him dress behind a Chinese screen. They reminded Fitz that Sarah Thorndike was undoubtedly wondering why he had not yet paid his addresses. They elucidated the cold temper of the Somertons and strongly hinted that the duke and duchess would brook no further delay. They then colorfully described the entire household waiting with bated breath for him to announce his engagement to Lady Sarah. They reminded him that a contract had been signed, and it was his duty to honor it. His parents insisted that he do so at once and, with a sigh denoting a final resignation to the hangman's noose, Fitz agreed.

Ten minutes after his capitulation, Maria Jenkins opened her mistress's door to find a pale—not to say green—Viscount Lyleton standing before her, hastily dressed in a lavender single-breasted coat and high-waisted loose-fitting white silk pantaloons. His black hair for once was simply fashioned (there hadn't been time to effect his usual elaborate coiffure). His black eyes were wide with terror.

"I would like a word with Lady Sarah," he managed.

"Certainly, my lord," Maria calmly replied, though she knew full well what this call meant.

She led him into Sarah's small sitting room—a pretty affair done in pale blue, sunlight warming and lighting it—and went to fetch her mistress. Sarah, like her future bridegroom, had dawdled as much as she could before her mirror. She had heard his voice. She knew what awaited her in the sitting room.

"The viscount, my lady," Maria said simply.

"Yes, I know."

"What are you going to do?"

"That I don't know." Sarah drew a shuddering breath and then flashed a grateful smile as Maria gave her shoulder a reassuring squeeze. Hands cold and clammy, Sarah walked into the sitting room, closing the door behind her. "Good afternoon, my lord."

Fitz turned from the window with panicky eyes. "G-G-Good afternoon, Lady Sarah."

Sympathy calmed her pounding heart. Poor boy. He had been hounded into this as much as she and was just as wretched. "Won't you sit down?"

"Thank you." Fitz waited until Sarah sat on the powder blue settee, and then sank down onto the matching chair opposite her. A moment later he was back on his feet. He seemed to be vibrating. He cleared his throat once. Twice. "You must give me leave, Lady Sarah, to tell you how much I admire you and . . . er . . . hope that you will accept my suit." He gazed despairingly upon her. "Will you do me the honor of being my wife?"

Sarah sat very still. Now that the moment was finally here, her thoughts were remarkably clear. They focused on a single phrase: the pursuit of happiness. She might not know where her happiness lay, or if she would ever find it, but she did know where she would find unhappiness if she did not do something differently and do it now.

Standing at the crossroads of her life, she looked Fitz right in the eye. "I want you to tell chivalry to go hang, Viscount. I want the truth out of you. Do you really want to marry me?"

"It would be an honor to claim so fair—"

"Piffle! No pretty speeches, if you please. Our futures are at stake. *I* think we'd make each other miserable if we married."

Fitz stared at her, openmouthed, and then heaved a grateful sigh. "Oh, so do I! We'd murder each other in our beds within a fortnight."

"Precisely. I knew we were of the same mind in this matter. The problem is: How do we get out of it? My parents are set on us marrying."

"My parents are awfully keen on the idea, too." Fitz paused a moment. "Perhaps," he suggested, looking green again, "if we showed them a united front—each of us refusing to marry the other—they'd back down."

Sarah considered this a moment and then shook her head. "Your parents might back down, but my parents have every reason not to. Besides, there is the money to consider. You are independent, but I am not. If I refuse to marry you, I strongly suspect my parents will threaten me with complete impoverishment until I change my mind."

"I hadn't thought of that," Fitz said glumly as he sank back down onto his chair. "I've blunt enough, of course. But the Lavesly fortune is nothing to toss aside. What are we to do?"

Sarah rose and, hands clasped behind her back, began to slowly pace the room. "If only they hadn't already signed the marriage contract."

"We're doomed," Fitz said, his head sinking into his hands.

"No! I won't give up. I won't be made miserable just to satisfy *them*. There must be a way out. There—" Sarah suddenly stopped and turned to regard the viscount, a plan beginning to bloom in her brain. "*They* are the ones who are keen on us marrying, just as you said. But what if they weren't keen on it?"

Fitz regarded her with puzzled eyes. "But they have everything to gain by our marrying. Why would they lose interest?"

"Because we . . . *we* would make them lose interest! Don't you see? We must make them wish they'd never thought of marrying us off. We must make *them* tear up the marriage contract!"

"But how can we do that?"

Sarah was trembling now. "I'm not quite sure. Let me think a moment." She paced the room twice and came to an abrupt halt before Fitz. "Oh, of course! We'll run a rig. All we have to do is give them a disgust of us. You must make my parents loathe you, and I must make your parents despise me, and together we must make them want only one thing: for us never to marry or even see each other again."

Fitzwilliam Hornsby, the eighth Viscount Lyleton, stared up at Sarah Thorndike in wonder. "That is brilliant!"

"Thank you," Sarah said, dimpling and dropping a quick curtsy, "Now, everyone must know that you have called on me this afternoon. They must be expecting our engagement. So we will give it to them."

"What? But you said—"

"It will only be a temporary engagement, I assure you, my lord. We must seem to give our parents what they want, and then make them lament that they got it."

"Yes, of course. I place myself wholly in your hands. What do you propose?"

Sarah bit her lip, frowning a moment as she contemplated the course she had so recklessly decided upon. Never before had she openly defied her parents. They would not take kindly to this plot. A small voice suggested the guillotine awaited her for such treason. Sarah took a gulp of air. Liberty or death. She had already chosen her course. "I suspect this will have to be a long campaign. It will take much to make our very determined parents change their minds. Are you with me?"

"To the end!" Fitz fervently declared, rising to his feet and warmly clasping her hand in his.

"Even though it means we will undoubtedly have to make complete fools of ourselves and in public?"

"The alternative is too horrific to contemplate," Fitz assured her. "Even if it means riding naked on a cow through the dining room, I will do it. How shall we start?"

"We'll leave the cow in the stable for now," Sarah said with a grin. "Do you like to get drunk?"

They spent the last hour before dinner hatching their plot. It seemed wisest to build slowly to a grand finale. What that finale was to be, they were not yet certain. The cow was held in reserve.

As the clock on the sitting room mantel began to chime the hour, a much happier Fitz led Sarah downstairs, her hand on his arm, their expressions equally grave. It took a quarter of an hour for all of Charlisle's guests to assemble in the dining room and take their seats.

"Shall I begin serving, my lord?" Jack inquired of Fitz.

"Not just yet," the viscount replied, rising from his chair. "Ladies and gentlemen, I have an announcement to make." The room was instantly hushed. All eyes were turned upon him. Jack was staring at him, still as a statue. It was only Sarah's calm presence at his side that gave Fitz the courage to announce their engagement.

The room erupted into a decorous chorus of congratulations as Fitz reclaimed his seat. The Laveslys appeared flushed with joy; the Somertons failed to hide their relief. Lord Pontifax and Beaumont Davis looked morose. Corliss Braithwaite sat pale and unmoving in her chair. Those seated nearest the affianced couple were telling them they had known how it would be from the start and what a highly suitable match it was on both sides. Jack turned away to attend to something on the massive sideboard.

Sarah and Fitz—their hands clasped together under the table in mutual support—withstood it all with something approaching smiles on their faces. They had very little to say. Charlisle's guests were saying it all for them.

Finally, with a nod from Fitz, the servants began to bring in dinner. Few at the table noticed that the affianced couple ate very little, and those who did notice were certain the excitement of so important an engagement had chased away all appetite. Fitz drank steadily through dinner. When the gentlemen finally retired to the library, he drank steadily there as well, laughing at the concerned expression on Jack's face when he called for more port.

In the drawing room with the other ladies, Sarah downed the last of a glass of wine, took a steadying breath, and was just about to march across the room and accost Lady Lavesly when Jack entered with a tray of champagne glasses and began to weave through the women. Sarah was distracted. She also thought a glass of champagne might be useful. She signaled the butler, and he approached, cool and impassive.

"May I offer my congratulations on your forthcoming marriage, my lady?" he said.

Sarah took a glass of champagne from his tray. "Don't start polishing the wedding silver just yet, Jack." Taking a sip of champagne, she marched off toward the Countess Lavesly. "Ah, my future mama-in-law!" she cried with forced gaiety. "Do excuse us, won't you ladies?" she said to Lady Danvers and Lady Winster, who had been congratulating the countess on her coup. "We two have so much to talk over."

The two women agreed with good grace. They were tired of Lady Lavesly's self-congratulatory monologue anyway. While they went off in search of better conversation, Sarah surprised the countess by wrapping her arm around her corseted waist and beginning to promenade the room with her. "I understand Lyleton and I are to have a fall wedding," she said without preamble.

"Yes. Your parents and we thought it best that—"

"Excellent. The summer would be too hot, and the winter would be too cold. Now, about your gown for the wedding. Do try, won't you, Countess, not to outshine me on the most important day of my life."

"I beg your pardon?" said Lady Lavesly, stiffening.

"Why, everyone in the ton knows how much you like to display your admirable figure with low-cut bodices and dampened muslins, and I don't blame you, for really you are a most striking woman. I, alas, am not. It would be too cruel if your dress was to outshine mine at my own wedding. Oh, and be sure not to dye your hair too close to the wedding date. You know how brassy newly dyed blond hair can look. Not at all the thing."

"Dye my hair?" cried the countess, angry pink stains in her cheeks. "I do not dye my hair!"

Sarah went off into a ripple of laughter. "Oh, of course you do! No woman of three-and-forty can claim such perfect golden locks without the able assistance of her hairdresser. Now, were you planning to invite your brother to the wedding?"

"Well, of course! He—"

"Oh, *dear*," said Sarah, biting her lower lip. "He's such bad ton, you know."

"I beg your pardon?" Lady Lavesly intoned, pulling them to an abrupt halt, her expression icy in the extreme.

"Now, don't get on your high ropes," Sarah said. "*Everyone* thinks a penniless baronet with an over-attachment to the muslin set is bad ton."

"How *dare*—"

The gentlemen burst into the drawing room just then, Fitz leading the pack. By anyone's standards, the amount of alcohol he had consumed that night must have made anyone drunk. But Lord Lyleton had a good head for liquor. Thus, he feigned being a good deal more jug bitten than he really was as he loped up to the Duke of Somerton and threw an arm around his shoulders.

"Papa!" he cried jovially, and planted a wet kiss on the duke's cheek.

The Duke of Somerton had a disgust of open displays of physical affection and did what he could to escape the viscount's embrace. Fitz was determined, however, and clung to the duke like a barnacle.

"My dear sir," he slurred. "My most estimable papa-in-law, we must celebrate the forthcoming union of our two houses. More champagne!" he bellowed above the dull roar of conversation in the room. "More champagne, damn your eyes. Magnums of it!" Footmen hurried from the room to fetch liquid reinforcements as Fitz stared lovingly at the duke. "I would drink champagne every hour of the day if I could," he solemnly informed him.

104

"Indeed?" said the duke. He was known for disliking the drink, thinking it more suited to deluding the masses than as anything worthy of a gentleman with discerning tastes.

"I daresay you'd be a much jollier fellow," Fitz continued, "if that damned harridan of a duchess of yours didn't keep you hopping so much. Bit of a grand Turk, 'ey what?"

The duke bristled and succeeded in removing himself from physical contact with his future son-in-law. "You, sir, are drunk."

"Not a bit of it!" Fitz happily cried. "Only half sprung. A little top-heavy at the most! You know, I once had my eye on that girl of yours—what was her name? Oh, yes, *Arabella*. Bit of a looker, 'ey what?" said Fitz, jabbing the duke in the ribs with his elbow. "Nothing like that girl I'm engaged to now." He concentrated a moment. "Shirley? Susan? No, no, no, *Sarah*! Well, beggars can't be choosers. If that son of yours, Gerald whatever-his-name-is, kicks off, does that mean I get to be the next duke?"

To Somerton's relief, they were interrupted by a wave of footmen moving through the room and passing out more glasses of champagne. To Somerton's chagrin, it was the only alcoholic refuge currently available in the room. He downed a glass with a shudder.

"You will find, sir," he snapped, "that Sarah will make you an estimable wife."

"Oh, no doubt. No doubt," Fitz said, swaying on his feet. "Bit of a worry as to whom our future offspring will resemble—*freckles*," he said with a shudder in response to the duke's outraged stare, "are very bad ton."

The duke—who had originally construed a very different meaning to the viscount's worry—would have been relieved if the Countess of Lavesly had not at that moment screamed.

All eyes in the room turned to stare at her and at Sarah, who had accidentally on purpose poured her glass of champagne into the countess's tight bodice. She was now ineffectually dabbing at Lady Lavesly's heaving bosom with a tiny lace handkerchief.

"Oh, I'm so sorry!" Sarah apologized over and over again. "Someone must have jostled my arm. I—"

"You did that on purpose!" the countess stormed.

"No, indeed," Sarah assured her. "Here, let me show you what happened."

"Don't touch me!" the countess screamed, backing away from Sarah.

Fitz, meanwhile, collapsed on the drawing room floor, in an apparent stupor.

There was a moment of stunned silence as everyone in the room turned from the aggrieved countess to goggle at Fitz. Who snored.

"Rawlins!" bellowed the apoplectic Earl of Lavesly. "Have my son carried to his room at once." Jack and two footmen leapt to the viscount and carried him from the room. Conversation among Fitz's guests resumed its normal tenor, though of course everyone was talking of him, except for the Duke and Duchess of Somerton. They claimed a far corner of the room and called Sarah on the carpet in furious undertones, informing her that she would grovel before the countess for the next sennight. Sarah agreed to this, repeatedly apologized for her clumsiness, and knew a certain satisfaction when she was finally released. The evening was going very well.

Her only mistake came just before midnight when she ventured into the library to find a book to help lull her to sleep. Unbeknownst to her, Mr. Beaumont Davis followed her there, making his presence known when he closed the door behind him and leaned against it, a look of feverish determination in his eyes.

"I must speak with you in private," he said, his voice urgent, his gaze rabid.

"Really, Mr. Davis—" Sarah uneasily began.

"You could not be so cruel as to refuse me this one small request?"

Sarah sighed heavily. No, she could not be so cruel. Besides, the conversation was inevitable. It was best to get it over with now as later. "Very well," she said.

106

"You are an angel of goodness!" Mr. Davis cried, and then began to pace the library in the utmost agitation.

"Mr. Davis?"

He whirled around upon her. "You must not marry that boorish, illiterate, inebriated miscreant!" he declared.

"Mustn't I?" Sarah said, hiding an unexpected smile.

"You are too good. You are too sensitive and fine to give succor to an ape-drunk. Lyleton is unworthy of you. He does not *deserve* you."

"Nevertheless, he will have me," Sarah said gently.

"No!" cried Mr. Davis, starting forward and clasping her shoulders in his hands. "It must not be so."

As it seemed that Mr. Beaumont Davis intended to kiss her, lost as he was to the heat of the moment, Sarah hurriedly disengaged herself from his hands and took a strategic step back. "Mr. Davis, you forget yourself," she said with some asperity.

"How can I not forget myself, when I am in your divine company?" cried Mr. Davis, throwing himself on his knees at Sarah's feet as he had often longed to do. "You inspire within me feelings that cannot be repressed, words that must be spoken, deeds that must be done. You are my muse, my burning light, my Arcadia. You must not be lost to me. Marry me, Sarah, and let me take you away from these cretins who don't know how to value you as you deserve."

"You are very kind, Mr. Davis," Sarah quietly replied. "I will always value your regard and your friendship, but what you ask is impossible. I cannot marry you."

"Do not let the bounds of social decorum keep you from the happiness you deserve!"

Sarah could not but smile. "I assure you, Mr. Davis, that I will not. But I must tell you that, despite your many compliments to my fine feelings, I am a very practical sort of woman. If I should take a husband other than Lord Lyleton, it would be for love"—she held up a hand before he could leap in—"and I do not love you, Mr. Davis."

He looked at her, wholly flummoxed. "You don't?"

"No," she said kindly. "I have daily tried to give you a hint as to my true feelings, but you would not heed me. I have no wish to pain you, Mr. Davis. Your admiration and goodwill deserve far better from me than that. Perhaps it would help if you could but see that I am not the angelic muse you think me. I am a plain, simple woman who delights in outdoor sports as well as literature. I quite like Donne and Dryden and Pope, and I fear, I am not an ardent admirer of Byron." She smiled as his green eyes widened in horror at this. "I think you deserve success in your career and happiness in your marriage, and by speaking honestly with you now, I hope that I am helping to assure both."

"You don't admire Byron?" Mr. Davis faltered as he struggled to his feet.

"No," Sarah gravely replied.

"You . . . you have no sensibility!"

"Very little," Sarah agreed.

Mr. Davis paled as the truth finally came to him. "You are only a bluestocking!"

"That is an accurate assessment."

"Oh! I have been deceived, misled, abused!"

"Mr. Davis—"

"That I could have been so blind! You must excuse me, Lady Sarah," said Mr. Davis stiffly, "but I cannot remain another moment in your company."

Sarah watched him beat a hasty retreat out the library door and sighed with a hint of wistfulness. She would never know such ardent admiration again.

She returned to her room and wrote a most apologetic note to the Countess of Lavesly, instructing Maria to deliver it along with a small posy of flowers the next morning. She finally climbed into bed with a feeling of satisfaction she had never known before. To rout both sets of parents *and* Mr. Davis in one night! She hadn't known she had it in her.

Chapter 9

SARAH TROTTED DUNE through an oak grove and emerged a half mile from Charlisle, the already hot sun making it sparkle in the early morning. There, leaning with his back against one of the older trees, was Jack Rawlins, impassively regarding her.

"Good morning!" she cried. "May I walk back with you?"

"Certainly, my lady," he coolly replied, pushing himself away from the tree and slipping on his black coat.

Sarah hastily sent her groom packing. She was alive with an excitement she had never felt before. Three mornings in a row could not be coincidence. Jack had watched her course, and arranged his own to meet her on her way back to Charlisle. It must be so!

But if it was, why was he now so grim and quiet as they walked together? Why was he so different from yesterday morning and the morning before that?

"It's a lovely morning, isn't it?" she commented.

"Yes, indeed, my lady."

Honestly concerned now, Sarah peeped up at Jack. "Are you quite well?"

"Perfectly, my lady. I trust you have recovered from last night's contretemps?"

"Recovered? Jack, I went to bed with a smile on my face for the first time since I came to this hellhole."

The butler blinked. "I beg your pardon, my lady, but how could you be happy when both the Somertons and your future in-laws were so very unhappy with you and the viscount?"

Sarah beamed. "Strategy, Jack. It's all in the strategy. I'm sure you noticed, for butlers notice everything, that my parents and the Laveslys were dead set on Lyleton and I making a match of it."

"I had detected certain matrimonial gleamings in their eyes, yes."

"Well, the viscount and I *don't* want to marry each other. We are, in fact, plotting to dissolve the engagement before it is even announced in the papers."

Jack was rendered speechless by a sudden confluence of emotions—relief, astonishment, exultation—which he could neither understand nor bring to order. He had thought her marriage to Fitz inevitable, and now . . .

The look in his eyes was almost that of wonder. "You are actually squaring up to your parents?"

"In a roundabout fashion, yes, though they must never know it."

"I am quite at a loss, Lady Sarah."

She smiled kindly upon the befuddled butler. "We intend to so badly alienate both sets of prospective in-laws, that *they* will insist on our never posting the banns in this or any other lifetime. That's why Lyleton pretended to fall down drunk last night, and that's why I poured the champagne over the countess."

"That is brilliant," Jack said, staring down at her with open admiration. "Flawless."

"Why, thank you," Sarah said with a startled smile. "Of course, I trust you will keep this in the strictest confidence."

"Consider any remark you make to me, Lady Sarah, as sacred as if made in the confessional," Jack declared, an unaccustomed hint of exuberance in his voice.

"Oh, you are good, Jack," Sarah said, impulsively reaching out and squeezing his arm. "Will you mind if we occasionally call on you for help? A third coconspirator could be necessary in this campaign."

"I would be honored to help you in any way, Lady Sarah."

"Thank you," she said happily, glad to see a tinge of warmth in his eyes. "With your help, I am certain to make my future in-laws loathe the very sight of me."

Something suspiciously like a chuckle escaped the butler. "You have certainly made a good start. If I might offer a suggestion, Lady Sarah?"

"I would be most grateful."

"The earl and countess are keen hunters, and while this is not the season, there will undoubtedly be a variety of riding parties formed during the summer. If you could show yourself to be less than an exemplary horsewoman, it would undoubtedly set their backs up."

"Why, how clever you are, Jack! They are bound to regard me as a wholly unacceptable connection if I display a bad seat and worse hands. The devil of it is, my horsemanship is the one thing I pride myself on. I'm not beautiful like Arabella, and I can't freeze someone in their steps like Frances, but by God, I can outride them and anyone else who cares to try me! Still, it's for a good cause. Any other crumbs you can throw me?"

Jack, his hands clasped behind his back, considered the matter for a moment, an unconscious smile on his face. To plant a barb in the Laveslys' flesh! Here was sport in abundance. "The earl and countess also strenuously oppose any negative emotional display, particularly at breakfast when neither, if I might be permitted to observe, are at their best. If you could contrive to pick a quarrel with the viscount during the morning meal, the resulting dyspepsia within the parental digestive tracts will undoubtedly turn them against you."

"It shall be as you say. I'll plot the whole thing out with Lyleton today."

"Never say die, Lady Sarah."

She grinned up at him, wholly entranced by the devilry dancing in his gray eyes. "I do admire your devious mind, Jack. I must repay you somehow." She thought a moment. An expression came over her that Jack had never seen before. "Charlotte Doherty has organized a concert for tonight," she said. "You might drop by for my performance. It should be highly . . . diverting."

"That sounds suitably ominous. You have become very determined of late," he observed.

"It's those devious American philosophers," Sarah said,

111

shaking her head. "They've spread their contagion through the world. I'm revolting, Jack."

He did not laugh, but he did grin at her, and that pleased Sarah more than she had expected.

Once back at Charlisle, Sarah hurried upstairs to bathe and change for breakfast, her mind awhirl with nonsensical torments for her prospective in-laws. Still, she was everything demure as she sat quietly beside Fitz—they had privately advanced to a first-name basis—at the breakfast table later that morning.

Lady Winster, however, appeared in high dudgeon. "Lord Lyleton," she intoned, "I regret to inform you that my ruby necklace is missing. It is a family heirloom."

"Oh, my dear Lady Winster!" the Countess of Lavesly gasped.

"Misplaced it, have you?" Fitz slurred. Although it was just ten in the morning, he appeared well on the way to being happily corked.

"No, sir, I have not misplaced it!" Lady Winster angrily retorted. "My maid has looked everywhere for it. It has been stolen!"

Fitz frowned. "Something's been pinched at Charlisle? Unthinkable! Unless, of course, your maid took it in the first place."

"Eggles has been in my employ these last eight years and more," Lady Winster snapped. "She did not *pinch* my necklace, as you so crudely put it. I am convinced those filthy Gypsies have taken it."

"Impossible," Fitz scoffed. "No one dressed so shabbily would be allowed to enter Charlisle, let alone burgle your room, Lady Winster. You must be foxed."

"I?" cried Lady Winster, her cheeks stained a bright pink.

"Lyleton, you forget yourself," the Duchess of Somerton intervened. "My own daughter has lost a bracelet, and I believe Mr. Braithwaite has lost a gold snuffbox."

"Not that thick piece with the double eagles carved on it?" Freddy Braithwaite demanded of his father.

"The very same," said Mr. Braithwaite.

"Good," said the undutiful Freddy. "I always thought that a hideous box. Not up to your standards, you know, Father."

"The point is," the duchess intervened once again, "that those Gypsies are stealing us blind, and I demand that you do something about it, Lyleton."

"Happy to oblige you, Duchess," Fitz replied, swinging a leg over the arm of his chair and letting it dangle there. "But they ain't to blame."

"Of course they are to blame," said the Earl of Lavesly, his tone harsh. "I warned you at the outset what would come of you letting those damned vagabonds camp on Charlisle land."

"You're all wet, Father," Fitz slurred, his black gaze unfocused as he regarded his fulminating parent. "Rawlins, have you seen any Gypsies lurking about the house?"

"On the contrary, my lord," Jack replied. "I have observed no one from either the village or the Gypsy camp anywhere near Charlisle. The Gypsies have been very careful to keep close to their caravans."

"There, you see?" Fitz said triumphantly. "Nothing to do with the Gypsies; Rawlins says so."

"What is the word of a mere butler when we are being robbed blind?" the Dowager Formantle bellowed.

Sarah observed Jack stiffen slightly, before proceeding to serve Mrs. Braithwaite.

"Now, now, salt of the earth is old Rawlins," Fitz assured the dowager. "You can trust him to the end."

"Be that as it may," Lady Winster fumed, "I demand that you take immediate action to investigate these thefts and return our belongings."

"Oh, very well," Fitz said with a weary sigh. "I'll send for the Bow Street Runners."

There was a clatter of silverware and china up and down the table.

"Good God, you can't be serious!" the duchess said in an awful voice. "Have those common louts moving freely among us? We would be murdered in our beds!"

She was heartily seconded by the majority in the room.

"Do but think, Lyleton," Sarah said in a tone of utter disgust.

"The Bow Street Runners are renowned for pocketing more than they recover to supplement their abysmal wages. Jewelry will be disappearing twice as fast with them in the house. And they never bathe. The stench would be unendurable."

"Trust you to kick up a dust over a jolly good lark," Fitz complained. "Very well, very well, no Bow Street Runners. I will attend to the matter myself. Now, I want some more of that dashed good ham."

Charlisle's increasingly worried guests had to be content with this unconvincing assurance as Fitz scooped several slices of ham onto his plate and called for another glass of claret.

Before he could settle in to well and truly hound the Duchess of Somerton—his assignment for that day—Fitz first had to repair to his bedchamber and change. He had been using an old schoolboy's trick at the breakfast table, tipping glass after glass of wine down his shirtsleeve when no one was looking. He was consequently drenched by the end of the meal, necessitating this change in habiliment. He left his valet's hands an hour later, looking trim as a trencher.

Sarah, meanwhile, set her sights on Lord Lavesly. She belittled the appalling shortness of his family tree, professing horror at being related to someone whose ancestors had but two centuries earlier been common soldiers with no tie to the land. She frowned at the earl's protestations of equality with her own family. She laughed outright when he sought to censure *her* behavior.

By this time, Fitz had attached himself to the Duchess of Somerton. Her sole aim in life was to impress the world with her superiority, and to look down on and denigrate anyone not of her standing. Yet here was this foppish simpleton *laughing* at her, *flirting* with her, and generally making a complete cake of himself in her company . . . and in public. Her cheeks were seldom free of a blush. She was nearly at her wit's end to find some sort of set-down that would put this upstart in his place and keep him mute in her company once and for all. But he seemed immune to even the most ruthless of snubs.

She took her place at the dinner table that night with a

tremendous sense of relief, for Fitz always sat at the opposite end of the table.

But not tonight. Tonight he had told Jack to place the duchess at his side. She watched with horror as he sat down beside her. The bile rose in her throat as she contemplated the interminable meal extending before her. She would have pleaded a headache and fled the room had she not remembered her position, her birth, and her purpose in this house. She would marry off Sarah and have done with it. Unfortunately, she had intended to marry off Sarah respectably, and she very much began to fear—as the dinner wore on and Fitz became more and more intoxicated, garrulous, and affectionate toward her—that respectability might be slipping away.

The half hour in which the ladies were separated from the gentlemen after dinner were, for the duchess, pure bliss. She was free from Fitz, she could take a hand in organizing the cherry-paneled music room for the concert that Sarah and Lady Charlotte Doherty had planned, and she could ignore her daughter and pretend, for a few minutes at least, that she did not have to look forward to a fall wedding at which the bridegroom would undoubtedly fall down drunk at the archbishop's feet.

With cunning born of desperation, she surrounded herself with a cordon of safety when the gentlemen finally entered the music room and took their seats for the concert. The duke was on her left, the Earl of Lavesly was on her right, the Danverses and the Braithwaites and the Winsters surrounded her. Fitz could get nowhere near her.

But she could not avoid noticing him. He seemed to all intents and purposes to be drunk as a wheelbarrow. He shouted bravos following Charlotte's excellent performance on the pianoforte, drowning out everyone else's applause. He stood up in the middle of Miss Braithwaite's moving recitation on the harp, and promptly fell over half the people sitting in his row, bringing the performance to an abrupt halt. He snored loudly through Lady Winster's aria, even though she was a talented mezzo-soprano, and then through Mr. Davis's admittedly tedious poetry reading. He demanded that Susan

Formantle provide an encore on the pianoforte before she had begun her first song and loudly commented on Miss Neville's regrettable lack of skill on the harp during that poor lady's performance.

And then there was Sarah.

She was the second to the last to perform. She walked to the front of the audience with such commendable calm and sufficient grace that her mother did not think of more than a half-dozen chastisements. She had chosen her gown well, a gossamer confection of pale green silk. Her red hair was simply but attractively arranged. Her freckles did not seem half so pronounced. All seemed well. Then she sat down at the pianoforte and, accompanying herself, began to sing in a clear, lovely alto:

Dear mother, dear mother, the church is cold;
But the alehouse is healthy, and pleasant and warm.
Besides, I can tell where I am used well;
The poor parson's with wind, like a blown bladder, swell.
Sing hey and a ho and a nonny, nonny no.
But, if at the church they would give us some ale,
And a pleasant fire our souls to regale,
We'd sing and we'd pray all the livelong day,
Nor ever once wish from the church to stray.
Sing hey and a ho and a nonny, nonny no.
Then the parson might preach, and drink, and sing.
And we'd be as happy as birds in the spring;
And modest Dame Lurch, who is always at church,
Would not have bandy children, nor fasting, nor birch.
Sing hey and a ho and a nonny, nonny no.
And God, like a Father, rejoicing to see
His children as pleasant and happy as he,
Would have no more quarrel with the devil or the barrel,
But kiss him, and give him both drink and apparel.
Sing hey, nonny, nonny, nooooo.

Half the noble jaws in the room had hit the floor. The other half, led by Fitz, were howling with laughter as Sarah rose from the pianoforte, gravely curtsied, and made good her escape, her heart pounding more with excitement than trepidation. She had done it! For the first time in her life, she had deliberately made a public spectacle of herself.

To avoid certain parental fury before going to bed, Sarah had planned to hide in a little-used parlor in the north wing until everyone had retired for the night. Instead, she found herself waylaid by the sound of laughter—masculine laughter—emanating from behind a hidden door in the wall of the first curve of the grand staircase.

Curious, she followed that muffled sound and opened the door. Cautiously peeking inside, she gasped, for there was John Rawlins, his arms wrapped around his torso, sobbing with laughter!

Sarah had never been more stunned, first because she had never seen a butler laugh before and Jack had assured her that butlers never laughed, and second because he looked so very attractive and so very much *not* like a butler as hilarity ruled him. He wiped his eyes with a handkerchief—"Oh, Lord!" he gasped—and suddenly realized he was not alone.

"No, no, don't stop!" Sarah said. She hurriedly stepped through the door, closing it behind her. A servants' staircase spiraled up before her. "You laugh so very well. It is a pleasure to hear you."

"Your pardon, my lady," Jack replied, "but it would be disastrous if anyone else *did* hear me." He tried to compose himself, then glanced at her and could not hold back a grin. "Where on earth did you learn such a Bartholomew's Fair song?"

"At Bartholomew's Fair, of course," Sarah promptly answered, still amazed at the changes laughter had wrought in the taciturn butler.

"No daughter of the Duke and Duchess of Somerton would be permitted to visit such low entertainment."

"Oh, of course not," Sarah answered a trifle giddily. "I was forbidden as soon as the words 'Bartholomew's Fair' left my lips. But I've got the most wonderful maid, Maria, and she agreed to chaperon me and my friend, Charlotte Doherty now, Charlotte Winthrop then, and offered to shield me from any

117

inquiries as to my whereabouts. So off I went. I had the most marvelous time! I was sixteen and quite agog at every sight. So much so, that I went a second time, and that is when I learned 'The Little Vagabond' quite off by heart. I discovered later that William Blake wrote it. *I* added the nonny nonny nos."

"Inspired," Jack stated, leaning back against the wall and regarding her with the aspect of one who had been truly amazed.

"Thank you," Sarah said with a grin. "I think it had the desired effect."

"You sang that song with an ulterior purpose?"

"Ye gods, yes! I don't go around shocking people for the fun of it. I'm not so cruel. No, I embarked upon that song with the sole illustrious purpose of putting my prospective in-laws off me for life."

"It is very likely that you have succeeded beyond your wildest dreams, my lady," Jack said, enjoying her hugely.

"I wish that were true, but the Laveslys are determined social climbers. They won't let the daughter of a duke escape their net so easily. No, I am in this for the long haul, Jack."

"Shall you sing another Bartholomew's Fair song tomorrow?"

"On the contrary," Sarah loftily replied. "I must bedevil the Laveslys with ever new tricks, attacking them from all sides until their only escape is to deny me any connection to their family." She looked around her. "But this is perfect! I hadn't thought of hiding in the backstairs. No one will think of looking for me here." She sat down on the steps. "I feel quite safe."

"Safe from what, my lady?"

"From my parents' wrath, of course! You can't think I would sing that song unscathed? No, no. I shall very likely be flogged if the duke and duchess find me this evening. But if we do not meet again until tomorrow morning, I shall likely come off with only a stern lecture."

"Then, you must by all means remain secreted here. May I fetch you a cup of tea?"

Sarah beamed. "That would be lovely, Jack. Thank you."

118

Supplied with tea and cakes, she stayed hidden away for several hours. When Jack finally assured her that her doting parents had given up their enraged search for their miscreant daughter and had retired for the night, she crept up the back-stairs to her room, unseen, unnoticed, and unscathed.

The next morning, however, she was but halfway through her toilette when her parents burst through her bedroom door and accosted her in a fashion that left her in no doubt as to their continuing feelings of outrage, fury, and humiliation. For a good hour they lambasted her for her crude performance of the night before, her lack of breeding despite her noble lineage, her willfulness, her gracelessness, her barbarism, her conceit. They charged her with the seven deadly sins, thrice, and were just gearing up for another go-round, when Sarah humbly begged their pardon and assured them it would never happen again. The concert had been such a solemn event, she said, that she had thought the audience would appreciate the introduction of a bit of levity. She had not meant to offend. Her parents informed her in no uncertain terms that she *had* offended.

"You will apologize to the entire company at breakfast," the duke stated, glowering at her.

"Yes, Father," Sarah meekly replied.

"You will be a pattern card of propriety for the rest of our stay in this house, Sarah, or I shall beat you myself!" the duchess declared.

"Yes, Mother."

Far from mollified, the Somertons finally abandoned their daughter to her maid and left the room.

Sarah considered her closed bedroom door for a moment. All in all, that had gone remarkably well. She was a little amazed at how calmly she had withstood their tirade. Had she grown braver, or simply more astute?

True to her word, Sarah humbly apologized to the company at breakfast and conducted herself as a model of decorum the whole of that day, though not from any sense of duty. She thought it best to lull the Laveslys into a false sense of security before striking again. Besides, she was quite certain the duchess *would* beat her if she was provoked too soon.

Fitz was also a bit more subdued. He pretended to drink himself into a stupor before lunch, and then took a nap stretched out on a chaise lounge in the drawing room while two dozen of his guests played cards on the patio. His stentorian snores did not go unnoticed by the Somertons, who shuddered and tried to concentrate on their game.

In truth, it was too hot to kick up much of a dust. The heat wave had continued, sapping energy and ambition for anything more than a cool drink and a quiet day.

"You must be so uncomfortable," Sarah said to Charlotte that afternoon as they sat together on a wooden bench beneath an ancient chestnut.

"Mother did advise me to avoid carrying a child in the dead of summer," Charlotte replied with a wry smile, her hand affectionately stroking her protruding belly. "But I've become quite adept at staying in the shade and moving as little as possible. Oof!"

Sarah looked at her inquiringly.

"The heir apparent is restless today," Charlotte said with a smile.

"Will it be a boy, do you think?"

"I think so, but Phineas wants a girl, and that would be nice because then I could name her after you."

Sarah flushed with pleasure. "My dear Charlotte!"

"Now, now, you are my dearest friend," Charlotte said, taking her hand, "even if you do know the most appalling songs."

"You laughed as heartily as anyone, and you know it."

Charlotte chuckled. "I heard Phineas laughing in his sleep last night. He was undoubtedly dreaming of you."

"I am happy to bring whatever dram of pleasure I can into people's lives."

"The Laveslys were not pleased. They were well and truly horrified."

"Good."

Charlotte brought out her fan and began to lethargically stir the air near her cheek. "This scheme of yours may not take as much time as you think to succeed. Another such performance, and I daresay the Laveslys will throw you out on your ear."

"I do have to be careful, you know. I can't be making rough game with the Laveslys, or the duke and duchess are bound to get suspicious. I've never really broken out before, you know."

"Much too well bred," Charlotte agreed.

"Much too timorous," Sarah corrected. "But I've tasted freedom these last few days, and I like it, Charlotte."

" 'Tis a dangerous feeling for a young woman in your position, my dear."

"I know it," Sarah said with a sigh as she leaned back against the broad tree trunk. "The problem is, it seems to grow with each new hour! It is becoming increasingly more difficult to recognize myself. I used to think I was the merest scrap of a mouse, yet here I am roaring away like a lion! It's all rather disconcerting . . . and problematical. Whatever am I going to do with myself when I finally leave Charlisle? I don't think I'll be able to go on as I've done before. The dissatisfaction with my life is too present in me now. I can no longer ignore it. But what is the alternative? How should I act? What should I do?"

"Perhaps this summer sojourn will give you the answer, or . . . You know, Sarah, it occurs to me that if you succeed in your current plan, the duke and duchess will not want you in their company for some time to come. I shall ask them to give you to me, so I may have you with me for my lying-in and for at least a few weeks after."

"Oh, you *are* good, Charlotte," Sarah said, kissing her hand. "I will be safe and happy for a few months, and perhaps that will give me the time I need to come up with some sort of life plan."

"There is nothing like attending to a woman in labor to encourage one to rethink her life," Charlotte wryly agreed.

Sarah finally returned to the house by way of the topiary garden, where she chanced to spy her father and the very pretty Lady Throwbright seated together, a ducal arm about the lady's waist, their heads close together as they conducted what appeared to be a mutually pleasurable conversation. Without missing a step, Sarah continued into the house. This was not

121

the first time she had observed her father flirting with a married woman. The Duke of Somerton was well known for his many affairs, which he conducted with the utmost discretion, unlike so many of his peers.

From all that Sarah had observed, affairs were a normal part of married life. Everyone engaged in them; everyone knew of them; everyone expected them. The Haute Ton within Charlisle's walls were probably already making wagers on who she would take for her first lover after she married Fitz.

"My dear Lady Sarah, I find you alone at last!"

She was just crossing the entry hall, intending to go upstairs and hide in her bedroom for an hour or so. But Lord Pontifax, coming downstairs, had caught her instead. He ran the rest of the way down to the hall and gazed adoringly into her eyes.

"I must speak with you in private," he said.

"Yes, of course you must," Sarah said resignedly. "The morning parlor would be suitable."

Lord Pontifax eagerly agreed and, clasping her hand in his, pulled her into the parlor, closing the door firmly behind them. He turned back to Sarah, carrying her hand to his breast. The steadiness of his heartbeat, Sarah noted, quite belied his ardent expression.

"My dearest Sarah, you must not marry that callow youth!" he exclaimed. "Lyleton is unworthy of you. Even his greatest friends agree that he is a featherheaded, caper-witted fool! He is not your equal in understanding or feeling. He is wholly ineligible."

"But he is the husband my parents have chosen for me," Sarah demurely replied.

"They have chosen the wrong man!" Lord Pontifax cried, regarding Sarah with a fervent expression that left her treacherously close to a giggle. "*He* can never make you happy. He has no strength for you to lean upon in times of trouble. He has no consideration of your finer feelings. He cannot touch your heart. Let *me*, dearest Sarah, let me be the one to chart your future course. Let *me* be your strength, your lover, your husband, your companion through the years!"

Sarah had never thought she would be grateful to her parents for insisting she become engaged to Fitz, but with Lord Pontifax pressing wet kisses to her most reluctant hand, she was more than grateful. She considered the engagement divine intervention.

"Lord Pontifax, you forget yourself!" she said sternly, retrieving her damp hand and taking a step to the side and away from the ardent lord. "If I have led you to believe that I regard you as anything more than a friend, I apologize. It was not my intention."

"Sarah, what are you saying?" demanded the suddenly pale Lord Pontifax.

"The truth, my lord," Sarah said, delighting in the calm she felt in the teeth of this unpleasant confrontation. "I do not love you. Though I do not love Lord Lyleton, I will not leave him to marry you instead. My parents, sir, would not tolerate the exchange. They would cut me off without a farthing. *I would have no fortune,* Lord Pontifax."

He became ashen. "But what is money . . ." he began weakly.

"It is a necessity, my lord," Sarah interrupted. "I am not some gaby filled with romantic notions. I understand the world all too well. Not only is a runaway marriage imprudent—and I believe that is what you are proposing—it is also foolish. We would only be ostracized by the ton, incur my parents' wrath, and be shackled together, penniless, for the rest of our lives. It will not *do,* my lord. You must see that. I thank you for your kind regard, but as I cannot return it, we must part now as friends and say no more of this."

Wiser after a week and a half in his determined company, Sarah bobbed a quick curtsy and made her exit before Lord Pontifax could find his tongue.

Flush with victory, she wondered what new dragons she could slay this day. She felt positively Amazonian.

Fate was kind to Sarah. This was the Earl of Lavesly's birthday, and a full celebration had been planned to follow a magnificent feast that evening. It was too good an opportunity, Sarah and Fitz both agreed, to ignore. They had Jack seat Sarah beside the earl at dinner so she could torment him. She had discovered that it took very little to upset Lord Lavesly. She launched into a monologue about the illustrious suitors she had had in the past, carefully insinuating her distaste in marrying down by marrying Fitz.

The Earl of Lavesly naturally bristled at this, defended his son's title and position, and found himself laughed at by (as he later described her) a freckled hellion with no more manners than a common footpad. When the dinner party adjourned to the drawing room for celebratory champagne, cake, and presents, the earl escaped her with an alacrity that left her chuckling for several minutes.

For the next hour, Sarah did nothing untoward, except drink champagne. Glass after glass of champagne. She soon found herself giggling at anything that was said to her. Walking a straight line from the astonished Freddy Braithwaite to the horrified Countess of Lavesly was impossible. Even standing upright became problematic. She had to lean on the lady's shoulder as the countess struggled with heroic hauteur to continue their conversation.

"Of course, Fitzwilliam is a wealthy young gentleman," she said, "and has no need of a career, but I have always thought he would do admirably in Parliament, perhaps even in the Cabinet."

Sarah went off into whoops of laughter. The countess turned a bright red, which made Sarah laugh all the harder. The Duke of Somerton materialized at her side with almost unseemly haste, his mouth grimly compressed as he glowered at his hysterical daughter. Nose in the air, the countess took this opportunity to make good her escape.

"Sarah!" hissed the duke. "What are you thinking of? What has come over you?"

"Why, nothing at all, Your Grace," Sarah tittered. "I have been socializing, as you are always after me to do, and listening to that absurd countess plot her silly son's ludicrous future. The Cabinet." She shook her head and then swayed against her father, grasping his lapel for support.

"You are drunk!" the duke exclaimed in the utmost horror.

"Am I?" Sarah said, blinking. "Impossible. No one can get drunk on champagne, can they?"

"Oh, of course they can, you stupid girl."

"Then, it's a wonder the whole of the Haute Ton isn't foxed from sunrise to sunrise. I don't know why you don't like champagne, Father," Sarah said, swaying before the duke and beaming benignly upon him. "It makes me feel so . . . effervescent."

"May I be of some assistance, Your Grace?"

Sarah owlishly stared up at Jack.

"You may," the duke tersely replied. "Help my daughter to her room and instruct her maid that Lady Sarah is to stay there until morning."

"Very good, Your Grace."

"But I don't want to go!" Sarah pouted. "I'm having the most marvelous time. Aren't you having a marvelous time, Father?"

"I have no more to say to you," the duke snapped, then hurriedly lowered his voice when he saw that they were being observed by everyone in the room. His wife's glare was particularly forceful. "You will go to your room at once, Sarah."

His youngest daughter woefully shook her head. "You just don't like having fun, do you? That's the nail on the head, that is. That's probably why you don't like champagne. It's so . . . effervescent."

"Rawlins?" said the duke grimly.

"At once, Your Grace." Jack got a firm grip on Sarah's elbow and steered her from the room.

"I seem to have dipped rather deep, Jack," Sarah informed him in a conspiratorial whisper as they charted an unsteady course across the hall.

"That was my deduction, my lady," he calmly stated.

"I have never in my life been drunk before." Sarah pursed her mouth. "My lips are numb."

"A symptom of an advanced stage of intoxication, my lady."

"Ah." She peered woozily up at Jack. "Have you ever been foxed?"

125

He regarded her with faux hauteur. "I would never forget myself so much as to become intoxicated."

Sarah sagely shook her head. "No, no, of course not. Still, you've missed out on one of life's more interesting sensations. Am I speaking clearly? I can't feel my lips."

"Quite clearly, my lady."

"Amazing. Whoa there, Jack," Sarah said, dragging the butler to a stop just before the stairs. "Tell them to stop capering about, or I'll not set foot on them."

Jack regarded her a moment and then shook his head. *"Tap-hackled,"* he said. Then he picked Sarah up in his arms and began to carry her upstairs.

"Jack! This is highly improper."

"True, my lady, but it is necessary."

"I *can* walk."

"No, you can't."

"You're laughing at me!"

"Not at all. I would never—"

"Forget yourself . . . Yes, yes, yes, I know the line by heart, Jack. But you *are* laughing at me. Your eyes are lit with it."

"I beg your pardon, my lady."

Sarah scowled at him. "Oh, you're no fun at all. Fitz is fun. He has many failings, I know, but he *is* fun. He makes a very good drunk, don't you think? Devil of it is, he can appear much more inebriated than he really is, whereas I . . ." Sarah sighed heavily and laid her head on Jack's broad, comfortable shoulder. "I'm afraid I've no head for champagne."

Jack had halted his ascent of the stairs and now stared at Sarah in some astonishment. She was fast asleep, curled trustingly against him as if he had always held her.

" 'O! The world hath not a sweeter creature,' " Jack softly quoted. Allowing the barest trace of a smile to grace his lips, he continued up the stairs and carried Sarah into her room. Maria looked up from the hem of an evening gown she was repairing, her brown eyes widening with alarm.

"Good heavens, is she ill? Is she dead?" she cried, jumping up from her chair and hurrying over to the bed on which Jack was laying Sarah.

"Neither," he reported, straightening up. "She is drunk."

"Lady Sarah?"

"Your mistress blamed the champagne."

Maria shook her head knowingly. "A sly drink if ever there was one. You go along like a house afire, and then suddenly find yourself in a dead stupor. I hope everyone was appalled by her performance?"

"Thoroughly appalled," Jack assured her.

Maria looked affectionately down at her mistress. "That's my girl. Thank you for bringing her safely to port, Mr. Rawlins."

The suspicion of a smile glinted in Jack's gray eyes. "You are most welcome. Good night, Miss Jenkins."

He left the room, closing the door behind him. Maria watched him go with a regretful little sigh. If only she was ten years younger! Then she turned back to Sarah and began to undress her for bed.

She returned to her young lady's bedchamber the next morning at seven, as was her habit, carrying a tray with hot chocolate, bread and butter, and a dish of summer melon. She closed the door with her foot.

Sarah jerked up in her bed from a dead sleep. "Good God, what was that?" A look of horror washed over her face. "Oh, my head!" She slumped back against her pillows, clutching her throbbing appendage with both hands.

"Feeling unwell this morning, Lady Sarah?"

Sarah cringed. "You needn't bellow! I can hear you perfectly well."

Maria's smile grew. "I beg your pardon, my lady. I forgot that champagne often has this aftereffect."

"Champagne?" Sarah's eyes suddenly widened with returned memory. "Champagne!"

"Precisely, my lady. Let me help you up."

With Maria doing most of the work, and Sarah all of the groaning, Sarah was soon propped upright amid her pillows, the covers tucked securely around her, the breakfast tray on her lap. She regarded it warily, and then began to turn green.

"Oh, please take this away, I beg you!"

Maria had just set the tray on the dressing table when there came a light knock on the door.

Sarah wrapped her arms over her head. "Who is shooting off cannons in the house at this hour of the morning?" she demanded.

Maria opened the door to Jack, who carried a small silver tray bearing a teacup and saucer. "Good morning, Miss Jenkins," he said in a quiet voice. "I took the liberty of bringing a little hair of the dog. I thought Lady Sarah might be in need."

"In the greatest of need, Mr. Rawlins," said Maria with a grin, which she carefully removed as she turned to her mistress and escorted the butler into the room. "Rescue is at hand, my lady."

Sarah considered Jack and the teacup, and shuddered. "I couldn't tolerate a sip of tea this morning, thank you anyway, Jack . . . I mean, Rawlins."

"This is not tea, my lady," Jack replied, setting the tray down on the bedside table. "It is a remedy for what ails you."

"How do you know what ails me?"

"In the course of my career, I have attended many a gentleman who has suffered from a singularly unpleasant hangover the morning after a night of revelry. This concoction has never failed to put them to right, and I trust you may find it similarly beneficial."

"So this is a hangover," Sarah murmured, closing her eyes against the throbbing in her head. "Death would be preferable."

"I do have an alternative."

Sarah opened her eyes and regarded the cup Jack held before her. She took the cup from his hands and stared suspiciously at its contents. "This looks vile."

"It tastes vile," he assured her. "But it is effective."

Sarah looked up at him pleadingly. "Are you sure death isn't preferable?"

A gentle smile touched his lips. "Quite sure. Drink up now."

Sarah drew upon the last dregs of her courage, took a resolute breath, and drained the cup in a single swallow. "Ugh!" she said, grimacing as she handed the cup back to Jack. "It's even more vile than it looks!"

128

"But it should allow you to tolerate breakfast within the half hour."

"Really?" Sarah said, brightening. "And the thundering herds in my head?"

"A mere whisper in the same period."

"You are a godsend," Sarah said feelingly.

Jack bowed, effectively hiding the humorous gleam in his eyes. Life had become vastly more enjoyable since knowing Sarah Thorndike. "I am always glad to be of service."

Sarah felt no compunction to rise and journey downstairs for breakfast. Her prolonged absence from the company would only drive home to the Laveslys her shocking conduct of the night before. Absence, in this case, would only make their hearts grow less fond.

She braced herself for the repercussions.

They were not long in coming. The duchess descended in high dudgeon, ordered Maria out of the room, and spent the next three-quarters of an hour raking her erstwhile daughter over the coals. All of the criticisms and invectives and exclamations of horror Sarah took meekly, as befit a contrite daughter.

"To think that I have reared a drunkard," the duchess said in an awful voice. "You will not partake of another drop of spirits for the rest of this summer, do you hear me, Sarah?"

"Yes, Mother."

The duchess finally left her daughter's room, serene in the belief that there would be no further outbreaks of freakish behavior.

Alas, she knew so little of Sarah's true character.

❋

Chapter 10

DETERMINED TO AVOID her parents as much as possible the next day, Sarah moved with considerable caution from garden to patio, from hall to room, and back outside again. She kept herself in company—with the Dohertys, with Freddy and Corliss Braithwaite, and with Lord and Lady Danvers—so she could not be accused of failing to do her social duty. Still, she was quite alone as she peered around a corner on the first landing in search of safe passage. She found instead John Rawlins with his back to the wall. Lady Winster was before him—almost against him, really—apparently holding him captive.

"I thank you for your generous suggestion, Lady Winster," Jack was coolly saying, "but I cannot accept."

"Of course you can." She pouted prettily. Her hand caressed his stern cheek. "All you have to do is say yes, and the rest is all delight. I always get what I want, Rawlins, and I want you."

"Again, I must refuse, Lady Winster. Now, if you will excuse me—"

"Do you know to whom you are speaking?" her ladyship demanded, her voice becoming brittle. "Do you know who it is you are refusing?"

"Perfectly, my lady."

"I would reconsider, Rawlins," Lady Winster advised, an index finger circling a button on his waistcoat. "I have the power to ruin you if I choose."

"I sincerely doubt that, my lady."

Lady Winster's expression was now grim. "You will do as I bid or I shall have Lyleton sack you, and then I will insure that no one in England hires you as anything more than a common stable boy!"

"You must, of course, do as you think best, Lady Winster."

She slapped him then, the sound ricocheting off the walls. "You will regret your insolence."

"I trust not. Was there anything else, my lady?"

Sarah, her ears red, her heartbeat a little rapid, stepped into the hall. "Rawlins! Rawlins! Oh, there you are," she said, walking up to the duo as if she had observed nothing untoward. "Rawlins, my dear man, you must help me. The ladies want to make a shopping expedition into the village tomorrow, and I have been deputized to make all the arrangements. We are to lunch at some inn, but that dullard Lyleton cannot for the life of him recall its name. And then there are the carriages to order. Oh, hello, Lady Winster. Will you be accompanying us?"

"There is nothing in a village shop that could interest me," Lady Winster snapped. "You will reconsider your decision, Rawlins," she commanded before sweeping off down the hall.

"What a thoroughly unpleasant woman," Sarah said as she and Jack watched her go.

"She is, I would say, typical of many in her class," the butler calmly replied.

"No wonder you don't like us."

"Oh, there are some of you who have a few redeeming features," Jack said. "Did you just rescue me?"

"I know you didn't need it," Sarah said, quite dazzled by his smile. "You're the most capable fellow in the world. But I was growing nauseous."

"And the shopping expedition?"

"I have Earnshaw arranging everything. He's a most enterprising young man. The name of the village inn, by the by, is the Nag's Head. Mother will be appalled."

"But I believe the Nag's Head is known for putting on a good meal. Perhaps the duchess can be reconciled."

"Perhaps. Mother *has* always prided herself on her excellent appetite. It seems," Sarah said with an arch smile as she began to walk away, "that Lady Winster suffers from the same pride."

She heard a masculine gasp behind her, and her smile broadened. Men were so easily shocked. But her smile soon faded. She disliked the knowledge that Lady Winster had ordered Jack to her bed. She disliked Lady Winster's certainty that she would succeed. She disliked that so common an occurrence should upset her so greatly.

She was saved from having to examine her feelings when Freddy loped across the entry hall just as she was walking downstairs.

"There you are!" he cried happily. "I've been looking all over for you. Lord Danvers is organizing an archery contest, and you are to be my partner."

"I am? How is this? I don't recall being recruited."

"*I* claimed you first thing. Danvers insisted I participate, and you know, Sarah, that I can't hit the side of a barn. You, however, are devilish clever with a bow and arrow. I depend upon you to save me from disgrace."

The archery contest had the efficacy of diverting Sarah's thoughts from more troubling considerations and lessening in a small measure the continuing outrage of her parents, for Sarah was talented and acquitted herself quite well. She had considered, briefly, "accidentally" shooting the wonderfully ugly hat off Lady Lavesly's head, but decided it would do her plans no harm to have one day of relative peace. The hat was safe.

Lengthening shadows drew the party back indoors to dress for dinner. When Fitz actually volunteered to escort Sarah upstairs, the Laveslys looked upon this with the greatest relief. Their relief would have been far less if they had overheard the conversation between the affianced pair. Sarah and he were plotting their next attack.

At dinner, Fitz pointedly ignored Sarah and spent the whole of the meal conversing with Corliss Braithwaite, who was seated on his left, happily basking in this unexpected attention. When everyone adjourned to the drawing room for cards later, it was Fitz who insisted Freddy and Corliss Braithwaite share a table with him and Sarah. And it was Fitz who insisted on partnering with Corliss, not Sarah, at whist.

They let the game go forward unscathed for half an hour, then Sarah started laughing at Fitz's play. He retaliated, and the argument escalated from there. Fifteen minutes later, everyone in the room thought it perfectly reasonable for Fitz to storm out of the drawing room. Lady Sarah Thorndike had a surprisingly cutting tongue, undoubtedly a trait she had inherited from her mother. She remained at the table, fanning her warm cheeks.

"Sarah?" Freddy tentatively asked. "Are you feeling quite . . . all right?"

"Never better," Sarah said with a serene smile.

When the party at last reached a general consensus on retiring for the night, Sarah rose demurely from her chair and climbed the stairs to her room. She only had time to remove her jewelry when the duchess stalked into her room to deliver what was now a nightly diatribe. Her outraged mother gave full vent to her spleen—would tolerate no excuses—and then swept from the room very far from being mollified.

"She's beginning to repeat herself" was Sarah's only comment to Maria before she began undressing for bed.

If Sarah was restless in her bed that night, it had nothing to do with the duchess and everything to do with the heat, which had not abated with the rising of the moon. She tossed, she turned, there wasn't an inch on her bed that was comfortable. Her thoughts jaunted off on paths she preferred to avoid. She could, at any unexpected moment, recall Jack's laughter of two nights before and how much younger and happier it had made him seem. There had been no bitterness or unhappiness in his gray eyes then.

"Oh, this is ridiculous!" she exclaimed as she threw aside her covers and slid from her bed. She opened a window to find the night air wonderfully cool and inviting. Far off, she could just hear the faint sound of music rising from the Gypsy camp and enticing her outside.

She pulled on her slippers and a dressing gown of emerald silk, and hurried downstairs to freedom. Once outside and uneasy at being so near the house and people she did not want

133

observing her, she struck out through the eastern gardens, happily breathing in the cool night air, enjoying the weird shapes and shadows the moonlight made of the topiary garden.

She had always preferred to be outside. She loved trees and flowers and hedges far more than she did wing chairs and chaise lounges and carpets. In a house—particularly in Charlisle—she could easily become claustrophobic. Outside she was free and unself-conscious.

She could dance a little jig in the moonlight—as she did now—and not worry about making a fool of herself. She could tilt back her head and stare up at the stars thick above her, letting her heart swell with their beauty, and never worry about having to explain herself to some stocky young man or, God forbid, her mother.

Thinking of the duchess pushed Sarah through the gardens and onto a wooded path that curled and dipped and slowly led down to Charlisle Lake. She could feel the air grow cooler as she drew near the water, night sounds all around her: crickets and frogs singing their chromatic chorus, the muffled flap of wings in the air, the soft snap of a twig as an animal passed nearby.

She came at last to the lake and took in its vast black expanse. This was peace. This was happiness. She began to circle the lake, all sound of her passing absorbed in the soft earth beneath her feet. Reaching the narrow dock that extended out into the water, she walked across its wooden planks, which creaked, and sat down at its end. She pulled off her slippers and dangled her feet in the cool water. "Lovely," she murmured as she leaned against a wooden post on her right.

The quiet of the lake at night made her think of Barlow, a small estate her father owned in Berkshire. The Jacobean house had only twelve rooms, not counting the servants' quarters, a pretty park, and a lake nearly as large as Charlisle's. She had only visited there four times in her life, but it had made a strong impression on her. Of all her father's properties, Barlow had felt more like home than anything else she had known. Unbeknownst to her parents, she had learned to swim in that lake. That had been freedom indeed!

She considered Charlisle's lake in the light of the half-moon and had just made up her mind to remove her dressing gown and slip into the water, when a sound that was not of the night made her suddenly turn her head.

There, just to the left of the dock stood Jack, dressed only in trousers and a white shirt, his feet actually bare!

"Good evening," she said.

"Good evening, Lady Sarah," he gravely replied.

How long had he been standing there? "Couldn't you sleep, either?" she asked.

"No, the heat—"

"Precisely."

He turned, as if to leave.

"Don't go!" Sarah called to him. "That is . . . You meant to dabble your feet in the lake, did you not?"

"Well, yes, my lady. But I had no intention of intruding—"

"Pish tosh. Come sit with me. There is plenty of room for two." She saw that he hesitated. "You don't want me to feel guilty for depriving you of the same pleasure I sought, do you? Come along, now. I promise not to tell anyone of such unbutlerlike behavior."

"Very well." Jack walked down the dock and lowered himself beside her. His feet slipped into the water.

"There you are," Sarah said happily. "Not a soul is demanding to lop off your head. You see? There are more pleasures in life besides cribbage."

"Of course there are. Backgammon springs to mind."

Sarah laughed. "Now, now, none of that nonsense, for you are quite found out. You have walked barefoot over cool evening grass. You know more about pleasure, John Rawlins, than the majority of those trapped in that hell house we have just escaped."

"You must, of course, believe what you choose, my lady."

Sarah grinned at him. "You are a rogue, Jack."

"A butler a rogue? I think not, Lady Sarah."

" 'Every inch that is not fool is rogue' . . . and you are no fool, Jack."

"You would turn Dryden against me?"

"I am coming to use everything that will serve my cause. Rebellion is a treacherous thing, Jack. It touches every conversation and charts new courses undreamed of even moments earlier."

They were silent for a few minutes, slowly dabbling their feet in the water, staring out across the lake. It was odd, Sarah thought, that of all the people she had wanted to escape in the house, the one person whose company she truly enjoyed should come upon her so unexpectedly. The gods must be favoring her.

She regarded Jack sitting only a foot from her side. That she should be so comfortable with him after so brief an acquaintance no longer surprised her. He was everything delightful, from his thick hair to his sensual hands, to his beautifully shaped feet lazily rippling the water.

Blushing unaccountably, Sarah turned her head and stared up at the moon, trying to collect her wayward thoughts.

It was Jack who finally broke the silence. "May I commend you, my lady, on your argument with the viscount earlier this evening? It was masterfully done."

"Why, thank you!" Sarah replied, her cheeks cooling. "I thought it went off rather well. But it wouldn't have been half so successful if Fitz hadn't been equally inventive. Calling me a mawworm. Inspired! I didn't know Fitz had it in him. I like him more and more."

"Perhaps, then, you should reconsider marrying him."

"Good God, no!" Sarah expostulated. "Were he my husband, I would become one of those harpy wives forever finding fault in everything poor Fitz does. And he would find me wholly incomprehensible, not to say irritating. Fitz and I do well as friends and that is all."

"The question arises, however, Lady Sarah, as to who you *will* marry if you don't marry the viscount."

A little knot formed in Sarah's belly. "Yes, well, I once had my heart set on an obscure knight."

Jack stared at her. "And who was the lucky man?"

Sarah sighed wistfully. "No one at first. He was more my ideal. You see, I thought a knight was as far down the social ladder as I could get. And the knight had to be obscure, for I long to be obscure as well. I was not made to be the darling of Society. My sister, Arabella, essayed that role for two years and did it splendidly; even the redoubtable Frances was considered a success, but I haven't got it in me. My first Season passed. No prospect appeared. I thought my case hopeless. But then one day, I actually met and liked an obscure knight."

Jack went very still. "Did you?"

"Yes. Sir Geoffrey Willingham. The wonder of it was, that he actually liked me, too. He even asked me to marry him. I know you will find this hard to believe, Jack, but I'm a very practical sort of woman. I wasn't looking for love or romance—which is fortunate, for neither existed in Geoffrey. Still, he was a good man, and I believed there was a reasonable chance we would at least be comfortable together, the most that I had ever hoped for in marriage, certainly. But Father soon made short work of *that* dream."

"He objected to Sir Geoffrey?"

"Vehemently. It seems I had miscalculated. The duke informed me that I must marry for position or wealth. There is no middle ground. A knight holds no standing with my parents. He might as well be a shop clerk as a Sir Anything. Even a baronet is unacceptable. At least, a *poor* baronet is unacceptable. That was the rub, you see. Geoffrey lacked a decent title, but that could have been overcome if he was rich, only he wasn't rich. He had a modest income only *and* a widowed mother to support. Father nearly set the dogs on him."

"Quite understandable, of course," Jack said quietly. Though he sat only a foot away from her, he seemed to have removed himself several yards hence.

"Yes," Sarah replied, looking at him curiously, but she could not decipher his expression. "That was two years ago, and I've yet to find any other man I could tolerate as a husband. My doting parents, therefore, became restive, hence this patched-up engagement with Fitz. I was so sure I would have met someone by now, but . . ." Sarah sighed. "Timing was never my forte. It's the oddest thing, really, because I've been remarkably successful in marrying off my brother and sisters."

Jack returned to swirling his feet in the water as he stared down into the lake. "You took an active hand in those affairs of the heart, my lady?"

"Well, someone had to," Sarah remarked as she leaned back against the wooden post once again, longing for the comradeship that had inexplicably evaporated between them. "I made a good job of it, too, if I do say so myself. Gerald was the first. I am very fond of my brother, for all he's a bit too punctilious. It seemed to me that just because he's got to be duke someday was no reason for him to marry a great block of ice like Lady Gertrude Bertram-Smyth. *That's* the bride my dear parents chose for him, and he was going along with it like the dutiful fathead that he is, but I soon put a stop to that."

"You were not being presumptuous?"

"It was a life-or-death matter. Lady Gertrude would have had Gerald pontificating worse than Father!"

"A fate to be avoided at all costs," Jack gravely agreed. He seemed to have moved a little closer again without moving at all. "I quail as I ask this, Lady Sarah, but *how* did you put a stop to their marriage?"

She chuckled with fond memory. "There was an engagement fete at our country place in Lincolnshire, toasts to the happy couple every night, engagement balls, the whole dreadful lot of it. Well, each night after everyone was asleep, I would crawl out my bedroom window and sidle along the outside ledge to Lady Gertrude's bedroom window."

"The ledge!" Jack gasped, his head jerking up to stare at her.

"Now, now, it was a good foot and a half wide and perfectly safe. Besides, I'd been walking ledges and climbing trees from early childhood. There was nothing to it, really."

"I begin to think it a very good thing that you are *not* marrying the viscount," Jack declared. "You'd undoubtedly do him out of a good ten years of life."

Sarah chuckled. "I have always been a trial. My parents have assured me of it often enough."

"And what was the purpose of sidling along the outside ledge to Lady Gertrude Bertram-Smyth's room?"

"Devilry, of course. I'd creep into her sanctum with a jar of spiders one night, two garden snakes the next, five mice after that, and leave the little dears on her bed. Lady Gertrude Bertram-Smyth did not let me down. By the time I'd left her with the sweetest bullfrog who ever croaked, she bore an uncanny resemblance to a screaming fishwife. She vowed she'd rather become the bride of Beelzebub than marry Gerald. She called the duchess a harridan. She called the duke a muffin-face. She called *Gerald*, who is naturally the apple of his parents' eyes, a twiddlepoop. And so the engagement was terminated."

"I begin to understand how you devised this current roundabout scheme to avoid marrying Lord Lyleton. I should not be surprised. History is littered with enterprising females: Salome, Cleopatra, Lucrezia Borgia—"

A gurgle of laughter escaped Sarah. "Thank you so very much!"

She felt Jack's smile in the night. "And who did you find to marry the marquis instead?" he inquired.

"That's the delightful part of it. Gerald found her himself. Helen is the sweetest girl who ever lived, and one, moreover, who still knows a good joke when she hears one. They've been married for three years, and they're still blissfully happy. Helen has teased a good deal of starch out of Gerald, and I couldn't be more grateful to the dear girl. She counterbalances my sister, Frances, you see. Frances decided to marry the Marquis of Riddlefield, who is, if such a thing were possible and unfortunately it is, even higher in the instep than she."

"And what did you do to end *that* engagement?"

"Why nothing at all! In fact, I did everything I could to encourage it. The marquis was just the sort of man to make Frances happy, inasmuch as she can be happy. She always wanted to follow in Mother's footsteps, you see and be a duchess in her own right. So, she got her marquis and, it looks like she'll be a duchess by the time she's thirty. Frances is in clover.

"Now, my sister Arabella was another matter entirely. She fell madly in love with Lord Stephen Harigote, and he quite reasonably fell madly in love with her, for she's quite beautiful and sweet and good and all the things *I* am not. But my parents had already chosen a husband for her, the Earl of Laradid, *twenty* years her senior, Jack, and reeking of brandy; and *she*, the big chucklehead, went along with it! Sobbing enough to soak the entire house—and it's a big house, Jack—she bid Baron Harigote good-bye and prepared like a Christian martyr to marry the earl."

Jack was thoroughly amused. "Somehow I don't think the earl ever met her at the altar," he said.

"He didn't," Sarah assured him. This was so much better. She had a mad urge to slip her arm through his and lean confidingly against him. "Gerald and Helen and Stephen and I formed a syndicate."

"A syndicate?" Jack weakly inquired.

"Yes. We raised enough money to bribe the earl's *chère amie* of the moment into breaking in on the engagement dinner—drunk—to publicly accuse the earl of his excesses, known and unknown. She did it beautifully, and Stephen, leaping into the horrified breach following my parents' denouncement of the earl and his subsequently hasty departure from the house, offered for Arabella, was accepted with alacrity, for he is vastly rich, and married her before a month had passed. They are expecting their first child in January," Sarah stated with a most satisfied sigh. "You can see how I was misled into believing that if the lovely second daughter of a duke can marry a mere baron, the unbeautiful third daughter of a duke should find no difficulty in marrying an obscure knight.

"I forgot—because I am always trying to forget—that I *am* a daughter of the Duke and Duchess of Somerton. There are standards to which I am held, staked out, as it were, as a tasty tidbit for any gentleman with sufficient fame or fortune—and preferably both."

"You should not rate yourself so low, my lady."

"I know my worth. It was taught me long ago."

"Ah, no," Jack reproved gently, mesmerizing her as his beautiful hand reached out and brushed an errant curl from her forehead. She lost her breath at the touch. "You learned only a

140

malicious fabrication. Can you not spare for yourself even a little of the generosity you give others?"

"I know my failings," Sarah managed.

"You know only that you are human. To be human is to be flawed, not the machine your parents require. I very much prefer the flesh-and-blood woman to the mechanical marionette they would have you be."

Sarah could scarcely hear over the pounding of her heart in her ears. "And I thought you were a man of some taste."

Jack pressed a finger to her lips. "Hush."

She could feel that bewildering touch long after he had pulled his finger away.

"Value yourself," he continued, "not as your parents do, but as . . . your friends do."

It took a moment before she could find her voice. "Do your parents value you, Jack?"

"There is only my mother, and she is fond of me. I have even on occasion been doted upon."

"Good woman. And what of your father? Did he dote on you?"

"Hardly. He considered me an inconvenience."

"Poor Jack. Have we that in common as well?"

She could not decipher his expression. "More than you could guess," he said, a hint of bitterness in his voice.

Troubled, Sarah looked away. "I look forward to standing godparent to Charlotte and Phineas Doherty's first child. It was conceived in love, and that must count for much."

"They are a happy couple."

Sarah smiled into the night, unaware that the moonlight was shining on her like a lamp. "Very happy," she agreed. "Neither will entertain a parade of lovers through their bedroom; neither will debase their marriage vows with indifference; neither will narrow their children's lives into rigid perfection." Sarah forcibly pulled herself back from dark thoughts. She disliked any hint of self-pity. "I have always had a fondness for lakes," she said with determined brightness. "There's something mysterious about them, for there is an entirely different world beneath the surface. I learned to swim in a lake. Can you swim, Jack?"

"Yes."

She suspected he was not deceived by the sudden change in topic. "I learned when I was twelve."

"I started when I was seven."

Sarah scowled at him. "And when did you begin to ride? You do ride, don't you?"

"Oh, yes. I learned when I was nine."

"Ha! I rode when I was four."

"Are we in competition?" Jack asked with a smile.

"No," Sarah conceded. "It is just that you have so much, Jack, that I will become quite dispirited if I don't find some area in which I can triumph."

"Why do you say I have so much? Do you think me rich?"

"In all that is truly important—family, ability, understanding, freedom—yes." She cocked her head, puzzled. "Don't you know the blessings in your own life?"

Jack stared out across the lake. "I had . . . forgotten them." He turned his head suddenly and smiled down at her with such warmth, that Sarah felt as if his lips brushed against her own. "Thank you for reminding me of them."

"You're welcome," she replied, badly shaken. Escape seemed suddenly of paramount importance. "I had better go back to my room. It's getting late."

She started to get up, but Jack moved quickly, rising in one fluid motion to his feet and holding his hands out to her.

Heart pounding in her breast, Sarah placed her hands in his and felt fire shoot from his fingers into her veins, flaming into her, heating her cheeks, pushing her heart into her throat as he pulled her effortlessly to her feet. She stood scant inches from him, gazing up into his night-darkened eyes and quite unable to look away. There was something in his expression and in the way he still held her hands that was quite unlike anything she had ever known before. It was lovely and frightening and . . . intimate.

She could kiss him now. She had only to rise on her toes, and her mouth would meet his.

142

Her face turned crimson. She hurriedly turned away, pulling her hands from his, and began walking up the dock. "Good night, Jack."

"Good night, my lady."

His low voice made her shiver. She moved faster back to the house.

She didn't see Jack turn roughly away from her. "Fool! Idiot!" he growled at himself.

How could he be in danger? He knew who he was. He knew what she was. With an oath, he stared out across the lake. Then, in one swift, violent movement, he dove into the water, hoping to wash away the insanity so suddenly and inexplicably ruling him in the moonlight.

✳
Chapter 11

SARAH SUFFERED A shock the next morning when Jack failed to meet her following her gallop as he had done now for almost a fortnight. Was he ill? She found him nowhere at Charlisle and was forced to buttonhole Mrs. Clarke, who assured her that Mr. Rawlins was quite well, merely busy.

Sarah should have been gratified by this information, but she was not. If not ill, why had he not kept their rendezvous? More questions plagued her as the day advanced. It seemed that Jack was avoiding her, though she could not point to any one occurrence as proof. Still, his absence impressed itself upon her. And when he did share a room with her, he seemed to have reverted to the cool, aloof demeanor of his first week at Charlisle.

What had happened? Alas, Jack sidestepped every opportunity for a private tête-à-tête. Sarah walked slowly up to her bedchamber that night troubled in mind and spirit.

After supposedly retiring, she finished *She Stoops to Conquer* and was still not tired. For some unaccountable reason, she was having great difficulty sleeping of late. Her appetite had also fallen off. More than once, Maria had asked if Sarah was coming down with something, but she was not. In fact, until today Sarah had never felt more invigorated in her life. Sliding off her bed, she walked downstairs and went to the library in search of further entertainment. She opened the carved oak door and stood stock-still, staring in amazement at the scene before her.

Fitz, still in his evening dress of peach-striped coat and white pantaloons, was kneeling before the library grate and feeding a piece of paper into the small flames. But it was Jack who made her stare. He was just settling Sir Marcus Templeton down on the carpet. Sir Marcus seemed dead to the world.

"Good God, what's all this?" Sarah cried, sensibly closing the library door behind her.

Fitz started guiltily and turned to regard her with wide, horrified eyes.

Jack, meanwhile, was counting what seemed a good many banknotes in an envelope. "Merely the resolution of a minor business matter, my lady," he answered.

"Is he dead?" Sarah demanded.

Jack looked up. His eyes were shuttered. "Merely sleeping," he replied.

Sarah's gaze hurriedly fled his to stare unseeingly at Sir Marcus. Unaccountable as it seemed, there were tears in her eyes. "An odd place for a nap," she observed. She looked at Fitz, who had stood up and was nervously brushing off his white pantaloons. "What's going on, Fitz? Come on, now, you know you can trust me."

The viscount glanced rather desperately at Jack, who nodded. "You must carry this secret to the grave," Fitz informed her.

"That was clear to me the moment I entered the room," Sarah said dryly. "What's all the to-do?"

To her surprise, Fitz blushed. "I'm afraid I've been rather indiscreet."

"No," Sarah murmured wickedly. "You?"

He grinned at her. "You are a shrew," he pronounced, "and I'm glad you don't want to marry me. It all began five months ago. I was on the cut one night, and I wrote a most . . . incautious . . . letter to a young woman of my acquaintance."

"Opera dancer or paphian?"

Fitz gaped at her. "How on earth—?"

"It wasn't hard to deduce. Which was it?"

"Opera dancer," Fitz replied, considerably more at ease now. The tale of the alluring Aldora Higgins and the blackmailing Marcus Templeton poured forth. "The deuce of it was," Fitz continued, "Rawlins couldn't find the letter anywhere."

145

"Rawlins?" said Sarah, turning to the butler.

"The viscount very kindly took me into his confidence," Jack replied with a wry glance at Fitz. "It had occurred to his lordship that I would have a greater opportunity to search Sir Marcus Templeton's rooms than he."

"But the letter wasn't there," Fitz said. "After making a thorough search of his room and ascertaining that Templeton had not given the letter to anyone else for safekeeping, Rawlins finally deduced that Templeton must keep it on himself at all times. Rawlins is the most clever cove. He said the most expedient way to get the letter off of Templeton was to drug him, so here we are."

Sarah gaped at the two men. "Jack drugged Templeton?"

"Most amazing thing I've ever seen in my life," said Fitz, warming to his narrative. "I had arranged to meet Templeton here to give him his money. I proposed a toast to the successful conclusion of our business, and that was that. Rawlins had drugged the claret, you see. There was Templeton the life and soul of the party one minute, and the next minute stretched out on the carpet, looking like a beached salmon and snoring fit to shake the rafters. Before I had a chance to take it all in, Rawlins was handing me my letter and advising me to burn it at the first opportunity. That," he triumphantly concluded, "is what I was doing when you burst in upon us."

"Brilliant," Sarah said admiringly. She was startled to see a faint flush creep into Jack's cheeks. "What happens now?"

Fitz looked blank and then turned to Jack. "Yes, what does happen now?"

"I believe, sir," Jack replied, "that it is time Sir Marcus packed his bags and decamped. The trouble, I fear, is that the drug will not wear off for many hours."

"Perhaps we should help him on his way?" Sarah suggested.

The mask did not slip. "An excellent suggestion, my lady. If you, my lord, will insure that no one stumbles upon Sir Marcus, I will order his carriage and have his valet pack his things. You will be rid of him within the half hour."

Sarah was not surprised to find herself thirty minutes later standing in the front courtyard and waving the Templeton carriage (and its somnolent passenger) good-bye.

"Thank God that's over," Fitz said with a hearty sigh at her side. "I shall sleep well tonight for the first time in months."

"It must have been a terrible experience," Sarah said sympathetically. "And *then* to find yourself saddled with a freckled fiancée when you hadn't even discarded the first—!"

Fitz grinned engagingly at her. "It's been a black summer. But now one trouble's gone and another's nearly done. I shall be a free man by summer's end, thanks to you and Rawlins."

"Now, now, we cannot take all of the credit; you've helped yourself a good deal, too. Your drunken advances toward Mother tonight were perfectly inspired."

"I never knew devilry could be such fun."

"Nor I."

Sarah returned upstairs to her room, while Fitz, heeding a discreet signal from Jack, returned to the library, closing the door carefully behind him.

"Success!" cried the viscount, advancing into the room. He heartily shook Jack's hand. "This calls for champagne."

"*Not* while I am on duty, sir."

Fitz grinned at him. "You make a damned fine butler, Jack. Both Lady Winster and Lord Merbles have tried to buy you away from me."

"I am glad you find my service satisfactory."

"Satisfactory?" Fitz cried. "My dear fellow, you've rescued me from a lifelong bleeding. I don't know how I'll ever be able to repay your goodness and your quick wits."

"You may begin by sending for Greeves. The sooner he reclaims his post, the safer I'll be."

"Safer?"

Jack frowned as he stared at the library door. "If there is any mercy in this life."

But it seemed there was none. It mattered not the many ways Jack found to castigate himself, he was happy only in Sarah's company. Avoiding their morning walk had been almost . . . agony. To do so twice required a fortitude he hadn't known he possessed.

147

To retain a grave and reserved demeanor when in the same room with her was nearly impossible now that she had broken out to alienate the Laveslys. Gone was the demure ducal daughter. In her place was a wholly captivating hellion only he seemed to appreciate, no matter how many times he told himself that he should not.

That Sarah, for some odd reason, enjoyed his company she had never tried to hide from him. That she needed the support of every friend if she was to survive the summer unscathed he knew only too well. He thought he had left guilt behind on the Peninsula. He was wrong.

When he found Sarah weeping on a wooden bench in the rose garden on the second afternoon following Templeton's abrupt departure, her head bowed, arms wrapped around herself, he felt something break within him.

"My lady!" Jack cried in a low, urgent voice as he hurried up to her. "What is wrong? What has happened?"

She raised her head, and he saw—to his amazement—that she was weeping, not from sadness, but from laughter!

"Thank God you've come." She gasped, brushing the tears from her cheeks. "This is too wonderful. It must be shared with the world!"

"What must?" Jack said stupidly, rocked off center and with no idea how to get back.

Sarah held up a letter she had mangled in her left hand. "My friend Lady Wainwright has just written me. It is all over London. You know of Beau Brummell, of course?" An entrancing smile danced upon her mouth.

Jack forcibly brought himself to order. He placed his hands behind his back; they seemed safer there. "Even a butler in the hinterlands hears of the leading arbiters of taste and fashion."

"Yes, of course. How silly of me. Well, as you may also know, the prince and Brummell have not been on speaking terms for a while. Prinny has even been openly hostile to Sir Henry Mildmay, one of the Beau's friends. That is key to the story, Jack."

"I am all attendance, my lady."

"Good man. Here is the gist of the matter: Beau Brummell,

Mildmay, Lord Alvanley, and Henry Pierrepoint recently won a substantial sum of money gambling at Watier's and—being the reasonable men that they are—they decided to spend all of it by celebrating with a ball at the Argyle Rooms. They sent out invitations accordingly. The thing of it is, they could not avoid sending an invitation to Prinny . . . and he came!

"There the four Exquisites stood, receiving their guests into the Argyle Rooms. In walks Prinny, decked out in all his finery. He shakes hands with Alvanley, with Pierrepoint, and *then* walks past Brummell and Mildmay without so much as a glance. The crowd gasps at this deliberate snub, but our hero is unperturbed. 'Alvanley,' cries out the Beau in a loud, cheery voice, 'who's your fat friend?' "

Jack stared down at Sarah, aghast, and then sank onto the bench beside her rocking with laughter. His legs would no longer sustain him. "Oh, the audacity of the man!" he choked. "The brilliance!"

"I have always liked him, for all his affectations," Sarah said, chuckling. "This will eventually ruin him in the ton, of course, but oh, the pure delicious effrontery of it all! He must go down in history, Jack, or there is no God."

They sat laughing together, shoulder pressed to shoulder, and for a little while Jack let himself forget who he was and who Sarah Thorndike was.

The second week of July began with three days of rain, which effectively broke the heat wave. Jack thought the deluge a godsend, for it provided a ready excuse not to partake of a morning walk with Sarah. Others were not so complacent. The rain considerably exacerbated the tension growing within Charlisle. Twenty-eight people trapped together under one roof was irritating enough, but when they were forced to bear witness to the increasing arguments staged by Sarah and Fitz, *and* clash with each other, *and* find that nearly a dozen pieces of jewelry were missing, Charlisle became a tinderbox that needed but a single match to explode, and there were a good two dozen people with matches in hand.

The first break in the clouds saw ten of Fitz's guests—

including the Winsters, the Throwbrights, the Merbleses, and Mr. Davis—scurrying away soon after sunrise, each of them privately vowing never to return again. They were not missed. The remaining gentlemen escaped to fish at one of Charlisle's best trout streams, a not entirely happy excursion, for Fitz kept up a steady, and occasionally insulting, commentary on the abominable fashions that fishing required, the mugginess of the day, the mosquitoes, and the general stupidity of the exercise when there was an excellent fish market in the village. He concluded with a rambling discourse on the superiority of Watier's to Brookes's and White's. As all of the gentlemen in the party belonged to one of the latter two clubs, Fitz succeeded in alienating everyone.

His loud and continuous monologue also alienated any fish that might otherwise have been tempted into biting. This last was finally too much for the Duke of Somerton. He was a Compleat Angler and prided himself on the artistry of his cast and the usually impressive size of his catch. He had no catch to boast of today and spent the whole of the walk back to the house lambasting Fitz for his insensitivity, poor judgment, lack of sportsmanship, and generally ungentlemanlike behavior.

Fitz responded by slinging an arm around the duke's shoulders, telling him he was the dearest man in the world, and kissing his ducal cheek with a resounding smack that elicited many a masculine titter from the group.

The ladies and the few gentlemen who had not gone fishing—including Freddy Braithwaite, who declared himself hopeless with a rod and reel, which he was—played at croquet on the lush western lawn, happy to be out of doors and away from the card tables. But all was not convivial. The Countess of Lavesly, who prided herself on her skill at croquet, found herself ruthlessly beaten game after game by Sarah Thorndike. The Duchess of Somerton's far from subtle hints to her daughter were of no avail. Not only did Sarah win each game, she crowed about each victory to such effect that Lady Lavesly finally threw down her mallet and stormed back into the house.

Sarah watched her go with the greatest satisfaction. It seemed to her that the Laveslys were close to breaking. If Fitz could keep up the pressure on *her* parents, she might be a free woman before many more days had passed.

But what then? The Somertons would undoubtedly insist on leaving Charlisle with all possible speed, but Sarah did not want to go. It was not that she was fond of the house—it was too large for her tastes—but she was fond of some of its denizens. She cast a surreptitious peek at Jack, who was gravely circling the group with a tray of lemonade.

While she was coming to take a perverse pleasure in harassing her parents and the Laveslys, smiled whenever she watched Charlotte and Phineas Doherty billing and cooing, and laughed outright at Freddy Braithwaite's endearing idiocies, Sarah found herself happiest when in John Rawlins's company. Even with his inexplicable reserve, which he now employed whenever he was in her private company, Sarah was content because the triumph was all the greater whenever she could tease him into a smile that went all the way up to his gray eyes.

If she could not talk with him, she could watch him, and there was considerable pleasure even in that. Tall, broad shouldered, his sober servant's dress doing nothing to disguise his muscular frame, he moved with a physical grace that was wholly arresting. Even when he stood perfectly still, he was a pleasure to observe, for she liked tracing the strong outline of his nose and the masculine planes of his face. She liked studying his eyes most of all, for despite his new reserve with her, they reflected a greater enjoyment in life. Sarah knew an absolute thrill whenever she looked into them.

He had become a full-fledged coconspirator in her plot to escape marrying Fitz. In the midst of all his many duties, he still found time to keep a strict account of the Laveslys' whereabouts so that he could act as informant whenever Sarah decided it was time to bedevil them once again.

Thus it was, when the gentlemen returned from fishing and the ladies retired from croquet, that Jack slipped into the morning parlor, where Sarah and Fitz were meeting to map out their final campaign.

"A few more days at most, and we have them," Sarah was saying. "Wouldn't you agree, Rawlins?"

"That is certainly my opinion, Lady Sarah," Jack replied.

"The fishing expedition was a brilliant stroke, Sarah," Fitz said happily. "The duke is ready to call off the wedding right now, I'm certain of it."

Sarah smiled. "Father has no tolerance of idiocy when he's fishing. But I think Mother is still recalcitrant. So it's time to bring out the heavy guns."

"I should perhaps warn you, my lady," Jack intervened, "that Lord and Lady Danvers have instigated a ball to be held at Charlisle in two days' time. Lady Lavesly insists on importing an orchestra for the event. Some of the neighboring families are being invited."

"Blast!" exclaimed Fitz.

"A ball can be a very romantic event," Sarah said grimly. "It will not do to have Fitz and me locked in each other's arms for half the evening."

"Precisely," said Jack.

"We could lose a week's worth of work," said Fitz.

Sarah drummed her fingers on the parlor mantelpiece. "I see a three-pronged attack: an argument at breakfast followed by my disgrace during the riding party tomorrow, mayhem at the ball the following night, give everyone a day to let the full horror of what we've done seep in, and *then*"—she beamed—"we'll have the coup de grâce."

"Yes, but what will that be?" Fitz demanded.

Sarah sighed. "I'm not sure yet. Any ideas, Rawlins?"

"Some vulgar display by the both of you should do the trick, my lady."

Fitz brightened immediately. "Something vulgar? That sounds like fun!"

"But within the bounds," Sarah cautioned. "We must outrage, but in character. I mean, you couldn't try to ravish me on the breakfast table, Fitz. It isn't like you."

Fitz uttered a bark of laughter. "Do you mean that as a compliment?"

She smiled fondly at him. "Of course I do, looby. Let us

152

cogitate on the vulgar display over the next day or so. Something brilliant is bound to come to mind. There is always the cow, of course ... or maybe *we* could be caught stealing the jewels!"

"*No*, my lady. It is best that the real culprits be apprehended in that affair. Too much has gone astray."

"Any clues as to who's doing the deed?" Fitz inquired.

"A suspicion or two, my lord. I require a little further investigation to be certain."

"Fitz hired you instead of the Bow Street Runners?"

"It seemed a more appropriate and effective method of finding the thieves," Jack answered.

"Very sound thinking," Sarah said approvingly. "Very well, we've settled things for now. We'll propose the riding party at dinner tonight and be sure to rope in both sets of parents, whatever their objections."

"Bung ho," said Fitz, and they decamped.

Despite their fears, the suggestion of a riding party was warmly received at dinner. That it was proposed by both Sarah and Fitz seemed to their beleaguered parents a good omen. If Fitz had not flirted outrageously with the duchess throughout dinner, and if Sarah had not shrieked with laughter at Lord Lavesly's declaration that the Prince Regent was an exemplary husband and father, the Somertons and Laveslys might have thought that for once a meal had come off tolerably well.

✳
Chapter 12

SARAH FOUND HERSELF increasingly restless as the evening hours laboriously ticked by. She could not settle at cards, or among the small musical group gathered around the pianoforte, or even with Phineas and Charlotte Doherty when they called to her to join their conversation. She wanted to be outside and doing, not trapped inside with her mother's baleful eye watching her every step.

Waiting until the duchess was momentarily distracted by her hand of cards, Sarah stepped onto the patio, imagining she could see the faint Gypsy music floating gracefully up to the moon.

Escape, whispered again and again through her brain. The stirring voice of a Gypsy violin tugged at her heart.

"Sarah? Sarah, come in at once before you catch cold," her mother sharply commanded.

Reluctantly, Sarah turned back into the room, but her mind was already filled with a wholly brazen scheme. Brummell had been audacious. Why not she?

When she finally retired for the night to her room, she had Maria put away her nightclothes and instead removed from her wardrobe a simple cotton gown, the bodice of striped blue, the skirt white. Stout walking shoes soon followed. Then Sarah ordered Maria to bed so that, should she be discovered, her maid would not be considered culpable. To her credit, Maria argued against the entire scheme, but Sarah was adamant. She would have a few hours of complete freedom or die trying.

She sat up reading for an hour after the last bedroom light had been extinguished. Then, listening carefully, she peeked up and down the outer hallway and slipped out of her room. Glancing left and right and behind her until she thought her head would spin off, she crept downstairs. But four stairs from the entry hall, she was suddenly arrested by the low murmur of voices emanating from the morning parlor.

"The Laveslys have asked to be awakened at seven tomorrow," Jack was saying, as he and Earnshaw walked out of the parlor. Sarah hurriedly sat down on the stair and tried to efface herself in the wall. "But, as you know, the countess likes to take an inordinate amount of time at her toilette and will hold the riding party back an hour if she can. So start them up at six-thirty."

"Yes, sir," said Earnshaw.

Jack spotted Sarah, pretended not to see her, and then steered the footman away down the hallway.

Sarah waited five minutes after she could no longer hear their voices, before she stood up and made it safely to the front door.

"And just what, may I be so bold to ask, are you up to now, my lady?"

Sarah turned guiltily to find Jack, arms akimbo, stoically regarding her not more than six feet away. "I'm off on a lark, and don't you dare try to stop me," she retorted.

"As if I would forget myself so much," Jack replied, walking toward her. "Have you a secret assignation?"

A gurgle of laughter welled up within Sarah. "No, of course not, you rogue. I simply decided that if I'm to make a complete fool of myself on horseback tomorrow, then I deserve a treat tonight. I'm off to have my fortune told."

Jack paled. "You cannot seriously intend to go to the Gypsy camp unattended at this hour?"

"I'm sure they're perfectly lovely people who wouldn't dare harm a hair on my head as long as they're camped on Charlisle land. And I needn't go unattended. You could come with me."

Jack gaped at her, and then drew himself up into his most imposing height. "A butler would never demean himself by entering into such disreputable company."

"Yes, but you also told me once that butlers don't laugh, and *you* do, so that won't fadge. Do come with me, Jack, it will be such fun!"

"On no account in the world."

"Well, on your head be it. If I am kidnapped and held for ransom, you'll only have yourself to blame."

"Are you blackmailing me?"

"Of course I am! But it's for a much more enjoyable adventure than joining Lady Winster in her bed."

"I would not let myself be blackmailed on that occasion, and I have no intention of letting you do so now."

"Very well," Sarah said, opening the front door. "Stay locked up in this house if you want. *I'm* going to have some fun." She closed the door firmly but quietly behind her. She had not gone more than a half dozen yards when she heard a very unbutlerlike epithet and then footsteps—grim footsteps—following her. She understood Jack well enough by this late date to know that he would feel compelled to assure her safety by escorting her to the Gypsy camp. "Isn't it a lovely night for a walk?" she said.

"You," John Rawlins retorted, not mincing matters, "are a meddling mooncalf!"

Sarah laughed. "Of course I am! But no butler would ever forget himself so much as to tell me so."

"I have been bullied into it," Jack said peevishly as he drew alongside her. "I doubt if even the Somertons' butler was ever this aggrieved."

"True, but that's because Millikin, for all his grim exterior, has a heart like soft butter. He's used to slipping me chocolates or shillings at the least provocation and turning a blind eye to all of my escapades."

"Corrupted, utterly corrupted," Jack said with a sad sigh. "You are a bane to all butlers, Sarah Thorndike."

"Perhaps, but they tend to have a good deal more fun whenever I'm around."

"Butlers are not supposed to enjoy themselves!"

"But *people* are. Own the truth now: Aren't you glad to be free of Charlisle and your onerous duties for a little while?"

"I shall enjoy all the freedom I desire when Greeves returns."

"Greeves?" Sarah questioned, startled. She felt a sudden chill. "I had forgotten him. Does he return to Charlisle soon?"

"Yes."

"Oh."

They continued for several minutes in silence, crickets serenading them on all sides. "Jack?" Sarah asked, finally rousing herself from her melancholy contemplation of the near future. "What is your age?"

"I beg your pardon?"

"How old are you?"

She thought he stiffened beside her. "Now, now, it is women who are supposed to be recalcitrant about telling their age, not men. Cough it up, Jack."

"I am seven-and-twenty."

"Really? You seem older."

"That is not generally considered a compliment."

"I did not say you *look* older, only that you seem older. Perhaps it is because of the unhappiness that still lingers in your eyes."

Jack stumbled slightly. "I am not unhappy."

"Yes, you are, though it is a different unhappiness from when we first met. Why must you find new ways to be sad?"

"Does not Proverbs tell us that 'every bitter thing is sweet?' "

"Yes, but only to the 'hungry soul.' Why is your soul hungry, Jack?"

He stopped and studied her with an intensity she had never felt before. "It has not known where to find proper nourishment."

"The directions are simple enough. 'Serve God, love' . . . life," Sarah hastily amended, for Shakespeare's Benedick had said "love *me*," " 'and mend.' "

" 'Tis easier done than you know, my lady."

Sarah, by this time, was blushing furiously. If only she was illiterate! She took Jack's arm—not noting his surprise—and hurried forward.

157

"Is it?" she asked distractedly. "Then, why don't you do it?"

"Prudence has ever been my guide."

"You are being inscrutable again. You are often inscrutable, you know, and you are wretchedly parsimonious when it comes to dispensing information about yourself. More often than not, I am thrown onto my own resources, and I fear they may be lacking."

"Lady Sarah, from everything I have observed, your resources would carry you safely away from an Arab horde and back to a proper English tea if you so chose."

"Why, thank you!" Sarah said, with a startled smile. "That's the nicest thing anyone has ever said to me." They were but two hundred yards from the Gypsy camp now. As the music grew louder and began to thrum in her veins, Sarah grew bolder. "Will you be so good as to remove one conundrum?"

"Generosity may strike me."

"A thin hope, but I will persevere. Since you are only seven-and-twenty and have already achieved tremendous success in your chosen profession, why haven't you yet married?"

"That is a very personal question, my lady."

It was, but Sarah was determined to bluster her way through. "Oh, come now. I've told you why I haven't married, the least you can do is return the favor."

Jack sighed. Sarah Thorndike was undoubtedly the most determined female he had ever met. "I have thus far been pre-occupied in my life with neither the time nor the inclination to look about me for a suitable wife."

"No inclination?" said Sarah, mulling this over. "But surely your family expects you to marry and father an heir to carry on that imperturbable Rawlins reserve we've all come to know so well?"

"I believe there is still time to fulfill my duty to my family. I am not quite in my dotage."

"True." Sarah walked by his side a moment, considering. "What sort of qualities do you seek in a wife?"

"Lady Sarah!"

"Oh, come, how is that too personal?" she demanded. "The

standard answer for anyone not in my class is: a comely person unafraid of hard work with a decent dowry behind her."

Jack shook his head. "How did the youngest daughter of a duke ever come to so well understand the ways of the world?"

"Nurse Beecham, Maria Jenkins, Bill Regis, and Henry Jenkins taught me much. They're a better family than most people can boast, I believe."

"How are they your family?" Jack demanded.

"They have loved me, cared for me, taught me life's lessons, and passed on those values they deemed important. Is that not what a family does?"

"But your parents—"

"Paid for them."

Jack was silent a moment. "There are times, my lady," he said quietly, "when you seem far older than your one-and-twenty years."

"And you have not answered my original question."

"That is because I have no answer. I have never considered the matter."

"Never?"

"Never. There seemed no point to the exercise."

"Why is that?"

"I was concerned with other matters."

"Ah, yes," Sarah murmured. "So you said." She realized in this moment how little she knew of Jack, while he had almost her entire life history. She knew nothing of his family save that they were servants. She knew nothing of his childhood or youth or how he had come to be so well educated. She knew nothing, in short, of his life before Charlisle. How had he kept so secret with her, and why?

They had reached the outskirts of the Gypsy camp, seven brightly painted caravans pulled into a broad circle in a meadow at the edge of a dense park. Each caravan had its own campfire. In the center of the camp was a large bonfire. Here the musicians sat and played violins, concertinas, tambourines, and a flute. A young woman danced sinuously through them and the throng of villagers (mostly male) who had paid their shillings for the entertainment.

Sarah's grip on Jack's arm tightened in her excitement. "She's wonderful!" She was mesmerized by the woman's red skirt swirling around her, her long black hair flying as she tossed her head this way and that, her arms fluidly moving to the music. Another young Gypsy woman joined her, similarly attired, equally skilled, and then two of the younger men. The crowd cheered and clapped in time to the hypnotic music. The bonfire seemed to blaze taller and brighter.

It was a thrilling scene. Standing utterly still, Sarah felt more a part of this midnight world than any dancing girl.

"A shilling for the dance," piped a young voice.

Sarah and Jack looked down to find a ragamuffin of perhaps eight years and undetermined sex holding out its hand.

"The lady wishes her fortune told," Jack said.

"Oh. Then you want Grandmother."

"And where may we find her?" Jack asked.

The urchin pointed a thin finger at the yellow-and-green caravan on their far left.

"Thank you, child," said Sarah, pulling a coin from her pocket and pressing it into a happy hand.

Still holding onto Jack's arm, she began to walk toward the fortune-teller, though her eyes never left the bonfire. The music strummed in her veins, her heart beat to its intoxicating rhythm. She had a mad desire to pull Jack into the wild dance and forget utterly who she was.

Then she saw the Gypsy matriarch. The woman sat before a small table studying the cards she had laid out before her in the light cast by a lantern hanging from the caravan beside her. She was shorter than Sarah and plump, though that might have been an effect of the voluminous folds of her blue skirt and the huge shawl draped around her. Her hair was black with a white widow's peak. Her eyes were also black and large and knowing as she studied her approaching guests. Her face, browned by the sun, bore deep grooves around her eyes and mouth, but whether they were lines of happiness or sadness, Sarah could not tell in the lantern light.

"Good evening, sir, my lady," said the Gypsy with a regal nod of her head. "Come to have your fortune told?"

160

"Yes, Mother, if you please," Sarah replied.

Again the Gypsy studied them both. "It will be a pleasure. Who desires to be first?"

"He does," Sarah said hastily.

Jack looked down at her and smiled. "Pudding-heart! I'm the blackmailed escort, you're the seeker of adventure, remember?"

"There is much I could tell you, sir," said the Gypsy.

"Indeed?" asked Jack with the lift of one dark brow. "Anything of interest?"

Sarah thought the Gypsy matriarch smiled in the shadows. "A good deal, sir," the woman replied, gathering up the cards on the table.

"Very well," Jack said, drawing a coin from his pocket, "I shall abandon the scruples of my hallowed post and submit to having my palm read."

"I read more than just palms, sir," the Gypsy said, nodding to the opposite chair at her little table.

"Of course," Jack replied, sitting down. "You read the future."

"And human souls," the Gypsy said, lighting a candle.

Somehow the flame cast her into even greater shadow as it illumined Jack's face. Sarah thought the Gypsy must see, as she saw, the doubt and amusement and interest warring in those handsome features. But what else did she see?

"Your hand, sir," the Gypsy commanded.

Jack gave her his right hand. She studied it intently in the candlelight, her brown fingers lightly tracing the lines there. Then she turned it this way and that and finally released it. She then took his left hand in hers and examined it with equal intensity. Releasing it as well, she stared into his eyes for a long silent minute, then sat back in her chair with an amused smile.

"I knew this night would bring me entertainment."

"I am happy to oblige you, Mother," Jack replied with an answering smile. "What did you see?"

"You are not what you seem. Many are deceived as to your true character and purpose."

Jack's eyes widened in surprise and—could it be?—unease.

161

"Ye gods," Sarah murmured, "are we harboring a cutthroat in our midst?"

"No, my lady, you are quite safe with the gentleman. At least, you need not fear losing your money or your life."

"Testimonials are always welcome," Jack remarked.

"That, sir, is a lie," the Gypsy retorted. "You care nothing for what others think of you. You follow your own star. It has led you through a time of great danger—"

Jack started.

"—and will soon lead you through a new trouble. Consider that others in your ken are also not what they seem and act accordingly."

Jack was silent a moment. "And what of fame and fortune?"

"You ask me of things that do not concern you. Ask instead of your heart, if you dare."

Again Jack paused. He studied the woman as acutely as she did him. "Very well," he said.

She leaned toward him. "You've a long life before you, sir. You must learn what is important and claim it, whatever your fears, whatever the obstacles. The happiness you seek is within your grasp."

"That is impossible," Jack said roughly.

"You are already blind," the fortune-teller retorted. "Do not deafen yourself as well, or the prize you seek will slip forever from your grasp."

"Is it that ephemeral?"

"No, sir, that elusive. Navigate the dangerous shoals within yourself, and those that others set before you. Keep your wits about you, and you may succeed."

Jack suddenly stood up. "Do not offer false hope to one too familiar with the ways of the world," he said coolly.

The Gypsy smiled in amusement. "You are not as knowledgeable as you think, sir. It is your turn, my lady," she said, turning to Sarah.

Sarah scarcely heard her. She was puzzling over the cryptic reading, which both the Gypsy and Jack had seemed to understand, but she could not decode. How was John Rawlins not what he seemed? Had she been mistaken in the qualities she had seen in him? That seemed impossible. What danger had he passed through and what trouble was coming? And why had he questioned the Gypsy, not with humor, but with earnest intensity?

"My lady?"

Sarah jumped and then hurriedly sat in the chair Jack had vacated. "Sorry," she mumbled.

The Gypsy smiled knowingly. "You think too much, my lady. You should trust your heart more."

She held Sarah's hand with a light grip that was both dry and hot. Her larger, rough fingers brushed lightly over her palm. Sarah forcibly held back a shiver. The woman was no crank. The Gypsy then examined her left hand in minute detail. Sarah only began to breathe again when she released her hand.

"You've a strong heart, my lady. One that embraces life despite the walls others seek to place around you. Trust in its strength. Trust in the truth it whispers to you late at night when you can't sleep." Sarah could not hold back a blush. "I see a long life before you divided into three roads," the Gypsy continued. "You must choose one. Your choice will be buffeted by fear and exhaustion, beaten down by opposing forces, seduced by the promise of escape. You must follow only the dictates of your heart if you are to find the happiness you seek."

"You speak in riddles, Mother. Can you not tell me anything more certain?"

"You have already met your future husband," the Gypsy retorted.

"Oh, no!" Sarah cried, appalled. "Surely not. You must be mistaken!"

"I am never mistaken."

"But this is awful!"

"You will have four children."

"Four?"

"One daughter will become a noted writer of books."

"But—"

"*If* you follow the road your heart dictates, you will find happiness lies on that road. As for the others, they lead to despair," she said with a shrug. "In any event, you will be long-lived.

163

They say that Hell is eternal torment. A long life of despair is very akin to Hell. Think on that before you take your next irretrievable step, my lady. You should consider breeding horses."

"Horses?" Sarah asked dazedly.

"You'd be very successful at it."

The Gypsy rose, and Sarah stumbled numbly to her feet, handing a shilling to the woman as if in a dream. "Thank you," she murmured as she turned, unseeing, and began to walk from the camp, Jack at her side. She felt that he was as removed from her as she was from reality. The woods soon swallowed them up. All was darkness. A chorus of crickets surrounded them.

"An . . . interesting excursion," Jack said at last. "Not quite what I expected, though."

"Oh, this is horrible!" Sarah burst out. "I don't *want* to marry any of the men I know. They're shallow or pompous or foolish or cruel, and I'd be miserable with any of them! In fact . . . " Sarah turned the possibilities over in her mind. "Why trap myself at some stupid man's side when I've money enough to live comfortably as a spinster?"

"Now, now, my lady," Jack said sardonically. "You would not be so cruel as to deprive the world of a noted novelist?"

"What?"

"The literary daughter among your four promised children."

"Oh, Lord," Sarah said, her hand covering her face. "I'm doomed."

"Not necessarily," Jack replied. "The Gypsy held out the possibility of happiness if you will but follow your heart."

Sarah was grateful that they were in a dark wood and the moon was presently obscured by the clouds overhead. She very much feared her heart was in her eyes as she looked up at Jack and then hurriedly turned away.

"No, that is quite impossible," she said woodenly. Her heart could only promise despair. She would not listen. They continued walking back to Charlisle in silence.

*

Chapter 13

SARAH HAD TO forego her habitual ride with Henry the next morning to avoid overtiring Dune. The riding party would require that both keep their wits about them. She was grateful for this abstention. She would not be disappointed when Jack again failed to appear for their morning walk. His continuing absence had left her spirits more and more depressed and that—combined with last night's adventure—left her oddly uncertain as to how to act with him and what to say. Her heart was nettled as Jack held out her chair for her in the breakfast room, grave and imperturbable as he always was in company.

Still, it provided a certain inspiration. The quarrel Sarah staged with Fitz at breakfast that morning was a masterpiece that created a severe attack of dyspepsia in more than the Laveslys' interiors. She turned to Jack, hoping he would silently applaud a job well done, but he did not.

Dispirited, she left the table. "Wish me luck, Jack," she whispered as he held open the breakfast room door for her.

"Certainly, my lady."

She bit her lip, hurt by this reserve that would not melt away as it once had only days ago. To gain the front courtyard and fresh air was a blessing. Her head hurt. She had slept but little last night. The Gypsy music had hummed in her veins, the fortune-teller's words had snaked through her brain again and again until she thought she would go mad.

Three roads to choose from and only one promising happiness. That one included marriage and children—and horses. But that seemed impossible. If she had truly already met her future husband, then she must be unhappy in marriage, for

165

none of the marriageable men she knew touched her heart or stirred her soul or even valued the things she cared about. Marriage was not the road to happiness, despite the literary daughter. It was one of the roads to despair. Two other roads were left, one of them treacherous. What could they be?

Sarah shuddered as an image of her living as a spinster in her parents' house came to her. Yes, that was a real possibility and a horror to be avoided at all costs. But what was the third way? Oh, if only the Gypsy had been more specific! If only she had told her how to avoid despair.

To follow the dictates of her heart was no advice, for her heart had no discernment. Her heart knew nothing of her lofty social position.

No, her heart was a treacherous guide. Better to trust to whatever wisdom she had acquired and her knowledge of the world. Jack thought she had the resources to escape an Arab horde. Surely, they could also help her escape a lifetime of despair.

A horse's neigh startled Sarah. She turned to find several grooms leading horses toward the courtyard with Henry Jenkins, of course, leading them all, Dune cheerfully shambling beside him.

"Good morning, Henry!" she called as he drew near.

"Good morning, Lady Sarah. A fine day for a good gallop."

"Yes, it is," Sarah said as others in the riding party began to advance into the courtyard. Henry bent over to toss Sarah into the saddle, but her hand on his shoulder brought him upright. "I am going to disgrace you today, Henry," she whispered in an urgent undertone, "and I am sorry, but it is vital I do so. I will explain all in a few days, I promise."

"You must do as you think best, Lady Sarah," Henry stoically replied. He tossed her up into the saddle. "I'll give Dune an extra apple today to appease him for your disgrace." He winked at her.

Sarah leaned down and clasped his hand in hers. "*Dear* Henry."

"Sarah!"

Sarah jerked upright to find the duchess bearing down upon

166

her on one of the Somertons' famous black Arabians. She stifled a sigh and planted a smile on her face. "Yes, Mother?"

"I have told you and told you that you must not be familiar with the servants, particularly with those from the *stable*." This last was said with a world of disgust.

"I was not being familiar, Mother, merely polite. Somerton manners are renowned throughout the ton."

"Do not think you can cajole me into finding an innocent meaning in that statement and your guileless expression. I am, as I have told you every day this summer, extremely displeased with your conduct. You will strive today to make every observance of civility to the Laveslys, you will attach yourself to Lyleton throughout this morning's ride, and you will say nothing to shock or embarrass the company, is that clear?"

"Perfectly, Mother," Sarah replied, a hint of color in her cheeks.

She limped through Charlisle's front door a half hour later, the Duchess of Somerton's arm around her waist to support her.

"Of all the stupid, inelegant, unfathomable things to do!" the outraged duchess was saying, continuing a chastisement that had lasted all the way back to the house. "How could you be so singularly graceless as to fall off your horse right at the Laveslys' feet?"

"It was an accident, Mother." Sarah winced. "I was distracted by something Lyleton said and quite forgot what I was about. I am just as embarrassed as you, I do assure you."

"Lady Sarah!" Jack cried, rounding a corner and perceiving them. He strode into the entry hall, the shock of seeing Sarah in pain demolishing his now-habitual defenses. "You are hurt!"

"Of course she is hurt!" the Duchess of Somerton snapped. "She has fallen from her horse and sprained her ankle. *You* shall help her upstairs to her room and *you*," she said to Earnshaw as he emerged from his duties in the morning parlor, "shall go to the village and fetch a doctor. I require refreshments."

"There is a buffet set out in the morning parlor, Your Grace," Earnshaw said.

"That will do for now," said the duchess, sweeping off.

Jack, meanwhile, had started Sarah up the stairs. "I do not recall that injuring yourself was a part of your plan," he said accusingly, an arm around her waist, her arm looped over his broad shoulders.

"But I am not hurt."

Jack paused. "You did not sprain your ankle?"

"Good God, no!" Sarah scoffed, deliciously aware of the strong arm that supported her. "Give me some credit, Jack. I know how to fall off a horse! No, it came to me that a feigned minor injury would serve two useful purposes. First, it will only increase the disgust the earl and countess already feel for me. How I wish you had seen their faces when I fell off jumping the merest bump of a log! Second, it means I don't have to stand up with Fitz at the ball tonight and have everyone comment to our parents about how well we look together, for unfortunately, Jack, we *do* look well together."

"So I have observed, my lady, but only in a brotherly sisterly fashion."

"That is what I think, but that's not how the duke and duchess see it. Was ever a daughter more plagued by dithering parents?"

A chuckle escaped Jack. "*You* are a plague to all butlers, Lady Sarah," he sternly informed her.

"Am I?" she asked looking up at him, her heart bumping against her breast when she saw the warmth in his eyes.

"Decidedly. You would test the countenance of a Horse Guard."

He thereupon scooped her up—quite ignoring her gasp of surprise—and carried her the rest of the way up the stairs to the first landing.

"I can walk, Jack!" Sarah protested, afraid of the ease with which he carried her and how much she liked it.

"Not according to the duchess," he retorted. "Remember, my lady, the play *is* the thing."

It was wonderfully disconcerting to find her mouth so close to his. "You wouldn't carry the Dowager Formantle if *she* sprained her ankle."

"Very true. I would *shoot* the Dowager Formantle and put her out of her and everyone else's misery."

Sarah giggled the rest of the way to her room.

As the Duchess of Somerton had never in her life attended one of her children in a sickroom, Sarah was able to speak privately with the village doctor. She bribed him with a winning smile and a guinea, and he obligingly wrapped her foot and ankle, then gave her a wink. She watched him depart with the greatest satisfaction. Her secret was not only safe, she could count on the good doctor to assure the Charlisle party that she would be limping for the next sennight. Now all she had to do was remember to limp.

Despite the success of this newest venture, however, Sarah regarded herself in her dressing mirror that evening with little satisfaction. The lavender ball gown she wore was lovely. Maria had done her usual superb job with her red hair. The slim diamond and amethyst necklace around her throat glimmered in the candlelight. She would make a good showing tonight, but she would not dance, could not dance if she was to continue this important masquerade. The problem was that Sarah loved to dance. It was her next favorite activity after riding. If her future was not at stake, she would have thought it very hard to give up such pleasure as tonight's ball promised.

"What a bore this is going to be," she said, rising from her chair. She wore sandals tonight, for none of her shoes would fit over her bandaged foot.

"Now, now, my lady. The viscount is bound to provide some entertainment," Maria replied, handing her a fan with an intricately painted scene of cupids frolicking in a verdant countryside.

"Yes, there is that," Sarah said with a smile. She examined the slim red mahogany walking stick Maria now handed her. "Left hand for the left foot, you say?"

"That's right. Put your weight on the stick when you walk."

Sarah limped from her room. Holding onto the stair railing with one hand, Maria on her other side supporting her and carrying the walking stick, Sarah hopped downstairs to the entry

169

hall. Maria handed her the stick at the foot of the stairs and returned to her room as Sarah began to hobble across the hall.

A delightful frisson on the back of her neck made her turn slightly to find Jack regarding her with carefully veiled amusement.

"You were born for the stage, my lady."

"You always know just what encouragement to give me." She hobbled into the drawing room, where the party had gathered before dinner. Two dozen other guests from the neighborhood would be supplementing their company at the ball later in the evening. She had limped but two steps into the room when Freddy spied her and hurried forward to claim her hand.

"You're looking dashed pretty tonight, Sarah," he said, leading her to the nearest chair. "Though from what the Laveslys have been saying, I was certain you'd be black and blue all over."

"The Laveslys perhaps thought my fall worse than it really was," Sarah murmured, sitting down. She hurriedly hid her smile with her fan. Fitz could be heard on the opposite side of the room loudly declaring to the elder Mr. Braithwaite that a female who couldn't sit a horse was a pox on any company. The Laveslys—with open reluctance—now approached the pox. They appeared wholly unmoved by Sarah's profuse apologies for disrupting the riding party with her poor horsemanship. A bad seat was tantamount to total depravity. She saw it in their faces. It was all she could do to hold back a triumphant shout of laughter. They escaped her not thirty seconds after entering her company. Sarah turned with a grin back to young Mr. Braithwaite. "I have disgraced myself, Freddy."

"Yes," said that young gentleman with an unusually knowing look. "And I'd give my best snuffbox to know why."

"I'll tell you anon."

"Thought you'd been acting cagey. It's not like you to go falling off horses, let alone be so unguarded with your tongue. There's been times this last fortnight that I've practically blushed for you."

"It's all for a good cause, Freddy, and don't you dare say a word to anyone."

"As if I'd go bashing about one of your schemes," said Mr. Braithwaite, clearly affronted.

Sarah smiled affectionately at him. "You are a dear. Promise to talk to me at least once during the ball so I don't die of boredom?"

"Count on it, old girl. I don't care how pretty these neighboring girls are, I shan't forget you."

The party soon moved into the ballroom, noted for its pale pink marble floor and the three cut-glass chandeliers brightly illuminating the room. Fitz—with a hint from Jack—signaled the musicians and a polonaise wafted into the room.

As it happened, the better families in the neighborhood had a bumper crop of pretty girls. This was all to the good as far as Fitz and Sarah were concerned, though the rest of the women in the Charlisle party were not so enthused.

As Fitz was the master of the house, it was his duty to receive each new guest as they walked through the ballroom door, Jack announcing them in a clear voice. Fitz had his assignment—indeed, he had thought of his assignment—and derived a good deal of amusement from leering at every female who entered his house, married or no. Snubbing his own party, he proceeded to dance every dance with each of the new crop of beauties, flattering them mercilessly until they blushed and stammered and could not look him in the eye.

Everyone in the ballroom observed Fitz kiss Miss Marlow's hand with a good deal more warmth than mere politeness dictated. Everyone saw the ardent expression on his face as he danced and conversed with the admittedly beautiful Miss King. No one could miss the intimacy that quickly developed between him and Miss Temple, his dark head and her fair one nearly touching as they conversed in low tones, occasionally laughing, their gazes locked rapturously together.

All were aware that Fitz had not gone near Sarah during three hours of dancing, music, and conversation. They noted with secret glee that the Lavelyys had adopted glacial masks to hide their acute embarrassment. None could ignore the Somertons as

171

they silently seethed on the gilt-edged chairs they had claimed at the top of the room.

"It's going rather well, don't you think?" Charlotte whispered in Sarah's ear. They were seated together at the opposite end of the room.

"Splendidly," Sarah assured her, quickly averting her gaze from her parents' baleful glare. "I haven't seen them this incensed since the Earl of Laradid's *chère amie* interrupted Arabella's engagement dinner. If only *I* had a Lord Harigote to step to the fore and claim me."

"He'll appear someday, never you fear. You've too large a heart not to find someone to love."

Sarah quickly looked away. "Arabella was made for a knight in shining armor, not me. I'm not the sort of female who inspires ardor in a man's breast."

"Oh, come, now, I won't have you disparage yourself so! Only look at Mr. Davis and Lord Pontifax. They spent almost a fortnight trying to throw themselves at your feet."

"Now, there's a pair of swains anyone would be proud of. Pay me no heed, Charlotte. I've given into a fit of the blue devils because I can't dance tonight, and everyone seems to be having such fun."

"*Particularly* Lord Lyleton."

The two women chortled together like schoolgirls, displeasing the Somertons no end.

Charlotte was replaced by Freddy, as he had promised, and he was replaced by Lady Danvers. The chair beside Sarah was then temporarily vacant. But she had seen Lord Pontifax casting her determined looks during the quadrille. He had begun to be more attentive as it became clearer that she and Fitz were not suited. Poverty often lent determination to a man's character. She was not safe. As he continued to dance with Miss Neville, Sarah hurriedly limped out of the ballroom and into the adjoining salon, where card tables had been set up for those revelers who did not choose to dance.

"George, you sap-skulled dimwit, *clubs* are trump!" bellowed the Dowager Formantle.

There was no pleasure to be had here. Sarah hobbled from

the salon and out into the eastern gardens. The moon was nearly full tonight, bathing the flowers and fruit trees and hedges in shimmering white light. A few couples, including Fitz and a pretty girl whose name she could not recall, were standing on the terrace just outside the ballroom taking in the fresh air and the moonlight, their conversations hushed. There was no pleasure to be had *there*.

Cautiously maintaining her limp should anyone glance her way, Sarah followed a brick path through the gardens, the music and laughter from the ballroom following her. The walkway led her into the topiary garden, green giraffes and bears holding perfectly still in the moonlight.

Quite safe now from all scrutiny, Sarah leaned her walking stick up against a topiary cat and began to dance to the jig the orchestra was playing. She could not go through the entire night without once moving in time to the music. It just wasn't in her.

"Your pardon, my lady— "

Sarah jerked to a stop, a blush flooding her cheeks as she whirled around to find Jack Rawlins impassively regarding her.

"The Duchess of Somerton requests your company," he continued.

"Don't you dare laugh at me!" Sarah threatened, waving a finger at him.

"I'm not!"

"Oh, yes you are. I see it in your eyes, you scoundrel. I deserve one dance tonight to compensate me for my noble self-sacrifice, and you shan't talk me out of it."

"As if I would be so forward."

Arms akimbo, Sarah shook her head at the butler. "Do give over, Jack. There isn't a timorous bone in your body, and you know it. You'd bind and gag me if you ever thought I was doing something idiotic." An idiotic idea suddenly burst into Sarah's brain. "Dance with me!"

Jack's mouth fell open. "What?"

"I must have one dance tonight. Just one. Fitz is too busy, and you're the only other man who knows my sprain is a sham. Please dance with me, Jack."

173

He took a wooden step backward. "Lady Sarah, it would be wholly improper for a man of my station to—"

"Don't read me chapter and verse, John Rawlins, I know it by heart. One measly little dance will do no harm. No one can see us."

"Nevertheless, I cannot—"

"You can, or I'll write Lady Winster and tell her you're longing for her return to Charlisle."

The butler regarded her sternly. "Blackmail does not lighten a man's heels."

"*Don't* come over all stodgy, Jack," Sarah implored, impulsively stepping forward and capturing his large hand in both of hers. "You were born to dance; anyone can see that."

He seemed suddenly confused. "It has been years since—"

"The orchestra is playing an *écossaise*. Babes in arms know how to dance an *écossaise*. *Please*, Jack?"

His face was inscrutable as he stared down at her. He seemed to sigh. "Of all the daft notions. Thank God Greeves returns soon." He bowed. "May I have the honor of this dance, Lady Sarah?"

"Sir! You are too good."

Sarah placed her gloved hand in his, and they began to dance. His height seemed to complement her smaller frame. His hand, whenever it clasped hers, was big and strong and disordered every sensibility. Moving in time, mirroring each other's steps, made Sarah feel wonderfully effervescent, as if she had just consumed several glasses of champagne. For all his protests, Jack danced with grace and precision. He was the perfect partner.

"Do you waltz?" she asked, as they moved together and stepped back in time to the music.

His eyes would not meet hers. "No, though I have seen it performed."

"Mother won't let me learn. She thinks the dance too scandalous. There is not a higher stickler for propriety than the duchess. Even Almack's accepted the waltz last year, and you know, Jack, it would still insist on the minuet if anyone would dance it."

174

"It is a conservative institution, I believe."

"Dull as dishwater. Thank God there are a few hostesses in London who know how to have fun."

"You do not sound as if you enjoy city life."

"I was made for the country, with a few larks now and then to keep things interesting. The rest of my family delights in London."

"Ah, yes. You are the black ewe."

Sarah smiled up at Jack for remembering one of their first conversations . . . and became quite transfixed. He was gazing down at her with such warmth that she forgot to breathe. The moonlight brought all the planes of his face into sharp relief and seemed to make him taller and somehow lighter, as if the world was not weighing on him for this moment at least.

She did not blush. She felt positively ashen as she stared up at him, unable to look away, her heart beating in her breast and insisting upon a truth she had tried to avoid.

The music ended. She curtsied automatically, still looking up at Jack, mesmerized. Dizziness pounced. She swayed toward him. He was leaning toward her, as if to meet her halfway.

Then he blinked and jerked himself back, his face bloodless. "May I take you to the duchess now, my lady?"

Reality crashed into Sarah. She hurriedly turned and found her walking stick. "Yes, please."

He was several feet behind her, his voice cool in the night air. "I hope you were able to derive some enjoyment from your one dance this evening."

"Yes, thank you," Sarah woodenly replied, beginning to limp back to the ballroom. She had enjoyed the dance far more than was good for her.

*

Chapter 14

SARAH DISMISSED HER maid for the night the moment her head cleared her nightdress.

"But your hair—" Maria began to protest.

"I am fully capable of brushing and plaiting my own hair. You must have been longing for your bed these last two hours and more. Off you go."

"But, Lady Sarah, you don't appear at all well. Let me just—"

"I am fine, Maria. I am only weary. The sooner you go to your bed, the sooner I can claim mine."

Maria had attended Sarah for nearly nine years now, and she knew that determined look all too well. Her mistress meant to stay mute. Maria could only bid her good night and return to her own much-smaller room in the garret. Perhaps on the morrow, Lady Sarah would be more communicative.

But Lady Sarah was feeling very far from communicative as she sat down at her dressing table and began to brush out her hair. She was exhausted in mind and spirit, and wanted no dialogue with anyone, particularly herself. But her thoughts would not be silent. Her brush stilled. She stared bleakly at herself in the mirror—face bloodless, red hair a mad jumble, blue eyes huge—then let her brush fall and dropped her face into her hands.

In love. She was in love for the first time in her life, and whom had her heart chosen for her life's mate? *A butler!* Not even a cleric or a baronet, who would have been equally ineligible of course, but a *butler*.

"Oh, you wet-goose. You mutton-headed, idiotic, cockle-brained *clunch*!"

She thought she had been miserable in the past, but to love without hope was a far greater misery than even her parents could impose. The pain now stealing her breath was shocking in its scope. She understood now how ardently she had tried to protect herself by hiding from the truth. How brutally she had numbed herself to her heart. But the truth was stronger than all her defenses. There was no escaping it. She had fallen in love with John Rawlins soon after arriving at Charlisle. Her love had grown every day since then. "Oh, what have I done?" she whispered.

Her parents, of course, who had refused Sir Geoffrey Willingham for lack of funds *and* a decent title, would never consent to her marrying a servant. Far worse was the knowledge that Jack would never consent to marrying her, for he would never consider falling in love with a "superior." However much he might like her company, he could not, would not, love her. If he could . . . Oh, if he could, she would brave even a Gretna marriage for him! But he could not.

To discover love and heartbreak in the same moment seemed more than she could bear.

Numbly, she rose from her chair, snuffed out the candles in the room, climbed into bed, and pulled the covers tight around her as she curled into a miserable ball. She had been used to thinking she had a high threshold for pain, but no longer. Jack had seen to that. Warm tears began to slide down her cheeks, but she would not sob or weep. She would not. Nor would she acknowledge how right the duchess had been to warn her away from becoming familiar with servants.

You must follow only the dictates of your heart if you wish to find the happiness you seek.

Sarah shuddered under the covers. Her tears became more profuse. The dictates of her heart had barred all roads to happiness. She was undone.

Sarah awoke miserable as Maria pulled open the bedroom drapes and declared that it was another beautiful day.

Sarah's first coherent thought was that she must not reveal her love to anyone. For the first time, she would keep an important secret from Maria. For the first time she would lie to her friend.

You were born for the stage, Lady Sarah.

She would now have to prove Jack right. It was not, she thought dispiritedly as she got out of bed, a particularly good omen that she could recall every word he had ever said to her.

Though her stomach roiled, she drank her habitual cup of morning hot chocolate to avoid creating suspicion as Maria brushed out her hair. She made herself listen to an account of a servants' hall conversation in which Fitz's scandalous antics of the night before played a prominent part. Maria had it from several servants that her parents were furious and openly considering the wisdom of continuing the engagement.

"Fitz is working wonders," Sarah said with a forced smile. She hurriedly stood up and turned away. "I think I'll wear the floral-printed cambric morning dress."

She had no appetite, but she felt the need of escaping Maria's piercing scrutiny. And it would be wise to make some sort of appearance this morning in company. So, heavy-eyed and listless, she limped downstairs with her walking stick.

Most of Charlisle's revelers were recuperating in their bedrooms, from their exertions of the night before. George and Susan Formantle were her only companions in the breakfast room, and to distract herself from the pain, which seemed now to be in her bones, Sarah began to converse with them and found, without the dowager's presence, that they were a delightful couple: intelligent, sweet, and very much in love. It was a pity that their lives were dictated and hounded by the formidable Dowager Formantle.

Sarah turned their conversation to the lawn party and concert the Marlows were hosting that afternoon, which most of Charlisle's summer guests were attending. It was a happy suggestion, for just then Jack entered the room, and Sarah could think of nothing further to say and knew not where to look. Fortunately, Susan Formantle was fond of music and eagerly discussed the prospect of hearing the Italian soprano the Marlows had promised.

If Sarah had held out the tiniest shred of hope that she did not really love Jack—that it was just an infatuation, or merely lust—it evaporated now as her heart thundered in her breast, a blush crept into her cheeks, and excitement coursed through her veins.

"Good morning, Lady Sarah."

"Good morning, Rawlins," she managed. He stood at her elbow. She could feel every inch of him in her marrow.

"Is everything satisfactory?"

"Yes, thank you, Rawlins."

"May I ask how your ankle is doing?"

"It is . . . healing nicely, thank you." She stared intently at the slice of buttered bread on her plate. She could not look up.

"The Duchess of Somerton asks that you attend her in her room."

"I'll go at once." Sarah gratefully hobbled from the room. That she would prefer her mother's company to Jack's! Oh, she *was* far gone.

She managed to avoid Jack for the next several hours. The conscious knowledge of her love was yet too new to withstand his company so soon. House-bound as she was with her supposed sprain, she could still hide in the library, and with the Dohertys in the music room and, when things got difficult, in her own room.

Word came at lunch that Fitz would not be one of the Marlow party. He was unwell. Everyone took this to mean that he was hungover. All eyes in the dining room fixed on Sarah to see how she would take this news.

She shrugged. "I'm not surprised" was all she said. Then she took another bite of salmon.

But this was enough to satisfy the other diners. As far as they were concerned, the writing was on the wall. If the marriage actually did come off, it would be a miracle of God (or one of Sarah's undoubted future lovers) if the Lyleton line continued beyond Fitzwilliam Hornsby. Having lived her entire life among these people, Sarah knew very well what they were thinking and was satisfied. At least one aspect of her life was going well. If some of the greatest members of the Haute Ton considered her forthcoming marriage doomed, her parents could not be unaffected.

If only she could be unaffected by Jack's presence as he glided cool and reserved through the dining room, ascertaining that every need was attended. But she was affected, and in the worst possible way. In the midst of all these toplofty ladies and gentlemen, she wanted John Rawlins to smile at her with the warmth he occasionally allowed himself to show when they were alone together. He seemed so very grave today that she longed to utter some quip to make him smile. She wanted to feel his strong arm around her waist once again. She wanted to clasp his large warm hands in hers and drink in some of his confidence.

Instead, she sat mute and still, though her eyes followed his every move until he finally left the room. How was she to survive three more weeks in his company if she could not even withstand three minutes?

No, this was impossible. She could not continue like this. She had to take herself in hand, be realistic, think things through, chart her future course without lamenting a hopeless love. She would not marry Fitz. She could not marry Jack. She could not continue with her parents. She could not even hope to die young. The Somertons bred for longevity. So what was she to do with herself?

Two roads foretold by the Gypsy were now denied her. What was the third?

Perhaps someday she could come to love another and marry him and have those four children the Gypsy had promised her.

Her heart reproved her for this infamous suggestion. There was no other man in whom strength and tenderness were so devastatingly mixed. There was no other man whose gaze could warm her fifty feet across a room. There was no other man of such intrinsic honor and courage. There was no other man with such sly wit and boundless intelligence. There was no other man who felt, as she did, the joy and contentment bequeathed by the natural world of forests, rivers, and gardens. There was no other man with whom she wanted to sit in the moonlight beside a still black lake.

There was no other man her heart would welcome.

So what was the third road?

She had no answer as she saw most of the houseguests off that afternoon. They were a merry party as they set out for the Marlow estate. She was glad to be rid of them.

The Dowager Formantle had also stayed behind and was now ordering Freddy—who had an abhorrence of Italian sopranos—to a card table in the drawing room. He cast Sarah one last desperate glance before being dragged off to his unhappy fate. The Danvers joined him with far greater cheer.

Sarah was quite alone.

Grateful for this status, she hobbled upstairs to her room and spent the next hour finishing Catharine Macaulay's *Letters on Education*, which had unaccountably been shelved in Charlisle's library. When that was done, however, she found herself at somewhat of a loss for anything else to do. As a rule, she would be walking outside or riding across a meadow on Dune. But these delightful activities were denied her because she had been too clever by half and now had to maintain the myth of her sprained ankle. She was not in a mood to converse with anyone. She considered the card table in the drawing room with horror. She was not even hungry.

With a sigh, Sarah collected her book and limped from the room. There was always the library.

But in the library, she found not the book she sought, but Fitz, looking far from hungover as he lounged on the red leather chaise, idly flipping through *Gentleman's Magazine*.

"You have sunk yourself below reproach," Sarah said in a quelling voice.

He looked up at her and grinned. "There is something to be said for being a once-a-week beau."

Sarah smiled at him in turn, a real smile, not the painted expression she had worn all day. Fitz was the dearest boy. "Everyone has been condoling with me over your triumph last night. You performed your role admirably. Even Charlotte looked shocked at one point. I was so proud of you."

Fitz nodded graciously. "I never had so much dashed fun in all my life. A little further effort, and blessed freedom is ours."

"From all the gossip I have overheard, I think you're right. Shall we welcome back your guests this evening with an argument?"

"Yes. Let's!"

Their argument three hours later came off splendidly. Alerted by Jack that the house party had once again returned to Charlisle, Fitz and Sarah slipped into the library and left the door open. Hearing voices in the entry hall, they began to raise their own voices.

"How *dare* you humiliate me in such a public manner?" Sarah cried.

"I didn't humiliate you," Fitz retorted with equal volume. "I was merely being polite to my guests."

"*Polite?* You practically ravished Miss King on the dance floor!"

"At least *she* knows how to hold a fellow's interest."

"Aha! You say I bore you!"

"*And* bedevil me. You're like a gnat: always flying around and accomplishing nothing."

"An apt description, sir, of your *parents*," Sarah said, well aware that the Laveslys were among the party so shamelessly eavesdropping in the hall. "They fly about madly trying to improve their position in the ton and only succeed in garnering ridicule and disdain."

"Don't you *dare* say a word against my parents!" Fitz shouted, happy in the contemplation of days without parental censure, thanks to this inspired defense. "They at least do everything in their power to advance their only child in the world. *They* do not sneer at an honorable title and an important estate. *They* know the worth of their neighbors and acquaintance. *They* do not vex everyone to death whenever they walk into a room!"

Fitz, Sarah decided, was a good deal more clever than people gave him credit. With one speech he had brilliantly slandered her parents while seeming to defend his own, as a dutiful son should. Thus pressed to even greater endeavor, she retorted by calling him a lobcock and a loose fish. Not to be outdone, he caller *her* a knaggy, hard-hearted ape leader. She replied in kind.

"How dare you threaten me with your stick?" Fitz erupted.

Caught off guard, Sarah hurriedly recollected herself and shouted, "You are a mangy cur, Lyleton, and shall be beaten as one!"

This had long ago become too much for the Duchess of Somerton. She curtly informed those around her that it was time for them to retire and change for dinner. As they began to reluctantly mount the stairs, she swept down the hallway and burst into the library with righteous fury.

"How dare the two of you behave in such a low manner?" she demanded. "You are a disgrace to both your families. *You*, sir," she intoned, glowering at Fitz, "will leave us to change for dinner. I have a few words for my daughter."

Cowed, Fitz cast an apologetic glance at Sarah and slunk from the room.

"You," the duchess said brutally, slamming the door behind Fitz with such force that it sounded like a cannon exploding in the room. "You vile affront to decency!" She began to grimly advance on Sarah. "You despicable harridan!" She slapped her daughter hard, and then a second time to drive home her point. "Have you become lost to all decorum? All propriety? All *dignity*? Can you forget your family, your position, and yourself so entirely that you screech at the master of this house like a common fishwife? That you actually threaten him with physical violence?"

"Your Grace—" Sarah began, her cheeks burning from her mother's blows.

"Don't even think of addressing me! You disgust me. I loathe the very sight of you. I disown you. I disavow you. I am done with you from this day forward! If I see you at the dinner table tonight, I will throw you out of the house myself! You will pollute no one with your company. You will instead sit in your room tonight in quiet contemplation of the hideous nature

of your character, the lowness of your morals, and the complete and horrific lack of any goodness, obedience, or sense of duty within your corrupt soul."

The duchess turned on her heel and swept from the room, slamming the door behind her.

It was only when she was certain her mother had left that Sarah broke down. She turned from the door. The walking stick fell from her hand as she wrapped her arms around her torso and doubled over, racked with sobs. She had behaved badly, she knew, but that her own mother should despise her so!

Her hand went to her mouth to try to quiet her weeping.

"May I be of some assistance, my lady?" a gentle voice asked behind her.

Sarah turned slightly and saw, through a blur of tears, John Rawlins standing beside her. It was the compassion in his gray eyes that undid her.

"Oh, J-J-Jack!" she sobbed. She took an unsteady step toward him, and in the next moment found herself enfolded by strong arms that held her safe, her cheek resting against his broad chest. The strong beat of his heart beneath her ear was inexplicably comforting. She cried all the harder.

"My lady, my lady," Jack murmured against her red hair, "do not torment yourself so."

Sarah wept wholeheartedly. To live each day knowing her own parents loathed her, that they had loathed her from birth, seemed too much to bear. She felt more than heard Jack's low, soothing voice speaking words of comfort as he cradled her, somehow containing her pain and lessening it. Still, it was many minutes before sanity began to reawaken in Sarah's brain, and she realized that she was being held by the man she loved and that the man she loved could not love her.

She hastily broke free from his warm clasp, taking a few steps back and blindly accepting the handkerchief offered to her. Embarrassed now that anyone, particularly Jack, should have witnessed her giving in to such weakness, she hurriedly dried her eyes and cheeks and blew her nose.

"I'm sorry," she managed through her constricted throat, "I'm acting the complete thimblecap."

184

"On the contrary, you are acting like a woman who has been wounded too many times in her life."

Sarah shuddered as his gentle fingers brushed the remaining tears from her cheeks, and hurriedly turned away. "Don't be nice to me, Jack, I can't bear it."

"That is only because you are unaccustomed to it."

"Oh, what is wrong with me?" Sarah cried. She walked to the windows overlooking the lush western lawn, but there was no comfort there. There was comfort only in Jack's warm, compassionate gaze. Troubled in heart and soul, she steeled herself and then turned to face him once again. "Is it selfish to seek one's own happiness or at least to avoid unhappiness?"

"It is the most courageous quest any of us can undertake," he quietly assured her.

Candlelight cast his shadow large upon the paneled wall behind him. Her stuttering breath sounded loud in her ears.

"I don't feel courageous. I feel unnatural. Gerald, Frances, and Arabella all toe the mark in their fashion, but I cannot even *find* the mark. I used to think Mother must have had an affair with one of the footmen; it was the only way I could explain my freakish nature. But as I grew older, I realized, of course, that Mother would never lower herself to common carnal passion. Indeed, it's a wonder she's had any children at all! Then again, it's not. Mother is frightfully keen on doing her duty. Oh, why am I so different, Jack?" Sarah burst out, her hands clenched before her in impotent despair. "Why can't I be satisfied with my generous lot in life? Why can't I conform and be dutiful and obliging and fit into the mold that others, like Frances, seem to relish?"

He was standing before her. His warm fingers tilted her chin up so that she must gaze into his gentle eyes. "Perhaps because you have a larger spirit that cannot tolerate diminution," he said softly.

It was hard to catch her breath. "You don't think it's just pure obstinacy?"

He smiled then, and his smile went all the way through her, warming her, comforting her, cheering her. "A little of that, too, of course," he said, releasing her. He took a step back and

185

seemed deliberately to assume the mantle of servant once more. "Would you like me to send a cup of hot chocolate liberally laced with brandy to your room?"

She smiled for the first time since her mother had accosted her. "Thank you, no. I'm actually feeling tolerably better." She glanced down at the mangled square of linen in her hand. "I've ruined your handkerchief, you know."

"I have others."

Ah, it was so tempting to stay here, forever enveloped in that generous gaze. "You have been very kind, John Rawlins," she said formally. "Thank you."

He bowed with equal formality. "You are quite welcome, my lady."

He held the door open for her, and she walked from the library as if nothing untoward had ever occurred . . . as if she did not feel his gaze tracing every inch of her.

*

Chapter 15

SITTING IN HER room that evening and contemplating, not her vile nature, but love and John Rawlins and the three different roads her future might take, Sarah quite missed out on the coup de grâce to her engagement. Now convinced that his parents longed to deny the banns if only the Somertons would also concede, Fitz cornered the duke in the drawing room after dinner.

The topic he wished to discuss was a most exclusive brothel in London that the duke was known on occasion to visit. It was one of those pieces of information that the duchess and most of Polite Society professed not to possess, though of course it was common knowledge. Everyone knew everyone else's business in the ton. It was just that they all had the good taste not to openly discuss it when a powerful woman was involved. But for Fitz, when it came to a choice between a fishwife and *his* freedom, there was only one course open to him.

"Is it true they've got the prettiest girls in all of Europe housed there?" he loudly slurred, pretending to be drunk as he placed a comradely hand on the duke's shoulder in the over-heated drawing room.

"I wouldn't know," His Grace replied, trying to turn away. Fitz firmly held him in place.

"Course you know!" he happily bellowed. "You're practically a founding member."

"Lower your voice, sir!"

"Thing of it is," explained Fitz with a hiccup, "I'm *not* a member, and if I'm going to marry that shrewish daughter of yours, I'd dashed better *become* a member if I'm to have any sort of an ... er ... outlet. You've got to recommend me to Mrs. Hill."

"I will do no such thing."

"But you must! One man to another, future father to his son, that sort of thing. No need to be parsimonious with the ladies' favors, old man. I won't cut you out. Word of honor."

"You, sir, know nothing of honor!" The duke succeeded in turning his back on his inebriated host and began to converse on his right with Lady Danvers.

Delighted with himself, Fitz summoned a footman to refill his wineglass, and then began stalking the duchess, who stood white and rigid not six feet away. Her companion, Mrs. Elinore Braithwaite, scurried off to safety as soon as Fitz looped his arm around the duchess's waist and began to wax poetic on the joy he would know upon being related to such an august personage. In his exuberance, he began to enumerate the many reasons he doted upon her, including her wholly adequate bosom and her wide, tempting mouth. With a suddenness that caught her off guard, he then swept her into his arms and kissed her.

Having never in her life been manhandled, not even by her husband, the duchess screeched—there can be no other word for it—when Fitz finally let her come up for air. "Barbarian!" She then slapped him with all the force her outrage demanded. Fitz tumbled to the floor as if Gentleman Jackson himself had planted him a facer. "Maggot!" she shouted down at him. "I'll see you in *Hell* before I let you marry my daughter!"

She stormed from the room. The duke took a moment to order Fitz never to approach his wife again, before hurrying after her.

Fitz sat up on the carpet, gingerly feeling his jaw. "This calls for champagne!" he declared, as everyone in the room regarded him with astonishment and the delight that comes from witnessing one of the truly great scandals of the year.

The Laveslys, in the earl's room, and the Somertons, in their sitting room, reached the same conclusion that night after everyone else had retired for the evening. However unsavory

188

the repercussions, they must for their own sanity call off the wedding.

Neither couple slept well that night. Both arose early the next morning, a trifle haggard but determined. As soon as propriety permitted, they sent each other notes requesting a private audience. They selected the library for their rendezvous. Jack was the only one who knew of their meeting, and as soon as they had dismissed him, he hurried upstairs to wake first Fitz and then Sarah, to give them sufficient time to prepare themselves for whatever was to come next.

"But how is this?" Sarah demanded, still in her dressing gown as she joined Maria at her bedroom door.

Jack succinctly described the previous evening's debacle.

"Oh, clever, clever, Fitz!" Sarah happily cried. "I am free, and the summer isn't even over. How I wish I had been there to witness his performance."

"He was, if I may be permitted to say so, my lady, superb."

"Blessed boy! We won't have to resort to the cow after all. I must dress and congratulate him at once!"

As it was, Sarah had but five minutes to find and hug Fitz. She had just professed him to be the best former fiancé she had ever known, when Maria rapped upon his door to announce that Sarah had been summoned to the library by her parents. A moment later Jack brought a similar summons for Fitz.

"Be of stout heart," he abjured them, and won a shy smile from Sarah for his concern.

The supposedly contentious couple walked gravely together into the library, Jack closing the door behind them. The Countess of Lavesly sat upon a settee, the earl standing behind her. The duchess sat opposite the countess in a wing chair, the duke standing beside her. They all wore the same forbidding expressions. It was the duchess who spoke first.

"Honor, prudence, and family interest require that we end the engagement subsisting between you both," she stated.

Fitz and Sarah wisely held their tongues. They did not even smile.

"Disagreeable as this decision is," the duchess grimly continued, "your marriage would be far worse, for we are now

189

convinced that, rather than bringing the hoped-for benefits of property, connection, and advancement to our families, your union would ruin us all. You have both behaved in an abhorrent fashion from the moment you met. I have been seriously displeased by your conduct."

"I beg your pardon, Mother," Sarah said with a demure curtsy.

"You have behaved badly, Sarah," said the Duke of Somerton, "but you are far from entirely to blame. This . . . This *miscreant*," he said gazing at Fitz distastefully, "has acted so disgustingly from first to last that we could not tolerate his alliance with our family."

"You will not place the blame on *my* son!" the Countess of Lavesly cried. "*Your* daughter has behaved no better than a *doxy*!"

"How *dare* you?" seethed the Duchess of Somerton, as she rose to her feet. "Your son has gone out of his way to insult me with every word and deed!"

"Your *daughter*, ma'am," said the earl, appearing a trifle flushed, "has comported herself with such a lack of decorum that I wonder you even claim the relationship!"

"Father—" said Fitz.

"Sarah may on occasion have acted badly, but at least she is not a *drunkard*!" stated the duchess.

"Mother—" said Sarah.

"No, she is a hoyden," pronounced the countess, blond curls shaking with fury.

"And *your* son is a libertine," said the duke.

"The pot calling the kettle black, *I'd* say," said the countess with a sniff.

"Oh! How *dare* you?" the duchess said. "The duke is one of the most respected members of the ton. He possesses a family and fortune that you can never hope to aspire to."

"Saying you're too good for us?" demanded the earl. "Too good for *us* when you have *that* for a daughter?"

"Your son, sir, exhibits all the worst traits of your all too humble beginnings," said the duke. "I shudder to think that we ever considered aligning ourselves with such an ill-bred line of *commoners*."

Sarah and Fitz looked haplessly on as full-scale warfare broke out between these two august couples. They tried to intervene more than once, but were so ruthlessly ignored that they finally decided that the wisest course was to beat a strategic retreat. They slipped out of the library, quietly closing the door behind them. They were not missed.

Sarah looked at Fitz. Fitz looked at Sarah. They grinned at the same moment and heartily shook each other's hand.

It fell to the duke, as the ranking member of the party, to make the announcement an hour later at breakfast. "We sincerely hope," he said, his leonine features so frozen that Sarah was certain he would crack open, "that this unhappy matter will in no way detract from your continued enjoyment of this summer sojourn. The end of this betrothal is entirely amicable, I assure you. The Laveslys and Somertons continue on the best of terms and hope to enjoy your further company."

This seemed ominous to Sarah. As the duchess was not yet speaking with her, she buttonholed the duke after breakfast.

"You cannot intend for us to stay at Charlisle?" she asked.

"We must," the duke growled.

"But the embarrassment—"

"Cannot be avoided. We will not have it said that the Somertons left Charlisle with their tails between their legs."

"But, Father—" Sarah pleaded.

His expression was cold. "The Somerton honor is at stake. I do not say that we must remain here all summer. On the contrary, the duchess and I agree that we need only remain at Charlisle another sennight."

"A sennight!"

He looked disdainfully down upon her. "You need not fear being trapped in Lyleton's company or even that of the Laveslys. I'm sure they wish to avoid you as heartily as we wish to avoid them. A certain discomfort must prevail, of course, but will soon pass. A sennight is not so very long, after all."

"Of course not," Sarah murmured. She watched her father

walk to the hall to join the elder Braithwaites in a morning promenade across the grounds. At the moment, a sennight felt like forever. She was certain she couldn't survive it.

"Sarah?"

She turned to find that Corliss Braithwaite had not left the room and was regarding her with some anxiety.

"Is it certain," said Corliss, her cheeks as pink as her gown, "that you will not marry Fitz?"

"Quite certain."

"You did not want to marry him?"

"And he did not want to marry me," Sarah assured her.

"Good," said Corliss with a hearty sigh of relief, "because I *do* want to marry Fitz."

"What?"

"I know he is not terribly clever; but, Sarah, neither am I. To me, Fitz is everything amiable, sweet, and kind. I am always happy in his company. I don't mind his wardrobe or his devotion to his stable. His goodness more than makes up for those paltry defects."

"You *are* sunk," Sarah declared, struggling hard to regain her equilibrium.

Corliss laughed a trifle giddily. "Completely, irrevocably, happily so."

"But, my dear girl, I must warn you: Fitz is the farthest thing from being ready to marry anyone, even you."

"Oh, I'm well aware of that. He needs a few more years of independence. But he will come around, Sarah. I will make him come around. I will make him believe that there is only one wife possible for him. I'm so glad you don't want to marry him."

In a bit of a daze, Sarah watched Corliss trip happily off to the gardens. This was a day of wonders.

"May I offer you my congratulations, my lady, on a campaign well fought?"

Sarah whirled around to see Jack standing gravely before her, his eyes shuttered. "We have been very fortunate in our allies."

"The courage and the audacity were all yours, however."

192

She blushed a little at the compliment. "I am not certain that audacity is an entirely desirable trait in the daughter of a duke."

"Not to the duke, perhaps."

Mrs. Clarke coughed discreetly at him from a few feet away. He bowed to Sarah and joined the housekeeper in a hushed conversation, and then left the room.

Sarah shook her head with disgust as she watched him go. Oh, what was she doing, mooning over the man, when she should be making every effort to forget him? How could she dream of him—as she had done last night—when she must resign herself to living without him? Why, in short, was she deliberately tormenting herself like this?

This would not do. She had a week to withstand his company. A week in which to stiffen her resolve, harden her heart, and get on with her life. She walked from the dining room, considering her past and her future with a clear eye.

As every other young lady of the ton had done, she had thus far lived her life at her parents' decree. She had accepted their decisions and their judgments without question . . . until this summer. Now that she had stood up in opposition to the most important decision they had ever made about her life, she could not go back to being the accommodating daughter she had tried to be before. She had changed somehow. She was no longer that meek Sarah who dreaded every word her parents uttered. She felt, in fact, almost as undutiful as they had always thought her.

This raised a host of problems, she realized as she slowly began to climb the stairs to the first landing. Just because the engagement to Fitz had failed didn't mean her parents weren't still determined to marry her off. She would not submit, could not submit. She would not marry to oblige them. Nor could she live out the rest of her life under their thumb. She would not be the despised spinster daughter encountering their censure every day for the rest of her life.

She had reached the first landing and was halfway down the hall to her room when her head suddenly came up. She stopped dead in her tracks. She had thought of the third road!

She had stopped beside a life-size statue of Diana at her

bath, amazed at the vision of what her life might become: independent, content, alone, it is true, and yet to be no longer hounded by her parents and the ton . . . there was no despair in that course! The Gypsy had been wrong after all. Some happiness might be had without a husband and the literary daughter.

She heard a door open and, not wanting to be seen and forced into conversation when her thoughts were madly dancing down the third road, Sarah stepped behind Diana and watched in growing amazement as first Lord Danvers and then Lady Danvers stepped out of Mrs. Elinore Braithwaite's room, peered cautiously up and down the hall, and then scurried off to the passageway leading to their own room.

No longer hearing their footsteps, Sarah stepped around Diana and stared down the hallway. Had she really seen what she thought she had just seen?

A servants' door in the white-paneled wall opened up, and Jack stepped into the hallway. He and Sarah quietly regarded each other.

"The Danverses?" Sarah whispered.

"So I have long suspected," he calmly replied.

"Good God. Can you prove it?"

"Not yet. I have only been able to make a cursory search of their room. I found nothing untoward."

Sarah clasped her hands behind her back and considered a moment. "Then, we must somehow make them incriminate themselves in company."

"We?"

Sarah looked up at Jack in surprise. "Yes, of course! You helped me escape an imprudent marriage. Why should I not help you catch a pair of jewel thieves?"

"You might be helpful at that," he conceded.

"You're too kind."

An answering smile lit his countenance, then quickly faded. "But come, we cannot be plotting in the hallway."

"No, indeed. Let us retire to my sitting room. They shan't stumble upon us there."

Sarah's painfully acute awareness of her feelings bitterly opposed this suggestion. To be alone with Jack was misery.

194

But she had promised her help. Besides, she had to withstand his company for another sennight. It was time to start hardening her heart. After all, she *had* found the third road.

It required only a few minutes for two intelligent people to decide on how they would expose Lord and Lady Danvers. But the plot required some of the stolen booty, and finding *that* required more earnest contemplation.

"The jewels must be in their room," Sarah said, slowly pacing before the sunlit window overlooking the rose garden. "But not where a maid or a valet might stumble upon them."

"The room lacks a safe, hidden or otherwise. Nor are there any secret hiding places in any of the furniture that I have been able to discover."

"Then, they must have brought the hiding place with them."

"A false bottom in a trunk, perhaps?"

"Exactly," Sarah said with a quick smile. The smile turned to an expression of pure astonishment. "Or in a decorative jar of snuff!"

"Of course! Pour out the snuff, place the jewels in the bottom of the jar, replace as much snuff as you are able, and there you are. How perfectly brilliant!"

"Thank you," Sarah said dimpling.

"I meant the *Danverses*."

Sarah scowled at him and won a most engaging grin for her pains. Ah, was there a more charming man in the whole of England? "From what I have overheard," Jack continued, hurriedly retracting his grin, "Lord Danvers always carries at least three jars of snuff with him on any visit and insists on filling his snuffboxes himself. Three jars could well hold what has already been stolen."

"Then, you know your course," Sarah said, rallying her wayward thoughts. "I can easily distract the thieves while you search Lord Danvers's room again."

"Yes, and it must be today. Lady Danvers informed me that they will leave Charlisle at the end of the week to keep a family engagement in Leicestershire."

"Then, let us act quickly. With luck, we may be able to expose them before dinner. What excuse shall I give to keep

195

the Danverses in my company for a good hour, so you may work undisturbed?" Sarah frowned in concentration. "A walk? No, I'm still supposed to be limping. I have it! Punting on the lake. I can insure that we take an inordinate amount of time walking to and from the lake—my sprain, of course—and then keep us at least an hour on the water. I'll say Freddy Braithwaite has broken his word to take me punting today. I shall appear quite desolate. They can't help but offer to take me in his stead."

"And what if Mr. Braithwaite stumbles upon your party?"

"Oh, I'll warn him off, never you fear. Freddy's the most obliging fellow. He never asks questions when you don't want him to."

"An admirable trait," Jack gravely agreed. "Very well, our course is set. Place yourself in the morning parlor and look suitably melancholy. I shall lure the Danverses into your company."

＊

Chapter 16

DESPITE THE COMPANY, or more likely because of it, Sarah thoroughly enjoyed her jaunt on the lake. She had never knowingly been in the company of out-and-out criminals before, and she found the experience exhilarating. Careful not to give a hint of her knowledge, or to disconcert the Danverses in any way, she managed to keep the conversation almost entirely on the subject of jewelry. She shared the delicious gossip about the Earl of Larchmont, who had recently purchased an impressive ruby ring, and it hadn't been for his wife; then she debated whether Lady Winster's pearl choker or the Countess of Lavesly's pearl choker was the superior in composition and grade of pearls, while thanking heaven that she had only had a bracelet go astray this summer.

The Danverses—just as interested in jewelry as she—conversed with the utmost equanimity, condoled with her over the loss of even that single bracelet, wondered why the Gypsies had not long ago been placed in jail for the thefts at Charlisle, and decided that the Winster pearls were the superior.

While continuing the conversation with a determination the Danverses could not withstand, Sarah yet had time to imagine Jack secretly rifling their room. It was rather thrilling to think of him in this nefarious employment. She grimaced. As if she needed any other excuse to think him the most intoxicating man she had ever known.

As no one could discuss the topic on everyone's minds—the ending of the Thorndike-Lyleton engagement—conversation during the afternoon luncheon turned (through a deft comment by Sarah) toward the recent jewel thefts.

"My favorite diamond necklace is missing from my jewelry box," Mrs. Braithwaite lamented. "I discovered it only this afternoon. It was my grandmother's. I have always treasured it."

"How terrible for you," Lady Danvers murmured sympathetically. "Only last year, a ring my mother gave me was stolen at one of the Jersey house parties. I cried over it for two full days." A footman offered her cold asparagus, and she took a healthy helping.

"I am amazed, Lord Lyleton, that you have not had those infernal Gypsies arrested yet," said Lord Danvers.

Forewarned by Jack, Fitz merely replied, "Oh, I have it on the best authority that arrests are imminently expected. I daresay we will all sleep safely in our beds tonight."

"Well, it's about time," the Dowager Formantle trumpeted. "I'm tired of carrying my jewels with me in my reticule everywhere I go."

"And I want my gold snuffbox back," stated Mr. Braithwaite with some ire. "It was a gift to me from the prince."

"Ow!" said Sarah.

Lord Danvers, on her left, turned to her with solicitous concern. "Is something wrong?"

Sarah had a hand clapped to her right eye. "There's something flown into my eye, and I can't find . . . My lord, will you lend me your handkerchief?"

"Certainly," Lord Danvers replied. He pulled his handkerchief from his coat pocket and with it came Mrs. Braithwaite's stolen necklace.

There was a universal gasp from everyone in the room.

"Good God, what are you doing with my necklace?" Mrs. Braithwaite indignantly demanded.

"I-I-I do not know!" Lord Danvers cried in all honesty. At first pale, he was now bloodless. "It is some trick. I am innocent!"

"If I may be permitted, my lord," said Jack to Fitz, "I have long suspected the Danverses' complicity in the recent unhappy spate of thefts in this house."

"Search them both!" Sarah cried.

This suggestion was instantly taken up. The Dowager Formantle swooped down upon Lady Danvers and searched her from head to toe, despite that lady's vociferous protests. Then she began to paw through her ladyship's reticule, dumping its contents upon the table. A lump of gold glowed amid the handkerchief, the small bottle of smelling salts, and a coin purse.

"My snuffbox!" roared Mr. Braithwaite, pointing an accusing finger.

A signal from Jack had already set footmen on either side of Lord Danvers, effectively placing him under house arrest. Lady Danvers was now similarly surrounded.

"No, no!" she cried. "There is some mistake. I am not a thief!"

"This is outrageous!" shouted her husband. "Unhand me at once!"

"May I suggest, my lord," said Jack to Fitz, who was enjoying himself enormously, "that my staff and I undertake a thorough search of the Danverses' bedchamber?"

"Have at it," said Fitz.

With the Danverses held prisoner in the dining room, Jack led six footmen up to the first landing. They were not alone. Most of Charlisle's guests scurried after them, eager to be in on the kill. Jack allowed his men to spend a good quarter hour making a thorough search of the Danverses' room. Then he signaled Earnshaw, whom he had taken into his confidence only an hour earlier.

It was Earnshaw who leapt upon the snuff jars with an eager cry and began dumping the contents of the first jar into a porcelain washbasin. Sarah's bracelet, Lady Winster's ruby necklace, Lord Merbles's jewel-encrusted stickpins, and several other items followed the snuff into the basin.

A great feeling of satisfaction settled over those crowded into the room.

"I have recently taken the liberty of making certain inquiries, my lord," said Jack to the wholly delighted Fitz. "It is my understanding that whenever jewels go astray at a house party, Lord and Lady Danvers are always in residence."

This was, of course, the nail in the coffin. Earnshaw sifted through the rest of the snuff, sneezing violently several times, and retrieved all of the stolen jewels. The entire party then trooped triumphantly back downstairs. Jack had already sent one of his staff to the nearby village to fetch back the local representatives of the law. With dubious help from Charlisle's houseguests, he provided these gentlemen with the essential facts of the case. The Danverses—despite their vociferous protests—were thereupon summarily hauled off for incarceration prior to their appearance before the local magistrate on the following morning. It promised to be a good show that every one of Charlisle's guests vowed to attend.

"Well done, Jack!" Fitz whispered, as Jack held out his dining room chair. "To think that the Danverses would be such clunches as to keep some of the booty on themselves!"

"They did not, my lord," Jack murmured. "I planted the jewels on them just before lunch to act as the necessary catalyst to their unveiling and arrest."

Fitz regarded him with awe. "You *are* devious!"

"Thank you, my lord."

Charlisle's guests could talk of nothing but the jewel thefts and the Danverses' capture. The Dowager Formantle insisted that she had suspected the couple from the start. The Duke of Somerton agreed. He declared that their characters had long been in question. Lord Lavesly said he had always thought the Danverses too eager to please. Mr. Braithwaite added that the Danverses had undoubtedly wielded their skillful flattery expressly to secure invitations to houses they intended to rob. Several others at the table thought this terribly clever of Mr. Braithwaite and congratulated him on his insight.

Sarah sat quietly by, free from all notice. Her ended engagement to Fitz was nothing to this, and she was heartily glad of it. She listened with utter contentment as the party praised Jack for his able help in unmasking the Danverses. She was glad that he should get his due, this one time at least. She preferred that no one know of her part in the Danverses' capture. She had never liked center stage.

* * *

"A most satisfactory conclusion," Sarah said to Jack as he inspected a buffet table in the drawing room. She had just come in to fetch the parasol she had accidentally left behind and felt that she must say something.

"Thank you, my lady," he said, adjusting some of the silverware. A small stack of china plates was straightened.

Sarah stood quite still. Something was very wrong. "You shall be lauded as Charlisle's hero for many days to come, I think," she remarked. "Will you be able to withstand so much attention?"

"There is not the necessity of it." He turned from the buffet table and regarded her impassively. "I will be leaving Charlisle tomorrow morning."

"Leaving?" she asked faintly.

"Yes. Mr. Greeves will be returning to his post tomorrow. I have some business of my own to attend to, and so I shall depart."

"But . . . the Danverses—"

"I have written a full account of the matter, which I believe the magistrate will find most satisfactory."

It was amazing to Sarah that someone could die and remain upright at the same time. "Then this is good-bye."

"Yes, my lady." Jack paused. "May I ask . . . What will you do once you also leave Charlisle?"

Sarah managed a shrug. "I shall rusticate with some semblance of independence. And what will you do?"

"I have a position waiting for me in Devonshire."

"Oh," said Sarah in a small voice. "I traveled through Devonshire once. It is very beautiful. I hope you will be happy there." She drew a shuddering breath. "Well, all that remains is to wish you Godspeed, and to thank you for all you have done on my behalf." She held out her hand. Jack clasped it in his and gravely shook it. For a moment, she felt the heat that always came when he touched her, and then they separated.

"It was a great pleasure, my lady," he said quietly.

Her throat now too constricted for breath, let alone words, Sarah turned and walked without sensation from the drawing room, her parasol quite forgotten. Somehow she found the

201

staircase through a thick blur of tears. All she could think to do was to flee, to run away, to hide.

She reached the first landing and turned blindly toward her room.

"Sarah?"

She continued walking.

"Sarah?" Two hands clasped her arms and held her still. "Good God, Sarah, what is wrong? Are you ill?"

She dimly perceived that it was Charlotte who had stopped her. "Please let me go," she whispered.

"I'll do no such thing," Charlotte declared. She pulled Sarah into the bedchamber she had just left. "You will come in here and tell me what has happened to make you look so ill."

Sarah heard a door close behind her. The numbness that had held her in thrall suddenly deserted her. Hot tears began to course down her cheeks. "Oh, Charlotte!" she gasped, and buried her face in her hands.

"My dear girl, what has happened?" Charlotte cried, nearly undone by her friend breaking down like this, for she had never done so before. She pulled Sarah into her arms. "Sarah, what is wrong?"

"I am in love!" Sarah said, as she sobbed onto her friend's shoulder.

"Are you?" asked Charlotte in the utmost amazement. She had had not the least suspicion of it.

"Yes. And it's useless. Hopeless."

"But why?"

"Because I am in love with Jack Rawlins!"

"Rawlins?" Charlotte blinked. "The *butler*?"

"Oh, don't say it like that," Sarah complained, pulling free of her friend and blindly searching her pocket for a handkerchief. "He is a man, the best man I have ever known, and I love him. He is leaving tomorrow, and I will never see him again!" She miserably dried her tears.

"But is that not for the best?" Charlotte queried, feeling very much out of her depth.

"Would you have said that if Phineas had left *you*?" Sarah hotly riposted.

202

"But Phineas is not a butler."

"I know that!" Sarah stormed, her hands clenched impotently at her sides. "I know all the reasons why I should not love Jack. I know all the reasons why he could never return my regard. I know all the reasons why the situation is hopeless, and oh, Charlotte, it hurts so much!"

This last was said on a sob that drew Charlotte forward. "My poor girl, come with me." She sat on a yellow brocade chaise and dragged Sarah down beside her. "There, there," she murmured, stroking through Sarah's hair until, at last too weary to remain upright, Sarah curled herself onto the chaise and rested her head on Charlotte's swollen belly. "These are hard times indeed."

"I tried, Charlotte," Sarah said through tears she refused to shed. "I tried so hard not to love him. You don't know. But almost from the first . . . I was lost."

"Yes, it was that way with me, too," Charlotte stated quietly, gently stroking her friend's brow. "My parents have never liked the Irish. I knew how violently they would object to Phineas. But love never considers the practical aspects of one's life."

"No," Sarah said with a sniff. She hurriedly dabbed at her eyes with her handkerchief.

"I have no balm to ease your pain. I will not say that you will eventually stop loving Rawlins, for I know your heart too well. Once it is given, it is given for good. But I do say that the pain will lessen somewhat as time passes."

"When I am stricken in years, perhaps," Sarah conceded. Suddenly, she yipped and bolted upright.

"Good gracious, what is wrong?" Charlotte demanded.

Sarah glared at her. "Your son, Charlotte, has just kicked me in the ear!"

Charlotte could not help but laugh. "How do you know it's a boy?" she demanded.

Sarah grimly blew her nose. "Only a boy would have so little consideration for a woman's misery. I will *not* stand as his godparent."

"No, no. Of course not."

Sarah blew her nose again and frowned at her friend. "You are a wretch."

That made Charlotte smile. "There, that is much better. A judicious use of spirit will help you through this lamentable period. Does he . . . Have you told Rawlins how you feel about him?"

"Good God, no! I am not such a ninnyhammer."

"Well, we can be grateful for that, at least. And if *I* did not know it, then no one else could have suspected it, either. You are at least saved from public censure and ridicule."

"That, of course, makes up for everything," Sarah said witheringly.

"Poor girl. This has been a most difficult summer."

"And my trials are not yet over." Sarah stared across the yellow bedroom at a small painting of a mail coach careening down a road in the midst of a storm. "I must first watch the man I love walk out of my life forever tomorrow morning, and then I must somehow force my parents into allowing me to chart my own course."

"What's all this?"

Sarah turned back to Charlotte. "I cannot continue as I have done. I can no longer play the dutiful daughter. Not after Fitz and . . . and Jack. You must see that."

"I begin to."

"So I must now follow a different road."

"To what end?"

Sarah clasped Charlotte's hand in her own and looked directly into her questioning brown eyes. "To a life not bound by despair."

*

Chapter 17

WITH THE DANVERSES' perfidy to distract them, Sarah knew she could keep to her room the rest of that afternoon and not be missed by any of Charlisle's guests. She had a good deal of work to do if she was going to present a wholly unremarkable facade to the company—and John Rawlins—that night. Her nose could not be red. Her eyes could not well with tears. She must not fall into weeping every time she glanced at the butler she had twice made laugh.

She must direct her thoughts to a less volatile subject and keep them there. The third road and the inevitable confrontation with her parents seemed the safest and most consuming course. Indeed, she could not have hit upon a better distraction. At dinner that night, Sarah had only to glance at her parents to be rescued from emotions threatening to overcome her every time Jack's movements caught the corner of her eye. The conversation around her required that she only say "Oh, yes" and "Indeed?" at suitable intervals. She was safe.

In the drawing room after dinner, she made herself play two hands of cards with the Dohertys and Lord Pontifax before pleading a headache and escaping to the sanctuary of her room. There Maria, long suspecting that something troubled her mistress, observed that she seemed unusually pale tonight and quiet, but she could not press. That Sarah would not confide in her seemed, to Maria, to be more than ominous. But it also seemed there was nothing she could do about it for now.

If Sarah slept that night, it was for no more than an hour or two. She abandoned her bed when the sky was still dark and the rooster had not yet crowed. Pulling a warm dressing gown

205

from her wardrobe and stepping into her embroidered slippers, she left her room. Walking noiselessly down the hall, she listened to the stillness all around her.

There was on the first landing a window and window seat overlooking the front courtyard. Sarah pulled aside the heavy yellow drapes and claimed this seat, hugging her knees to her chest, feeling cold and ill despite the comfort of her dressing gown and slippers.

She watched as the sky slowly turned gray. Nothing stirred. As gray turned to an azure blue and red began to rim the eastern horizon, Fitz's liveried coachman drove a gig into the courtyard below her. The bay mare that pulled the gig stamped now and then in the cool morning air as they waited.

A few minutes later, John Rawlins walked down the front steps toward the gig. He wore an austere greatcoat that enveloped him from shoulder to heel. His dark brown hair was covered by a top hat. He carried a valise in one hand and a small portmanteau in the other. These he secured to the back of the gig. He turned, as if he was about to take one last look at the house, but stopped himself. Instead, he strode forward and climbed into the gig. The coachman gathered his reins. The bay began to trot down the tree-lined avenue.

"Good-bye, my love," Sarah whispered, her hand pressed against a cool pane of glass. She watched until all she could see was Jack's hat. And then she could no longer see even that.

She had not known what desolation was until this moment. She could not even weep. She could only stare out at the growing dawn, seeing none of the exuberant colors, hearing nought of the increasingly vociferous chorus of birds, thinking nothing save "He is gone."

For another half hour she sat there, and then she could sit still no longer. She uncurled herself from the window seat, her legs stiff and complaining, and returned to her room. She changed into the first riding habit her hand came to, stamped her feet into her riding boots, and then ran downstairs and outside.

Two stable boys were forking hay into their charges' stalls when Sarah entered. They looked at her in amazement.

"I've come for Dune," she tersely informed them. "I'll ready him myself."

Five minutes were all that were required to give Dune's sandy-colored coat a quick brush and then saddle and bridle him. She led him out to the stable yard, climbed up a mounting block, settled herself in the saddle, and then set him out of the yard at a trot. She did not want Henry Jenkins's company. Not this morning.

Once beyond the stable yard, Sarah urged Dune to a gallop. Left cooling his heels in his stall since Sarah had supposedly sprained her ankle, Dune now eagerly raced across meadows and fields, unaware that it was Sarah who was running, running from a despair that threatened to engulf her.

She returned to Charlisle flushed and windblown a full two hours later, Dune's head sagging with weariness as he walked back into the stable yard. She jumped to the ground before a groom could assist her and would not even stay for Henry Jenkins's mild chastisement at the folly of riding unattended across a strange countryside.

She bathed and dressed in a white muslin gown, saying nothing to Maria, keeping her face expressionless, holding her tears at bay. There were still many hours of this day yet to be got through.

Acting as if all hope of happiness had not just died in her breast, Sarah joined the Charlisle party in the breakfast room and then rode with the Dohertys and Freddy Braithwaite in an open barouche into the village for the Danverses' appearance before the local magistrate.

The Charlisle party were not the only spectators. Word of the Danverses' crimes and capture had spread through the neighborhood in less than twenty-four hours. Half the population had come to bear witness to so momentous an event.

The magistrate, happy to sink his teeth into a meaty case after suffering through months of poachers and footpads and petty thieves, settled in to listen to anyone who cared to testify, which was most of the Charlisle party. Fitz explained his decision to use the butler to sniff out the culprits. Jack's letter was read into evidence. Earnshaw described his discovery of the jewels in Lord Danvers's jars of snuff.

Three hours after he had claimed his chair, the magistrate made his determination. The Danverses, to no one's surprise—save, perhaps, their own—were bound over for trial.

Lunch at Charlisle was a celebratory affair to which the magistrate was invited. He wholly enjoyed himself, for everyone wanted to question him on the case. It was not every day that a country justice of the peace could sit as the center of attention of the Haute Ton. He took second helpings from every dish that passed before him. No one noticed Sarah sitting mute in their midst. No one noticed that she touched none of the food offered her. They were full of the Danverses.

At the end of the meal, however, she did speak, requesting an audience with her parents at whatever time was convenient that day. Convinced that their youngest daughter finally meant to grovel at their feet as was her duty and beg their pardon for the hideous manner in which she had conducted herself the whole of the summer, the duke and duchess graciously granted her a half hour between the conclusion of their habitual game of whist in the drawing room and the hour set aside for them to dress for dinner that night.

At the appointed time, they sat in state together in green brocade armchairs in their sitting room, looking like royalty prepared to hear the petitions of their subjects. Sarah was uncowed. She had seen this performance too often to be swayed by it now. She stood before them calm and unrepentant.

"I've come to discuss my future," she said without preamble.

Her parents took a moment to recover from this unexpected beginning.

"Your future is certainly in doubt after your perfidy this summer," stated the duchess. She waited for an apology. None came. "How we are ever to live down this scandal, I do not know," she said, a hint of angry pink in her cheeks. "Your behavior, Sarah, from first to last has been abominable. It will be rectified. You will devote yourself during the London Season to exhibiting the utmost decorum so that hopefully this whole wretched summer will be forgotten by the ton."

"I am not going to London for the Season, Mother. I intend to settle at Barlow, our estate in Berkshire," Sarah said, calm and strong as her parents stared at her in disbelief. "I will take Maria and Henry Jenkins, and Bill Regis with me."

"You will do no such thing," the duchess snapped. "You will accompany us as you have always done to London, where we *will* find you a suitable husband. You will be married by Easter, Sarah, or face the gravest consequences."

"No, I will not marry by Easter," Sarah riposted. "I have gone to a great deal of trouble and put myself through the most ridiculous gyrations this summer to avoid a miserable marriage, and I have no intention of putting myself to so much trouble again. You may arrange whatever match for me you choose, Mother, but I'll deny each and every man at the altar, I swear it. My reprehensible conduct this summer must have convinced you that I am capable of the most desperate acts."

It had, and the Somertons' faces showed it.

"Sarah," said the duke disapprovingly, "what has come over you?"

"An absolute determination not to continue living as I have done thus far. I intend to settle at Barlow, Father, and spend the rest of my days there far away from Society and the Marriage Mart."

"I will not permit this folly!" the duchess declared.

"Oh, you will, or I can promise you a scandal that will make this summer seem like a dull tea party by comparison!"

The duchess gasped, and then rose with towering fury. "Why, you ungrateful, undutiful, little shrew!" she cried, walking up to her daughter and slapping her with all the vigor her outrage demanded.

There was a moment of shocked silence as Sarah unflinchingly met her mother's eyes. "That tactic won't work on me anymore, Your Grace," she said quietly. "You can denigrate, beat, and threaten me, all to no avail. You *will* pension me off to Barlow with the income from my dowry, or I promise to make your life a living hell. If, however, you agree to my terms, I promise to engage in no scandal and to live so quietly at Barlow that everyone in the ton, even you, will forget that I ever existed."

"It is . . . an interesting proposition, Amanda," the duke remarked into the stunned silence.

"Never!" his wife gasped, sitting back down suddenly in her chair. "I will never allow myself to be blackmailed by my own daughter."

"Then," stated Sarah, walking to the sitting room door, "you will suffer the consequences."

She left the room, quietly closing the door behind her. Though she was new at challenging her parents as an autonomous adult, she yet felt certain that she would win this particular battle. She had found weapons and a courage to use them this summer that even her parents could not withstand.

"Ah, good, Maria, you are here," she said, entering her room. She was quite amazed at how calm she felt. She sat down at the small rosewood writing desk, drew out a sheet of paper, dipped her pen in the inkwell, and turned to regard her maid. "You must help me draw up a list of the things we need to send for when we move to Barlow next week."

"Barlow?" Maria pricked herself with her sewing needle.

"Yes, I am moving there. It is to become my permanent residence. You and Henry will come with me, of course. Henry seems pretty set on marrying Miss Benton, the senior parlor maid here, and she seems a competent enough woman, so she may become my housekeeper. Bill Regis will attend Barlow's grounds. They don't offer as much scope for his imagination, but I believe he will be happy enough there. I'll need a chef, of course. I wonder if Rolbrook's undercook would be willing to leave such an august household? She's a talented young woman, and I've always liked her. I look to you for advice on which footman I should take with me from Rolbrook."

"Lady Sarah, have you run mad?"

"On the contrary. I am finally, blessedly, sane."

But sanity did nothing to lessen the pain she endured. She spent most of that night crying into her pillow over John Rawlins, rising the next morning pale and heavy-eyed. A headache lay thick and unmoving at her temples. Still, she had survived twenty-four hours without Jack. It gave her some hope that she might even get through this day.

Maria brought a note from her parents with Sarah's morning hot chocolate. The missive was brief and to the point. The duke and duchess had fully capitulated, stipulating only that they would announce Sarah's seclusion at Barlow to the ton as they saw fit. She had no quarrel with this. They could tell Society whatever they chose, as long as she was free to live peacefully at Barlow.

"My parents have sent to Rolbrook for a barouche to carry us to Barlow," she informed Maria. "We leave Charlisle in four days."

Not feeling up to meeting company this early in the day—despite so quick and momentous a victory—Sarah took her breakfast in her room, wrote to the Barlow staff, then to Sally Givens, the undercook at Rolbrook, and then to Evan Yates, a Rolbrook footman she and Maria had decided would best suit them at Barlow. She finally dressed. She then summoned Henry Jenkins and congratulated him when he informed her that Miss Benton had accepted his proposal of marriage. Lizzie Benton was then sent for and offered the post of housekeeper at Barlow, an offer she accepted with alacrity.

Her immediate future now settled to her satisfaction, Sarah finally left her room to join most of the party in the morning parlor. The London papers had arrived and were being perused by many. Conversation, needlepoint, backgammon, and whist made up the rest of the occupations in the room. Noting that her parents refused even to glance at her, Sarah settled herself with Freddy and Corliss Braithwaite, stoically entering into their discussion of Mrs. Radcliffe's *The Mysteries of Udolpho*, which Corliss adored and which Freddy refused to read.

The day crawled by with a fretful slowness that made Sarah want to scream. The next day was no better. Every minute was an agony. Until now, she had never fully understood that heartbreak meant skin that was oversensitive to any touch, frayed nerves that made her jump at the least sound, hot tears demanding release hour after hour and growing more determined the more determined *she* became that they would not be

211

shed. It meant a complete inability to find any pleasure in the beauty of a summer day or the absurd conversation of her secretly worried friends.

It meant a heart that throbbed with pain and would not be comforted.

Two days before she was to leave for her new home, she attended the simple wedding of Elizabeth Benton and Henry Jenkins. To sit through the vows nearly killed her. To smile and offer her congratulations at the ceremony's conclusion required a fortitude she had not known she possessed. To drink to the couple's health was treacherous, for any spirits could loosen the stranglehold she had on her emotions. She saw the happy couple off on the first leg of their journey to Barlow that afternoon with tremendous relief.

Her last day at Charlisle dawned with a brilliancy that was breathtaking. She knew, because she watched it, unmoved. Sleep came only a few hours each night now. Her appetite had long been impaired. Fortunately, those who still remained assumed her wan face had everything to do with what was clearly—for all the Somertons' fine words to the contrary—a break with her parents, and they thought no more about it. Fitz even went so far as to congratulate her on her courageous blow for freedom and to assure her that, once safely installed at Barlow, she would no longer feel the enormity of what she had done.

As she had for the last several mornings, Sarah sat quietly in the morning parlor with the rest of the guests. She heard the rustling of pages as the gentlemen perused the morning newspapers. She heard her mother debating with Mrs. Braithwaite the wisdom of allowing young girls to walk about town unchaperoned. She scarcely heard at all the conversation she was holding with Susan Formantle. She thought they were discussing gardening, but couldn't be certain.

A half hour had ticked slowly by when Greeves entered the parlor. *He* looked just as a butler should, Sarah glumly thought. He was of medium height, tended toward a portly frame, and boasted a head of carefully combed white hair. She found herself compelled to watch him as he walked across the room, finding in his many differences all too many painful reminders of his handsome predecessor.

Greeves offered Fitz a silver salver. Fitz, engaged in a heated conversation with Freddy Braithwaite on the many fine points of a gelding owned by the Earl of Klenych, absentmindedly took the calling card from the salver, barely glancing at it. Then he jumped in his chair and goggled at the card.

"Is this some hoax?" he demanded of Greeves.

"Not at all, sir," the butler replied.

"Well, well, this should be interesting," Fitz said, tapping the edge of the card against his nose. "Bring him hither, my good man, and announce him to the company."

Greeves bowed and exited the room. A moment later he stepped back into the parlor. "Sir John Rawlins," he intoned, and then decamped.

In his wake stood Jack Rawlins, but a Jack Rawlins Sarah had never seen before. He looked like a buck of the first cut. His dark brown hair was styled *à la Brutus*. He wore a dark green double-breasted coat with flapped pockets, a white cravat, pantaloons, and gleaming Hessians with gold tassels. In his hand he carried a top hat and gloves. The Beau himself would have applauded this elegant, gentlemanly attire. Sarah, however, was trembling on the chaise she shared with Susan Formantle. She felt numb. She was in agony. Why had he come? Why had Greeves called him *Sir* John Rawlins?

The question seemed on everyone's minds for they all stared at Jack with varying degrees of astonishment and censure as he walked up to Fitz.

"Jack!" Fitz said jovially. "My guardian angel. How good of you to call."

Freddy strained his neck looking from one to the other, thoroughly agog.

"Thank you for receiving me," Jack said, in the low voice Sarah knew so well.

Fitz grinned engagingly at him as he rose to his feet. "Welcome to my humble abode. I believe you know everyone?"

"What the devil is going on?" bellowed the Dowager

Formantle. "How dare you masquerade as a knight of the realm, young man!"

"Well said," humphed Mr. Braithwaite the elder.

"What do you mean by this, sir?" the Duke of Somerton haughtily demanded.

"An explanation is certainly owing," Jack said, turning to the company, never once glancing at Sarah. "I have been masquerading this summer, but as a butler, not a knight. That masquerade is now ended. I should perhaps begin by explaining that I have long been a friend of the viscount's—"

"My best friend," Fitz happily supplied.

"And he asked for my help with the Danverses."

Jack had arrested the attention of everyone in the room.

"The Danverses?" sputtered the Dowager Formantle. "Why would this cabbage-head need your help with the Danverses when no one suspected them of anything?"

"But the viscount did suspect them," Jack countered, cool and devoid of any emotion. It took everything Sarah had to regard him with a semblance of calm. "He was deeply concerned that Lord and Lady Danvers, let loose among so many eminent and bejeweled members of the ton, would quickly run amok at Charlisle. He asked me to come and collect the evidence necessary to accuse and convict them of their crimes. He thought it best that I be, not a guest, but a servant who would have access to every room in the house. I readily agreed to the scheme. I had recently left the army and was in need of some . . . entertainment."

"Good God!" the Duke of Somerton ejaculated, to everyone's further amazement. "You're not *Major* Jack Rawlins, the Savior of San Miguel?"

"I don't recall saving anything at San Miguel but my own neck," Jack replied, as the company goggled at him.

"I *knew* your name was familiar," said the duke, striding up to him and shaking his hand. Sarah blinked at this amazing tableau. "You showed those damned Frogs what the British are made of *that* day! I read of your knighthood in the papers. Well deserved, young man. Well deserved."

"Thank you, Your Grace," Jack said with a slight bow.

Fitz, Freddy, the duke, and Jack were now surrounded by the rest of the party, who eagerly questioned Jack on his war record, his knighthood, and his clever masquerade, which had fooled them so completely and led to the capture of the Lord and Lady Danvers.

Sarah could stand it no longer. She fled the room and then the house, which seemed to lack sufficient air for her starved lungs. She ran eastward across the courtyard and through the formal gardens, and then the topiary garden beyond. When she could no longer run, she walked, passing into a meadow that climbed slowly uphill to a stand of mixed beech and oaks. When she could no longer walk, she stood staring out across the vast Charlisle lands, seeing only a blur of green. When she could no longer stand, she sat down with a thump on a fallen log.

Her face was burning, not from the exertion of her recent exercise, but with horror. Her hands flew to her cheeks. A knight! A war hero! A friend to Fitz! She couldn't take it in. There seemed no way to comprehend the sudden upending of her world that left the man she loved so different from what she had thought him. *He* had been in battle. *He* had seen men led to their deaths. *He* had witnessed the body parts piling up in surgeries and the dead men rotting in the field. There was no mystery to his grief now. She knew him too well not to understand the unbearable pain war had inflicted upon him. Oh, how she had acted with him these many weeks!

Sarah groaned. What must he think of her? For many minutes, she could only huddle on the log, stunned and embarrassed and wretched.

"Lady Sarah?"

Sarah jerked to her feet and whirled around to find Jack standing not three feet away, the soft breeze teasing his dark brown hair. He might have abandoned his butler's disguise, but he still bore its grave imprint.

"Sir John." She seethed. All that she had suffered these last four days finally broke free, not in tears, but in fury. "Here is no butler calling on me, but England's newest hero! A knight! Undoubtedly Wellington's bosom bow!"

215

"Nodding acquaintances only," Jack murmured.

"Modesty does not become you! I daresay you have even been presented at court."

"Well, yes. The knighthood, you see—"

"And you are now undoubtedly Prinny's darling!"

"Letter friends only," Jack assured her. "But I should perhaps confess . . . "

"Yes?" Sarah asked witheringly.

"My . . . er . . . schooling . . . "

"Oxford?" Sarah brittlely inquired.

"University of Edinburgh," Jack stated, hanging his head.

"Oh! You are the outside of enough!" Sarah stormed.

"It gets worse," Jack said humbly.

"It couldn't possibly," Sarah informed him.

"I'm rather afraid it does. You see, though he will never publicly acknowledge it, my father is the . . . er . . . Duke of Merifield."

Sarah sputtered incoherently until outrage gave her words. "Oh, you are monstrous! Infamous! Horrid! To think that for nearly a month you have lied to me, deceived me, let me run on like a complete idiot and *despair* of ever . . . When I think what I have endured . . . When even Charlotte thought me mad . . . Oh! I can't talk to you!"

She whirled away from him, her arms wrapped around herself, overwhelmed by outrage and ecstasy, hope and a strong sense of ill-usage.

Jack sighed. "You would try the patience of a saint, Sarah." He sounded as if he stood but inches behind her.

"Oh, I'm awful, I know!" she said bitterly.

"Then, you know a pernicious falsehood, for you are the most wonderful woman in all of creation. It is a miracle I kept myself from kissing you before this."

Strong hands on her shoulders turned her around. Sarah regarded Jack with utter amazement as his warm hands now cupped her face. There was a look in his gray eyes she had never seen before, and his mouth was lowering to her own. Dizzy and uncomprehending, Sarah's eyes drifted closed.

His kiss was sweet and languorous and hot. It was nothing

she had ever known. It was everything she had ever wanted. But he pulled away too quickly. She stared up at him, for he seemed to have become a different man in those few brief delirious seconds.

He was not grave or impassive or imperturbable now. His heated gaze engulfed her. Hope and uncertainty and something Sarah was afraid to name warred in his expression. "Is it possible?" he said wonderingly, his thumbs brushing her cheeks in gentle hypnotic caresses. His eyes searched her face. "I thought it was hopeless. I have neither the title nor the fortune necessary to . . . You're the acknowledged daughter of a duke . . . I left Charlisle convinced I could not reveal the depth of my feelings . . . " He shook his head. "I had not gone two miles when I knew how impossible it was to leave you, to face a life without you. But I told myself there was no hope. I lack even the family Sir Geoffrey Willingham enjoyed, and *he* was refused. All summer long, I've had but one thought: to escape Charlisle and return to the sanctuary of my farm in Devonshire. But once there, I thought I would run mad. I had to come back. I had to discover if you could in any way return my regard. To learn if there is any hope—"

Sarah's emotions had undergone such upheaval during the course of this broken declaration that sanity now wholly eluded her. "I can promise you more than hope," she giddily vowed. "I can promise you absolute certainty of success!"

With a boldness that left Jack no hope of defense, Sarah captured his mouth with hers in a feverish kiss in which she intended to leave no doubt as to the depth of her own feelings. She was wholly successful. With a groan, Jack wrapped his arms around her, pulling her hard against him, his mouth devouring hers with a hunger that matched her own. Passion soared through her. She held him as fiercely as he held her, loving these drugging kisses that burned the world away.

"Oh, Sarah!" Jack moaned against her ear, holding her fast as the world danced madly beneath her feet. "I love you so much. There aren't words . . . But I have so little to offer. I can give you only the simple life of a farmer's wife far away from the Haute Ton, card parties, balls—"

Sarah grabbed him by the lapels of his fashionable coat and gazed wildly up at him. "That's right, offer me everything I've ever wanted."

Studying her rapt face, Sir John Rawlins saw everything he, too, had ever wanted and, being but human, swept Sarah into a kiss that left them both gasping for breath.

"My lady, my lady!" he moaned, kissing her temple, her cheeks, her soft throat. He felt her tremble in his arms. He dragged her mouth back to his, her sharp cry of pleasure pouring into him as his tongue claimed her mouth with a hunger that brought her arching against him. "We are both quite mad," he said with a groan several minutes later. "We must stop and be practical, Sarah. Your parents will never accept the grandson and nephew of butlers."

Sarah gazed somewhat sternly up at the man she loved. "I don't care. I've got a novelist daughter to produce, and, oh, Jack, you *are* the road to my happiness!"

Mesmerized by her shining blue eyes, Sir John recalled the Gypsy's prophecy, and he privately vowed to insure her future boasted all the happiness the Gypsy had promised. "You have given me back my life and love and laughter. Let me give you my life in return. Marry me, Sarah. Let me be your obscure knight."

Her smile was dazzling as her fingertips gently brushed against his mouth. But Jack wasn't deceived. He saw the mischief in her eyes. "But Father said that you're a war hero, Jack," she murmured. "You're the farthest thing from being obscure."

He grinned at her. "Never fear, my love. No one remembers a war hero's name, face, or deeds six months after toasting him from one end of Town to the other. As my wife, you shall enjoy all the obscurity you have ever longed for."

"Are you sure?" she whispered, her lips a breath from his.

"A butler never lies," Jack murmured, before claiming her mouth once again.

They spent the rest of that morning and the whole of the afternoon in each other's arms, repeatedly professing their love, agreeing to modify Sarah's Barlow scheme to his farm in evonshire, wondering how to convince the Somertons to gree to such a disadvantageous marriage, and resolving on iretna as a last resort.

But they had badly underestimated the Duke and Duchess of omerton. Horrified by their daughter's summer antics, humiliated by the ending of an estimable engagement, blackmailed ito letting Sarah have her way with Barlow, fearful of any furier outbreak of her freakish behavior, they were, to be blunt, grateful to get the wench off their hands. They accepted Jack with a hauteur that wholly belied their mutual glee.

It required a month to properly announce this new engagement and plan the wedding. During this period, the duke and the duchess were fully informed by Jack of his family background. This was a severe blow, but Jack's new title, the fact that his father—however unacknowledged—*was* a duke, and his firm promise to hide Sarah away on a remote farm for the rest of her life did much to reconcile them to his association with their family.

Thus, Lady Sarah Thorndike and Sir John Rawlins were married quietly to suit their own tastes and her parents' fears of exposure. There were no more than two dozen guests, comprised of her family, his family, Fitz, the Dohertys, the younger Braithwaites, and the Jenkinses. Sir John and Lady Sarah Rawlins then contrived to happily live the rest of their lives on an increasingly prosperous farm in Devonshire that became known for its exuberant summer house parties, the excellencies of its orchards, its ever-expanding stable of some of the finest horses in the country, and a female novelist of some note.